Praise for William Brewer's

The Red Arrow

"Brewer skillfully articulates the man's deep wells of pain and resentment in quick swings. . . . Coincidences occur again and again. The narrator meets them with joy and wonder and so the reader does, too. . . . *The Red Arrow* is more about enjoying the mysterious way these events unfold than understanding why things have happened the way they have." —*The Boston Globe*

"It's exhilarating to be a passenger on this wild ride. . . . It's to Brewer's considerable credit that he satirizes pretensions so deftly and so well." —*Alta Journal*

"Thought-provoking and stirring. . . . A notably bookish effort, a heady, inventive novel with intelligent things to say about mental illness, perception, creativity and psychedelic drugs. . . . For a novelist, it's no easy task to successfully employ books as plot engines (the narrator also has meaningful experiences with writings by W. G. Sebald, Giuseppe di Lampedusa and Geoff Dyer). Nor is it an opportunistic path to surefire best-sellerdom. Rather, it's the work of a confident writer who isn't beholden to convention or market considerations." —*San Francisco Chronicle*

"At turns delightful and demanding, William Brewer's debut novel is a serpentine ride that culminates in a moving encounter between art and science." —*Scientific American*

"A complex portrait of a struggling writer. . . . Through the narrator's preoccupation with literature, Brewer successfully creates a character whose internal struggles are complex and nuanced."
—*The Stanford Daily*

"[An] exceptional debut. . . . From the first page, the narrator teases with allusions to a 'treatment' he has had that he'll explain later, 'because if I do so now, I'll lose you.' . . . A first-rate work that intrigues and entertains." —*Kirkus Reviews* (starred review)

WILLIAM BREWER

The Red Arrow

William Brewer is the author of *I Know Your Kind*, a winner of the National Poetry Series. His work has appeared in *The New Yorker*, *The Nation*, and The Best American Poetry series. A former Wallace Stegner Fellow, he is a Jones Lecturer at Stanford University. He lives in Oakland, California.

williambrewer.net

ALSO BY WILLIAM BREWER

I Know Your Kind

The Red Arrow

THE

Red
Arrow

▸ ▸ ▸ ▸ ▸ ▸ ▸ ▸

WILLIAM BREWER

VINTAGE BOOKS

A DIVISION OF PENGUIN RANDOM HOUSE LLC

NEW YORK

FIRST VINTAGE BOOKS EDITION 2023

The Library of Congress has cataloged the Knopf edition as follows:
Names: Brewer, William, [date] author.
Title: The red arrow / William Brewer.
Description: First edition. | New York : Alfred A. Knopf, 2022.
Identifiers: LCCN 2021016802
Subjects: LCSH: Psychological fiction. | GSAFD: Suspense fiction.
Classification: LCC PS3602.R4816 R43 2022 | DDC 813/.6—dc23
LC record available at https://lccn.loc.gov/2021016802

Vintage Books Trade Paperback ISBN: 978-0-593-31443-2
eBook ISBN: 978-0-593-32013-6

Book design by Anna B. Knighton

vintagebooks.com

Printed in the United States of America
10 9 8 7 6 5 4 3 2 1

For Ry

I WANT TO SAY, first of all, that I am happy. This was not always the case. In truth, it was hardly ever the case—even when I felt happy I wasn't because I knew that was all it was, a feeling, an illusion that would soon be chased out by something I call the Mist. That I am happy now can be attributed to the fact that the journey worked, the *treatment* worked. I won't describe the treatment yet, because if I do so now, I'll lose you. What you should know is that I am thirty-three years old, of solid physical health (good levels of the new good cholesterol, low levels of the bad, proper pulse, no chemical dependencies), a professional failure, and am sitting solo on the Frecciarossa train waiting to depart from Roma Termini for Modena by way of Bologna. I am in Italy for my honeymoon; I was married in September, nine months ago, but we delayed the trip for better weather. Back on Piazza di Pasquino, at the very posh G-Rough hotel, a seventeenth-century townhouse converted into a temple of Italian design, Annie, my wife, is still asleep—as we both understand this trip is something I should do on my own—in the palatial king bed, an original piece by the famed furniture designer Guglielmo Ulrich, as is all the room's furniture, and after whom the room is named, and about whom I speak as if I've got a clue who he is. I don't.

I'm going to Modena to find a physicist. Because of the terms of my contract, I am not allowed to name or acknowledge him in any way, publicly or privately, until our project is complete and he has decided if he wants to credit me. For that reason, I will simply call him the Physicist, though if you're that curious it shouldn't be too difficult to find the one famous theoretical physicist native to Modena.

I need to find the Physicist because he owes me a story. *His* story, specifically; more specifically, the second half of his life's story, from our present moment all the way back to what he calls the "great realization," the moment when he had a "breakthrough in perception," as he describes it, after which he excelled in the study of physics, the result of which is his groundbreaking though still-controversial theory of quantum gravity. (I'm not allowed to name that either.) Everything from birth up to a year before the great realization I've already got, but it's the "realization" that matters: it is my ticket out of a sizable debt hole I created when I failed to write a book promised to one of our nation's largest publishers, publishers who paid me a rather sizable advance I can't pay back because I blew it all on things like four days in the junior suite of the luxury G-Rough hotel. Many dark-suited women and men in a Manhattan high-rise are eagerly waiting to give me a legal suplex if I don't deliver.

The good news is that, posttreatment, I'm able to forgive myself for getting into such a position, and I feel grateful for that. Yet no matter how profound the treatment was, how life changing— and it *was* those things—I realize I can't ignore that the debt is still very real, still my problem to solve, and, worse, that it haunts me beyond its financial implications. It's the last thorn stuck in my foot from years spent walking through thorns. Except not only is it keeping that time alive, and keeping me connected to it, it's also got the power to infect the new life I've been gifted. And so even in my happiness and clear mind I also feel anxious enough about the day's potential that I couldn't bring myself to eat anything from the G-Rough's impressive a.m. spread, not even a prosciutto slice or cube of melon to go with my morning cappuccino, which, now in the gut, has me feeling about as eager as possible for this train to come awake and race me closer to closure.

The solution is simple: all I've got to do is find the Physicist, get the rest of his story, and finish the job I was hired to do, which is to ghostwrite his memoir. Indeed, through a sequence of events that can seem either cruel or felicitous depending on which side of a life-changing treatment you find yourself, I found myself in a position where, by ghostwriting the Physicist's memoir, I could cancel my debt with my publisher. Whenever I turn in a new ghostwritten section, the money I'd normally receive in compensation is instead deducted from my negative balance. The more of his life I write, the more of my life I get back.

But then he disappeared. Vanished. All calls to voicemail. His email like a dead address. And nothing but stonewalling from his handlers. So where I'd thought there was some good old-fashioned professional collaboration and momentum, there is now only his absence, an absence that's not only thrown the project into a state of limbo, but also stands to resurrect my debt, a debt I cannot pay because I am worth approximately zero dollars, which everyone seems to agree on except the state of California, where, under its "community property" laws, I am *not* worth approximately zero dollars because I am married, meaning Annie—good, bright, unwavering Annie, whose love has been the one thing I've not screwed up, and whom I continue to adore more and more every day, especially after my treatment—could see her wages garnished or private assets seized should I be sued, a thought that sends my already hot stomach spinning like a Maytag.

Worse, I'm reminded of this fact nearly constantly by a guy

named Richards—that's his last name, he pronounces it "Ri-shard," I guess the *s* is silent? Richards is the editor on this memoir, an older guy from Montana with a JD who moved to New York and went into books but still talks like he hung a shingle in Bozeman. He's been in the game awhile, but from what I gather he's had a bad few years—mainly from him saying again and again, "I've had a bad few years"—and this book, the Physicist's memoir, for which he had to put his neck on the line in order to win it at auction, is his last big swing at saving his job. If that wasn't pressure enough, a recent regime change at the publisher has made it expressly clear that he's "the whitetail in their sights," to use his words. To say he was stressed about this project from the beginning would be putting it mildly. And then everything came apart. When I asked Richards early in the Physicist's disappearance if he was certain it was useless to try to explain the situation to his higher-ups, he just laughed a little pathetically into the phone and said, "Barking at a knot," whatever that means.

I feel for Richards, truly, but I fear he's beginning to crack. Or has cracked already. At first his correspondences were understandable: vaguely anxious emails asking if I'd heard anything, maybe once a day. I kept explaining that I've never actually had direct contact with the Physicist, so what could I do? But that didn't seem to matter. Then the emails picked up in frequency and desperation. He started peppering them with phrases like "What will I do?" which became "What will we do?" which evolved into the more personal "I'm sure you've got to be worried" before tipping over into "A situation like yours—I can remember from law school what it could mean for you and your wife, so unfortunate," and then back to "We'll be ruined" and "You'll be ruined" and, finally, "I'll be ruined."

Then he started calling once a day, sometimes twice, every time leaving me a voicemail where pretty much the only thing I can hear is this weird labored breathing sound he makes between clauses. It sort of sounds like he's sipping soup.

And then, just minutes ago, he took it to a whole new level when he decided to FaceTime me while I was in a cab on my way to the station. I know I shouldn't have answered, but it seemed so weird that he was FaceTiming that I convinced myself that maybe he was calling to say that contact with the Physicist had been made, all is well, I can enjoy the rest of my honeymoon. So I answered and there he was, his face looking how it looks in pictures online, red and kind of swollen, like a boxer's, and his head, which I've always described to myself as profoundly rectangular, complete with a flattop buzz cut of white hair, seemed even more rectangular when I saw that it fit so perfectly into the frame of the phone screen that it was like he wasn't talking to me through the screen but was the screen itself, like some disembodied digital personality from the future whom I was holding in my hand.

"Did you mean to FaceTime me?" I asked.

A heavy exhale scratched through the speakers. "It's been a tough ride," he said, talking to what felt like no one in particular.

"Is there news or something?"

"I just thought that it would be good for us to chat face-to-face." There was a looseness to his eyes, a shine.

"It's like three in the morning there—are you drinking?"

"Maybe I'm a little roostered up. It's been a bad few years. And it could get so much worse."

A deep and almost boyish loneliness emanated off Richards. It was undeniable. If this is what he wanted me to feel by FaceTiming, then his plan had worked. I did feel for him. Not least because he seemed to be calling from an emotional space I'd only recently been freed from myself. Even though he's always treated me less than kindly—he hated my involvement with the project—and more recently had become a badgering pest with designs, at times, to incite fear in me, even stooping so low as to mention my wife, all so that he might be less alone in his own uncertainty, I wanted to help this man. An opportunity to relieve suffering: that's how my mind posited it to me then in the taxi, holding Richards in my hand—a thought I can't imagine having had only a few weeks ago. A warm thought, a simple thought, a thought I was about to share with the real, vulnerable Richards reaching out to me from a place of elemental fear in what would be our most candid and unifying moment, except that just as I was about to speak his whole face hardened, and his voice dropped into a dry, edgy tone as he said directly into the screen, his digital eyes staring straight up into mine, "So much worse for you too, don't forget."

The screen felt hot. I looked away. Through the taxi's windshield I could see Termini coming into view, hard-edged and impersonal, and maybe it was because of what Richards had said, or maybe because the station's architecture is simply that austere in its modernism, but it looked to me like a prison through whose doors was the suffering Richards wanted me to join him in. I could feel it and I was afraid. But now when fear comes, it's like I can witness it. Not visually, but relationally, a charged cloud rising through me and expanding out in jagged waves, an event within, but not a part of me, no, just another thing that happens, and then it passed, and then before I was even cognizant of what I was doing I'd looked back at my phone, smiled, and said, "You know, Richards—it is what it is. I've got to go," and then I hung up, paid the taxi, and disappeared into the crowd, a mass of discrete events dressed in tailored suits and summer linens, gripping suitcases and smartphones, checking wristwatches, patting their pockets for tickets or a cigarette, each needing to be somewhere other than there, a blur from which I emerged onto the Frecciarossa 9318, car 8, seat 19D, where I am sitting now, waiting to begin a day trip north on the speed rail to Bologna, where I'll then transfer to a commuter rail and ride three stops up to Modena, the place where I believe, as of yesterday, I might find the one man who can cut the final thread connecting me and my past.

No one has joined me yet in my four-seat unit, which, before my treatment, I would've perceived as confirmation of my deep suspicion that I am despised by all people. Why despised? For many reasons. Whatever reason they want. Not least of which, I was certain, was that my very presence stirred up repulsion, as if just seeing me was like accidentally catching a glimpse of some abscess. That's what I was like, I thought—an abscess in the smile of reality. Of course I didn't think I looked like an abscess, but that was part of the horrid trick: there was some negative aura about me I could intuit but never see. Some days it seemed no nastier than a dour blur, but on other days, like today—a day when I'm really in the thick of confronting how I've failed and made a mess of everything and gotten myself into this position—it would be *raging*, like the demented glow of a bug zapper. But that's not how I feel: faintly in the window I see my red beard and freckled face reflected and know that I am perfectly ordinary.

Little TVs over the aisle show our route of Roma to Bologna as a red line up the boot with a speedometer resting at zero beside it and a clock above counting down to departure. As the seconds fall, I straighten my spine, open my lungs to the conditioned air, and begin simple, steady breaths. One, then another, following each with my attention until the rhythm settles first my stomach and then my mind so completely I can drop behind it and watch.

Through the speakers comes a prerecorded message, the only word of which I catch is "Frecciarossa," a name that was only a name to me until last night when I was dozing off in the Ulrich bed—one half of my mind still in this world, the other lost in early dreamlessness—and I heard a voice call out, "The red arrow," a phrase so empty of context that it felt like a spell from the cosmic beyond, or so I thought, letting sleep pull me deeper, not realizing it was Annie who'd said it from across the room at the midcentury secretary where she was sitting, still in her dinner outfit of black-on-black jeans and blouse with a green silk scarf for color, writing in her notebook these repetitive pages of Italian vocab she'd picked up throughout the day, along with notes on how and when the vocab stuck in her mind, a nightly habit she's maintained since we arrived in the country over a week ago, one expression of her commitment to learning the language that began when she was assigned to the development team for a new AI-powered language-learning program at the company where she works. "My task isn't just to learn a language," she'd first said of the project, "it's to pay attention to how I learn it, and when."

Now she collects vocab so obsessively she'll sometimes shout when a translation clicks in her mind, which is exactly what happened last night at dinner when we were quietly scanning the menus and she blurted out "Priest strangler" with enough force to make me straighten in my chair and look around. "*Strozzapreti,*" she continued, privately, "I remember *strozzare* from *Inspector Montalbano.* I bet that's it," and then she checked on her phone and smiled up at me. "I knew it. *Strozzapreti*—'priest stranglers'—great name for a noodle," and only then did I realize she was speaking about one of the pastas on the menu.

"The red arrow," I heard again in the bed, eerie and powerful, like some flare at the edge of the blackness I was draining through, but then abruptly the still-wakeful half of my mind latched hold of it and rustled me up to see Annie looking at me from across the room. "The red arrow," she said a third time, "when does it leave?" I blinked back, unsure if I was awake. "The Frecciarossa," she said slowly, dragging the syllables. "The train—what time do you have to be there in the morning? I hope you set an alarm. I've got my own plans for tomorrow and they don't include getting up with you." Frecciarossa, "the red arrow"—right then in my half-conscious state both ceased to exist in separate languages and instead were joined suddenly and forever in my own private tongue. A real physical feeling, solid and smooth, like well-cut and oiled watch gears interlocked and set spinning for the first time. Very pleasant. Then the tender darkness pulled me under.

And now, having just heard it from the speakers above, I can see the word floating in the anterior no-place of my consciousness, first "Frecciarossa," then "the red arrow," and then there's only "arrow," bright and serifed and softly vibrating like a magnet gathering new words around it, a sentence forming, the sentence the Physicist chose to start his memoir—the only sentence he specifically requested I include—a sentence he's used for years as a kind of catchphrase in lectures and interviews, a gate that's opened his thinking to countless crowded rooms, and that now opens the story of his life: "Time is not a line with two equal directions: it is an arrow with different extremities." And as I read it with my mind's eye and repeat it to myself, I feel the present shift, then soften, then bloom open like a flower with very long petals, each curling back to a point that got me here.

→

IT STARTED WITH A SUCCESS. A success with stories. I suppose it's only fitting—I'm just now realizing—that I must retrieve a story in order to end the hell that stories opened. The stories that did me in were stories I wrote. I hadn't intended to write stories. My plan had always been to paint. Growing up, I was the art kid. The one who could draw, then the one who could paint. I got to skip precalc in high school to do murals on classroom walls, which was a deal for me, because I was only an okay student, and horrible at math. After graduation I went to art school in the Northeast, then did an MFA. Moved to New York, as one does, and got an undersized and overpriced studio in Bushwick, as one does, and began an unsuccessful life as a painter.

I love painting. I miss it dearly. The physical labor, my grungy studio clothes, the look of my stained hands, how a friend could stop by and drink my beer while watching me paint and that counted as work *and* socializing. And yet, ever since the stories, I've never felt like I could return to painting. I couldn't ever say why. But now—I guess because I'm more honest with myself since my treatment—I'm prepared to say I wasn't any good at it. Sure, I was talented as a kid, but it isn't too difficult to appear artistically talented in a place like West Virginia. And then at art school I think I learned how to *appear* talented enough—I said the right stuff, praised the right contemporaries, tilted my head the right way during critique, and—most important—developed a style that "interrogates canonical aesthetics." I actually said and wrote that exact phrase more than once. It was a commendable performance. So good, in fact, that I believed in it too. But again, like with West Virginia, it ain't that hard in a place like art school. And then once it was over, I sold a few things here and there, almost all to one guy, and since then I've mainly kept myself afloat by art handling—hanging the pictures of successful artists on the walls of successful New Yorkers. Times got pretty lean. In my last five years of painting I sold exactly two pieces. So I guess painting was never especially good to me. But that's not entirely true, because if it wasn't for painting I wouldn't have met Annie.

It was six years ago, late summer of 2013, and Annie was working at her first tech job, a Brooklyn-based artificial-intelligence start-up that specialized in digital avatars. An artist-friend of mine linked me up with her firm about possibly doing some work with digital portraiture. I did not paint portraits, even my own—especially my own, which I've been unable to paint all my life—though of course I did not tell them this. Instead I took the meeting for the free coffee at a sterile Scandinavian café near my studio. Annie was the contact person.

I arrived early and waited at one of the squat Danish tables, scribbling in my sketchbook, trying to look how I imagined a tech person would want their potential artist hire to look: productive, focused, showered. And though my usual day wear of paint-stained Carhartt work pants and a many-holed T-shirt was completely acceptable in that northern corner of Kings County, I instead put on a paint-free ensemble. Why clean up if I knew I wasn't going to get the job? Because no one had taken me seriously in a very long time, so I'd take what I could get.

But after twenty minutes I was still sitting alone. Meanwhile the barista started openly glaring at me for hanging around without ordering, a problem I could've easily solved by making a purchase, except I couldn't because I was so confident that the coffee was going to be paid for that I'd left my wallet in my studio. Not that it would've mattered if I'd brought it; I was broke.

I could intuit the barista's disgust with me spreading through the other patrons. There was a young guy wearing a beanie and exceptionally large headphones rocking in place while typing on a Mac; another guy with an aggressive slouch and a stamped-on scowl who was also typing on a Mac, but with such percussive intensity I thought he might be screaming at someone in a chat thread, or not *at* someone but *about* someone, perhaps about me; then finally a young woman with a brown bob and oversize glasses marking up a paperback with a highlighter. Yes, there was no doubting it; they could all tell what was going on and wanted me to go. I could sense it in the way that they were maybe glancing at me whenever I wasn't glancing at them—I couldn't be certain because I couldn't bring myself to look at any of them directly for very long for fear I might see them looking at me, disgust beaming from their dark irises. On and on my thoughts went like this until I got so lost that I must've failed to pay attention to where I was staring, because when I came to, I realized I was looking right at the woman with the paperback, who was now looking back at me, having caught me looking at her, probably thinking I was checking her out like a perv, which I hadn't been. In fact, I'd made an earlier effort to *not* look in her direction because indeed I found her attractive, which I worried would cause me to look with genuine interest in a way that might unintentionally telegraph as creepy. So much for that, I thought, punching myself in the thigh as I watched her grab her purse, get up from her table, and start in my direction. In a desperate attempt to have an excuse for my unintentionally pervy glance, I started sketching her very quickly, thinking I could show her the drawing in both apology and defense, saying something about "inspiration." If this sounds exhausting that's because it is. That was my last thought as she walked toward me, a public lashing dressed all in black, not in a goth way or the default New York way but in a way that even then I could sense was expressive of certain convictions about aesthetic minimalism: *I am so tired.*

"Are you here to meet someone named Annie?"

I rose and shook her hand a little more intensely than intended. "I apologize. I didn't realize you were you. I was keeping an eye out for someone techie looking."

At this she drew back, her under eyes pinched. "What would techie looking be?"

Not so good looking is what I wanted to say but didn't. "I guess I don't really know." I stared down at my boots, which I would've liked to use to kick myself in the head.

"Right. Well, I blocked an hour for a meeting, so there's still time if that's okay." She offered to get us drinks on the company account, saying she was going to have a cortado, and I said that'd be great for me too, then deflated back to the table.

She returned with our coffees and, before she was even seated, asked if I'd signed the NDA, then launched into a description of the company and the work they were hoping to do, speaking with a confidence that called to me, even as the work she described filled me with terror. "You'd be contracted for something like two hundred portraits," she said at one point. "The portraits would be of twenty different models from whose images we feel we can dynamically compose almost any face. The goal is not facsimile— the uncanny valley is very real—which is why, unlike our competitors, we're banking instead on a looser look, something that's still realist, but more representational overall, with a style that hopefully leans into dynamic, analog qualities like brushstroke and texture. Postimpressionistic-ish. We're also considering filming a time-lapse of each portrait as it's being painted, should there be kinetic potentials worth mining, but we're still teasing out how we'd use that data. Ideally you'd deliver by Q4, which I know is a crunch, with Q2 already blurring past. But we can be somewhat flexible."

I wanted to pretend like I understood what she was saying, that I was thinking it over, but quickly I admitted, "I can't do it. I'm sorry if there was miscommunication from my friend, but two hundred portraits, it's not possible. I'm not your guy. And filming? I can't be filmed." She sipped her cortado and did not speak, dropping a hard block of silence between us that seemed not to bother her at all, but that made me squirm in my seat and feel like I owed her further explanation. "I worry about what an interruption like this would do to my current work," I added, even though I didn't have much work going, only a few stalled canvases I couldn't yet understand. Her hair had the same lacquered brown shine of the buckeyes that filled my backyard as a kid.

"That's fine," she said finally, her shoulders relaxing. "I appreciate the honesty. Most everyone we contact about contract work says they can do everything. Men especially. I appreciate you saving me the headache." Then she smiled for the first time, quickly but sincerely, and I felt a then-unknown warmth wave awake in me, like a pilot light between my lungs. She reached for her bag and looked around like she was making to leave, but I didn't want her to, not yet, so I asked her what it's like in the world of tech. Is her office a big open footprint with long tables and snack bars and all that? Guys in zip-up hoodies?

"There are definitely some guys in hoodies," she said, setting her bag down. "And yes, the office is an open floor plan, but not glamorous. It's a shitty old building that's almost certainly not up to code. We have to run space heaters in the winter. There are free snacks, but it's mostly tubs of candy from Costco. Also those barrels of cheese puffs. It's a start-up. Not my final destination, but I'm glad to have found the entry point. You know, everyone asks about the guys in hoodies, but what's more special are guys in black turtlenecks. My coworkers and I call them Stevies. Sometimes you'll catch two Stevies talking to each other and neither seems to realize that the other is wearing the same outfit."

"An aesthetic crime," I said.

"Indeed." She looked around again.

"Do you code and all that?"

"I can do a little if I need to. At a start-up everyone needs to do a little bit of everything. But what I am is a designer. I design the experience the code needs to express."

"I went to a school of art and design. I stayed on the art side though. Design felt a bit buttoned up."

"Interesting. I disagree. I mean, maybe I know what you mean in that it has a professionalized way about it. But maybe what seems buttoned up is just something that's been designed well, so it's clean. There's only what needs to be there. And that comes down to paying attention."

"So what is it you pay attention to?"

"As much as I can. Like this"—she lifted up her empty glass demitasse—"this is a well-designed cup. Some people get very turned off by coffee in clear vessels, which I get, but its clarity lets you see that the espresso has been cut in a way that's very pleasing to the eye, and the glass has a weight and thickness like ceramic, but unlike most glass it doesn't get hot, so you aren't going to burn your fingers or lips when you go to drink. It makes for good engagement. 'Engagement' is big in AI. That's what I spend a lot of my time thinking about. How does a person engage with a thing? And then how do you keep that interaction going in a way that feels natural?"

We continued like this well past our scheduled hour, long enough that the barista came by and cleared our glasses away himself, neither of us stopping to thank him as we talked. When we finally finished, I asked if she'd want to get together again, and she said sure.

A WEEK LATER we met at an Austrian restaurant near her apartment in Park Slope. We both ordered schnitzels as big as our faces and enjoyed two half liters of lager and were feeling altogether very joyful and in sync as we shuffled through our decks of personal history. She asked what West Virginia was like, admitting that she knew almost nothing about it, having never even met someone from there until me, and maybe because of the lager, or nerves, or both, I rambled briefly about how it's a beautiful but forgotten space, a no-place in the American mind, its people either ignored or relegated to caricature while its landscape is constantly defaced by industry, something my paintings tried to understand. After apologizing for getting swept away, I asked Annie where she was from, noting flashes of an accent.

"Northern vowel shift," she said. "I'm conscious of it. I'm actively trying to undo it. But sometimes it's an asset at work when we're testing bots." She said she was from a commuter town outside Chicago, calling it "the most suburban suburb of all suburbs."

"Maybe I don't know much about suburbs, but you seem very cosmopolitan for someone from the suburbs."

"Why do you say that? I mean, thank you, but—"

"I don't know. You work in AI. You have style. You're not plain, I guess is what I mean. When I think of suburbs I think of the plain neighborhood-world in *E.T.*"

"That is more or less what it's like. Maybe what you're picking up on as plainness is more a general placelessness in suburbs. I think they're designed to make place irrelevant, really. That's one of the perks for some people who move out there, like my dad, who was sick of being from a shit Polish neighborhood in the city. At least that's what he says. Where we lived, we didn't have to think about where we were from in the way it seems like you've had to think about being from West Virginia. The trade-off can be a kind of homogeneity, sure, but there's still a train that takes you straight to the city. And not *everyone* is the same. There are cool people. Like my grandmother, she was very cool. I spent a lot of my time with her. Maybe it's her energy you're sensing. She was a successful jeweler. She lived in the development over from ours and had a studio behind her house. That place was special. Lots of rugs all over the floor, workbenches. She even had a little foundry area. It was wild stuff. Dangerous for a kid, but she didn't care. She gave me things to do. Things to read. And even taught me some things. She'd take me into the city when she'd drop off new pieces at Saks. Then we'd have a bistro lunch and go to the Art Institute. She made these." She pointed to the burnished shards of copper hanging from her ears.

I admitted that all sounded much nicer than I'd imagined.

"Nicer than West Virginia, I bet."

I knew she was joking, and she wasn't wrong, but I said nothing.

"I'm sorry. That was dumb."

I let it drop. "Your grandmother—that's where you got your design sense?"

"Maybe, yeah. But I wandered backward into design. One thing my grandmother definitely did was get me to read a lot. That's why I was an English major. After college I worked in publishing for a while but hated it so I quit, then got into AI through personality design, which is just creepy industry-speak for writing a bot's character. Then that led to conversational design, then experience design. It's all design at the end of the day. I think really what my grandmother taught me was to just kind of go for it. See how something works. Give it a shot. Adjust accordingly." She finished the rest of her lager in a longer gulp than she'd expected, set the glass down, then half repressed a burp. "Do you want to share a cigarette?"

We smoked on a bench in the restaurant's front courtyard, our heads resting against the ivy-knitted façade, the sky sliding from indigo to black. A string of globe lights clicked on, throwing low-watt bronze over our bodies. A man with a Holga hanging from his neck stopped on the sidewalk to take a picture of the scene. He was our age but wearing a khaki Boy Scout uniform tucked into shorts that had once been jeans. His pale thighs glowed. We stared together into his dark lens.

"An aesthetic crime," Annie said once he walked off.

"Indeed. The patches on his shirt weren't even sewn on the right spots. And there was more than one rank patch, which makes no sense. No eye for detail."

And through this comment I revealed I was in the Boy Scouts. Not just in—I *was* a Boy Scout. An Eagle Scout. An achievement I'm proud of but hesitant to mention for the obvious proto-fascist sentiment it stirs up as of late. Luckily, Annie wasn't derisive. Maybe she was just being polite. Whatever it was, I ended up telling stories about my experiences, about how I spent so much time outdoors as a boy, and about the troop I was in, and eventually one story about how, on a backpacking trip into a West Virginia state park, we got caught in a dispute between environmental activists and state authorities in what some called a hostage crisis, but which to us mainly felt like camping with a group of environmental activists on one side of us and state authorities on the other. It was this story that returned to me later that evening. I was back alone in my studio, trying to work on a large curious painting of many small, brightly colored figures walking toward an erupting volcano, when I put my brush down and, thanks to extreme naïveté and a small bump of confidence from some cocaine left behind by an artist-friend, started typing that story on my laptop.

Why did I feel compelled to write it down? This is the question I'd later be asked countless times in Q and As, and always my answer was the same: I don't know. I couldn't explain how it happened. In art school I'd taken a beginning poetry workshop for one of my liberal arts electives, but I'd enrolled mainly in hopes that the small size of poems might also be reflected in the weekly workload. The class was fun enough. I wrote mostly landscape descriptions of the Monongahela River valley where I'm from, poems that seemed to interest no one. For another elective I took Rage and Relentlessness: On Post-WWII Art, Film, and Literature in the German-Speaking World, in which I developed a minor passion for Thomas Bernhard and W. G. Sebald, but it'd been a while since I'd read them. For years the only things I'd written were emails and applications for grants I never won; as for reading, there were articles and paperbacks, and sometimes I'd get swept up by something, but I never took myself as a reader, whatever that was— someone more disciplined than me, for whom doing what I was doing then at my laptop wouldn't have been strange. And while it did feel strange, there was also some element that felt faintly familiar, a deep call back to early boyhood when I'd burn hours filling notebooks with strange monsters and mutants—a kind of endless ballroom party of creatures spilling from one page to the next—and as I drew each figure my mind would coil out into the narrative of its life, traits, struggles, and finally its voice, which came right as I finished its image, and then I'd move on to the next.

That's a little like how it felt, that week I sat in my studio, typing away, tweaking the piece, letting the paints on my palette harden into a neon topography.

Then I did the most idiotic thing a young man can do when he's met the woman he believes is the love of his life: I sent her a story, asking her to read it. And she did. And then—as an English major, and as someone who worked in publishing briefly out of college before transitioning into tech—she gave me some seriously insightful feedback, saying things like "The pent-up aggression in this scene is very palpable" and "I love the rhythm of the sentences here" and "This is sloppy and I think you could do better," and didn't tell me I was a dope, and still wanted to see me. After I finished that first story about the troop, I wrote another, then another, focusing on, or even speaking as, a different scout in each story, and as the .docs piled up in a digital file called WFT (Weird Fiction Thingy), so did the hours Annie and I spent together, until a year and a half had passed and I'd moved into her place in the Slope, and it was there in our apartment one afternoon in March, on my twenty-ninth birthday, in fact, just as I was leaving to go kill myself, that my phone rang.

No one called me during the day except robo scams and political groups. I knew this, and yet, hearing my phone ringing in the apartment, I paused. I'd already locked the door for what I thought was my last time. My boots were on but not yet tied. I tried to stay focused on leaving this earth, having finally reached the point of action I knew I'd been journeying toward for so long. But for whatever reason, maybe *because* I was about to kill myself and wanted to hear one last voice before I was off to the great nothing, I quickly unlocked the door and hobbled in.

The call was from a number I didn't know from a part of the Bay Area I'd never been to and knew no one from. Another location scramble, I thought, before looking back at the phone and realizing the Bay Area town was home to a university whose English department housed a writing fellowship I'd applied to under Annie's encouragement, meaning I hadn't even heard of the fellowship until she'd told me about it, suggesting I apply, after which she made no mention of it again until one night when we were cooking dinner together and she asked in a very chill way if I'd sent in my fellowship application and when I said no, first having to think of what application she was even referring to, she turned to me, chef's knife in hand, and said, "Why the hell have you had me spend so much time looking at those stories if you aren't going to do anything with them? Was all that just a waste of my time?" The blade bounced and flashed as she spoke, its point transfixed on my torso like a cobra. I got the message. And now, months later, my phone was ringing.

I answered the call and was greeted by a stern North Shore accent—a voice that would come to mean so much to me—belonging to LD, the much-lauded fiction writer who runs the fellowship at the Bay Area university, offering me the fellowship, including two years of health insurance.

This began what I came to refer to as "the fluke years." I was not someone who won things. I lost. Continually. For almost twenty years the voice in my head, the same voice that almost caused me to get up and leave the coffee shop before I met Annie, said this every day, all day: *You are a loser, a fool, an illness, an unending source of pain for everyone you encounter.* And I believed it—hence my plans to step out. Therefore winning something was not supposed to happen, especially a fellowship in a field in which I had little experience, academic or otherwise.

That evening, when Annie walked the three flights up to our apartment after work, instead of finding a manila envelope con-

taining a letter for her and a separate letter for the police instruct-
ing them on where to find my corpse, she found me sitting by the
living room window, looking out over the damp pewter garden
behind our brownstone building, sipping a Japanese beer and looking very strangely elated. When I told her about the fellowship, she
told me to shut up, then screamed and bounced so that her brown
bob flowered out like a mushroom cap in a way that makes my
knees dissolve, cried a little, taking off and putting back on her
oversize round frames to wipe her eyes, and seeing how much joy
she felt for me was the great gift of this moment in my life, for in
that moment I almost completely believed that this person really
loved me.

"It works perfectly," said Annie, finally sitting down, the news
settling through her. For a moment I could see, in the way her
eyes looked out at nothing in particular, her head softly shaking
side to side, that she was watching in her mind a montage of all
the ways her career could grow by relocating. The Bay Area had
always been a potential move for her, an option that had begun
to orbit more closely as she outgrew her start-up gig. "There's so
much action there," she'd say, scrolling through job listings. "So
much growth potential." Which is exactly why, as I sat witnessing
her private joy, I felt ashamed realizing that I'd been at least partly
responsible for keeping that moment from her, all by holding on
to my failed life in the city, a stalled studio practice and piecemeal
art-handling work hardly being enough to justify sticking around.
In truth, what I always knew was that it was the city itself that
made those failures livable—sure, I'd done nothing, but I was sur-
viving in New York, and that had to count for something. Except
even that wasn't true anymore: my suicide note, now shredded
and buried in the kitchen trash, was grim proof. Shameful and

embarrassing. And yet the phone had rung, and I was very glad I'd answered it.

That night we spatchcocked the fuck out of a chicken and both felt very much like things were working out. (I was still in shock.) In the weeks after, we made a plan for packing, researched neighborhoods in the Bay; it turned out Oakland was the same price as Brooklyn, so we settled on that swiftly. We told our landlord. Told our friends. Annie started earnestly looking at all the job listings. I planned to sell my van and almost all my painting supplies, and the rest I boxed up and decided I'd drop in my father's storage unit in West Virginia when we passed through there at the start of August while driving across the country to our new home in California. I felt like I was happy.

But things seemed off. Everything was moving against the set rhythms of my life. Even on the first night, as shocked and excited and grateful as I was, I found myself awake in bed in the late hours, worrying about what was going to happen when it was discovered that I had no idea what I was doing, that I couldn't explain how the stories had happened, which led me to believe that maybe the stories themselves were part of a much larger and more elaborate plan to punish me in a way I'd never been punished before, a new and terrible level of punishment, which likely meant something bad happening to Annie.

And now, I've got to say, it's very strange: I remember having a thought like that—a thought that siphoned off so many hours of my life and made even objectively pleasant moments feel conditional and threaded with fear—and I feel nothing. Not even physically. Intellectually I know that that's how my mind worked, and that that's how I lived, but what I know more precisely, more intimately, is that it's over. And where vast swaths of my mental real estate were given over to rumination and dread, there is now a kind of emptiness, so that even as my memories slide by, I've also been able to simply look around and notice things with calm clarity, like how the Roman sun has, within minutes, gone from pleasantly ambient and out-of-sight to directly overhead and huge and now every rail across Termini's yard is shining like a bar of silver. I squint at them, my forehead against the window, then lean back—we've begun to move. The train is rocking cradlelike and smooth in a way that relaxes me into dual sensations of stasis and transit. I've got that very specific departure feeling one can get only in a great machine gathering its power, the undeniable start to something, a going *forward,* and yet as I look out again and see the old warehouses lining our way, each warm and glowing in various shades of mango and persimmon, I am sent back to my own warehouse studio in Bushwick on a hot day like this one, a day when I was tearing down my life to move, when I first learned about the treatment that would eventually save it.

$\longrightarrow$

I'D EMPTIED THE STUDIO of nearly everything and was painting the walls and floors a fresh coat of white when my friend Antony came in. Antony was, let me be clear, one of the smartest people I'd ever met. Tragically, he is no longer with us. Antony suffered from a rare pediatric cancer. He'd beaten it once as a teenager, but then it reared its head again in his twenties, only months before the golden cutoff point in remission, after which his chance of cancerless years would've grown exponentially. Antony was dying. He was dying and there wasn't anything anyone could do about it. Antony had the mind of ten men and the spiritual energy of twenty, yet he wouldn't live past twenty-five.

I met him shortly after he graduated from his MFA and started renting the studio next to mine in the building. We became friends the first afternoon he moved in because he sang bits of show tunes out of key nearly nonstop with the door open, which I tried to drown out by turning up my music, until he came knocking on the door of my studio and asked flat out if I was trying to drown out his singing, and I said I was, and within an hour I'd learned much of his life story up through when his cancer had returned his senior year of college, how he said fuck it all and decided to do an MFA anyways, ending in the present moment. And so began a long and fruitful and challenging friendship, of which I was always the lesser friend, the lesser mind, but happily so—I was lesser, but I was practical. "You cut through the bullshit," he used to say about me, meaning that whenever one of his monologues would spiral into a degree of abstraction and vocab I couldn't tolerate—which is to say I couldn't follow—I'd say as much. "You've had dirt under your nails," he'd say, which I think was his way of compensating out of pity for my lack of intellect by saying I had a kind of real-world grit. I know now, on some cellular level, that the stories also wouldn't have happened if it wasn't for Antony. None of this would have happened without Antony. He taught me, or at least reawakened in me, a kind of imaginative recklessness he was able to access with ease, in part because of his certain proximity to death. It left him fearless as a maker. He simply did not care if something was bad. He'd ask for my opinion on a canvas and if I told him I wasn't digging it he'd just shrug and begin again. Early on when I'd watch him work I'd sometimes ask what he was doing and always he'd say, "I don't know, so that's good." Still, though fearless in making, he was not fearless of death. We talked about it often; another reason we became close. I was one of the few people he knew who wouldn't run from the conversation. At that time, death was on my mind a lot too. And while it's maybe shameful to have admitted to a young man who was being robbed of a long life that I, a young man who had the potential to live a long life, very often thought about ending mine, he honored my pain for what it was.

This specific afternoon with Antony was during an especially hot day in early April, the kind of day when you can feel the first edges of summer and everyone in the city wants to quit their jobs and screw in the streets before the rains return with the last of the spring chill. I had the studio's factory windows open to let in the warm air and let out my joint smoke and I was listening to the radio when Antony came in, holding a rolled-up copy of *The New Yorker,* asking if I'd read it. I asked which article, acting as if I'd even opened that week's copy.

"It's from February," said Antony. "The article about psychedelics. I must've missed it, but I saw someone post about it this morning and I just went back through my pile in my studio and found it and read it. You need to read it. You know about these things, no? You've taken everything." He was the most energized I'd seen him in months.

I hadn't taken everything, just most things. It was true that I, like any good art-school kid, had done my fair share of psychedelics. And it was true that I had told him, as I'd told others, though with less and less frequency over the years, about how my first psychedelic experience on psilocybin mushrooms at the age of seventeen was in some part responsible for awakening me to the simple truth that I could leave West Virginia and pursue a life of art. I'd told Antony this story years ago, and he was genuinely interested at the time, though I couldn't have anticipated it resulting in him standing in my studio, in his vastly oversize, half-unbuttoned red lumberjack flannel, white-knuckling a rolled-up magazine. Antony was always telling me I must read things, and I'll be honest and say that most often those things—articles about archaeology on Crete or some little-known Beat poet—didn't excite me much. But I could tell by his tone this was different, and when I finally stepped out of the narrow frame of my own bullshit and looked at him, truly looked at him, I was knocked back by the sight of him bathed in a golden burst of spring sun, incendiary as a saint, and I knew I needed to hear whatever it was he wanted to share. "Read it to me while I finish painting these floors," I said.

He sat down on an overturned milk crate and proceeded to read me the entirety of "The Trip Treatment," a piece by Michael Pollan describing how doctors at NYU, just across the river, had been administering psychedelics to terminally ill cancer patients and seeing revolutionary potentials for palliative care. Case after case described how the terminally ill experienced "ego deaths" under high doses of psilocybin, and how these ego deaths were a kind of "practice death" that allowed individuals to confront their anxieties and fears about death so that they could live more fully for their final months or years. The personal accounts of these journeys and the results of the studies were astounding, as was the hope they presented for treating ailments like addiction, anxiety, and depression. By the time Antony was done reading I was sitting cross-legged on the floor, watching him like a kindergartner at story time, the paint roller long abandoned in the tray. And perhaps it was my lower vantage, or the way he was squatting on the milk crate so that his already long limbs looked grand and sculpturally exaggerated, as if for perspective, but in that moment, when he set down the magazine and looked at me, he was shot through with all the immense solemnity and wisdom of the Lincoln Memorial.

I'd been mesmerized by the article. I felt elated, hopeful. It was like I'd just learned that the prison I'd been locked in for decades wasn't a prison at all—you could walk right out the door. But my mind snagged at this thought, and not two seconds after Antony had finished reading, a thousand objections flooded in and snuffed out my belief, which my face must've betrayed, because as I felt the spell drain away, I watched Antony's face drain too.

"You don't believe it," he said.

"No, it's not that. It's just—I mean—you've got to admit, it sounds a little, I don't know . . . neat. Eat a mushroom and then *boom,* your mind is cured."

"Penicillin is derived from a fungus. It changed the world. Why can't this be like that?"

"Okay. I'll give you that. But what I mean is . . ." But then I was stuck, I lost my words.

Or maybe I was too embarrassed to say what I was thinking: that anxiety, depression, the fear of death—these aren't diseases. These are fundamental expressions of who we are. These are what it means to be the one primate that can talk. Life is suffering. I deserve the way I feel. This is what was chosen for me. This is me.

These were my real thoughts. *Deserve. Chosen.* I'm certain that somewhere in my mind then there was a part of me screaming out against this logic, but I couldn't hear it, not through the Mist, which, though I didn't realize it, was swirling like little storms in both my ears, whispering, *What would you be without me?*

"It's Michael Pollan!" said Antony, shocking me back from my thoughts. He'd stiffened into the tall posture of a threatened animal, one hand grabbing at where his hair used to be. "Don't you love him? You've read all his books. Organic food! Come on. He convinced you not to eat mutant corn, but this is where you draw the line? You've said yourself that a trip changed your life."

"You're right. I don't know. I'm not saying it's impossible. I'm just processing. Healthy skepticism."

"That's because you have the time and health to be skeptical," he said, staring straight at me.

I felt embarrassed, selfish, gutted.

"I'm sorry," I said. "That was stupid of me." And at this, my mind came untangled. It was suddenly clear and warm, like the air outside. Motivation surged through me. I started shaking my head. I cracked my neck. I could finally see him sitting across from me, how still he was. He who was never still. Only his flannel, big and loose, seemed to sway around his torso like a flag. I understood what was happening.

"I'm sorry. You're right. You're totally right. So what do we do next? Obviously we need to get you in there immediately."

"No."

"What do you mean? This is literally made for you. We could take the train to their office right now. They're on the other side of the bridge. Fuck it, we'll take a cab."

He looked at the floor. "I'm tired of clinics and studies. I'm done being a subject. No more poking and prodding. I want you to do this with me. We can take them together."

I tried to explain that when I did mushrooms it was recreational, under a way lower dose, with groups of people drinking beer and smoking weed and watching *The Wall*. "It's not even comparable," I said. "And the doses they're taking. I mean, I can't even get my mind around it. I'm no guide. I'd never even heard of a guide until today. You read the article. You need professionals."

Either a cloud moved over the sun, or his aura fizzled out. A cold guilt dripped through me.

"These chemicals are no joke," I said, pleading. "If you don't know what you're doing it could be hell. Four or five hours of pure hell. Why don't we call the clinic? They need you. And you—you're an artist, a brain. Imagine what you could see, what could be revealed to you. I bet they'd rush you into the study."

"No," said Antony again, shaking his hairless head. "You don't get it."

I thought that was the end of it, but he brought it up one more time, later that June, when Annie and I had dinner with him at his parents' apartment in Murray Hill, where he'd moved, too sick to be on his own. He'd declined rapidly since that day in the studio. He was gaunt, pale, weak, but still full of enough comedic and intellectual energy to answer the door with a napkin draped over his forearm like a butler, then later demand I explain why anyone would want to watch a documentary about any artist painting. "It's all shit on a wall!" he said. For dinner he'd ordered us spicy Szechuan noodles specifically so that the next day my asshole—his words—*would feel the "special tingle" from the peppercorns and I'd think of him.* At one point he asked Annie if she knew anyone who could preserve him in a bot. She did her best to laugh but could only look down and push her noodles around with her chopsticks. Later he pulled out a vape pen and started puffing it at the table. "Pardon the fumes," he said, in a Continental accent. "It helps me digest. Doctor-recommended indica. It's all the fun I've got to look forward to now. I did ask *somebody* to trip shrooms with me and be eternally healed, but he won't do it, so this is all I've got—weed and pain pills." I don't remember how I reacted to this—I must've laughed or made some jab or something—but what I do remember is that I suddenly felt very overwhelmed. I knew the meal was goodbye, not only because we were moving away, but something about Antony's joking, the finality behind so much of what he said, became too much, so I excused myself to use the restroom. But things weren't much better in there. When I flicked on the light I saw his collapsed wheelchair leaning against the wall beside a clothes-drying rack draped with towels used to clean his face when he'd get sick. I sat down on the toilet and covered my mouth so they wouldn't hear me. While I was crying for Antony, I was also crying out of shame—even all this, the wheelchair and rags and the withered young artist-brainiac wrapped in blankets at the table, wasn't enough to wake me up. Yet another confirmation that I didn't deserve to be alive.

At the meal's end, Antony became suddenly very tired. His mother must've been able to sense it, because right on cue she appeared, as if summoned, and suggested he get some rest. As we stood to leave, I was suddenly very grateful that Annie and I were moving away, because it allowed Antony and me to say goodbye to each other and even say, *I'll miss you,* all while pretending like what we were talking about was my departure to California. It was only when his mother showed us out to the elevator and squeezed my arm and said "Thank you" in a way I wasn't prepared for, right before I stepped between the parting doors, that I broke down again.

She was the one who called me two months later. It was our second day in California, and Annie and I'd taken BART south of San Francisco—we were staying in the city temporarily until our apartment opened in Oakland—to a car dealership in the peninsula city of Colma. Walking from the train, we quickly learned Colma is where San Francisco buries its dead. The town is nothing but a long strip of highway lined by immense cemeteries and mausoleums, punctuated only occasionally by a flower shop or car dealership. THE CITY OF THE SILENT read one graffitied overpass. Fitting then that it was there, sitting beside Annie on the other side of a salesman's desk waiting for paperwork to clear, that I got news that Antony had died.

Looking back now, I suppose it's obvious, but at the time I couldn't grasp the importance of that day in the studio, that I was learning about something that might save my life. With what Antony knew about my suicidal depression, I'm prepared to say that's why he read me that article, as much for my own life as for his. He said I had the time and health to be skeptical, but even then I must have sensed that while he was saying one truth, his stare, faintly jaundiced, was saying another: that maybe I didn't. Instead of telling me how desperate I was, he reflected it back to me using his own shortened life. That is why he was a better person than me.

BEFORE ANTONY DIED, before Colma, before Annie and I packed our remaining possessions in a moving truck and drove across the country, we spent a weekend for free in a house in Amagansett, owned by my friend Jules, a painter I'd been close with since our freshman year of art school who'd recently hit it big. It was Jules's success, in fact, that got him the attention of Annie's AI firm, which led him to recommending me instead (clearly out of pity). He'd offered us the place as a going-away gift. It sounded lovely. This is precisely why the prospect of the trip made me anxious. Only a few months ago I'd planned on being dead by now, and I hadn't yet gotten used to the fact of having been awarded the fellowship. I was certain that soon, very soon, something horrible would happen, a balancing of the scales. And where better for a reckoning than the Hamptons, a place I understood to possess so much cultural—and actual—capital that I assumed I wouldn't even be allowed in, literally: for years I thought the Hamptons was a single place with a single train station with a sign that read THE HAMPTONS, and were I ever to get off there, the Hamptonians would quickly turn me around and send me back. It was only when Jules bought the house in Amagansett that I'd learned otherwise. I'd asked where Amagansett was, and he looked kind of confused and said, "You know, on Long Island. The Hamptons," and then I must've returned his confused look with a confused look of my own as I tried to imagine Amagansett as a town within a town. Finally Jules took out his phone and showed me on the map, and while I tried to play it cool, I felt like a dunce. Moreover, I noticed that anytime I'd ask casually if he had any plans to go out to "the Hamptons" Jules would always say something like "Yeah, I'm headed out to Amagansett in a couple of weeks." Or if I asked, "How were the Hamptons?" he'd say, "Amagansett was great," which suggested Amagansett held a power I also didn't understand, further proof I didn't belong. But I didn't want to steal the opportunity from Annie, so I put on a smile, agreed to go, and spent the whole night before we left dreaming repeatedly the same dream in which she's standing by the water, smiling at me, and then is swallowed suddenly by an acrobatic great white shark that launches out of the surf and pulls her away in a single, wild loop of carnivorous perversion.

But of course, these being the beginnings of the fluke years, the opposite happened while in Amagansett: more good news arrived. Annie and I had been bodysurfing the frigid Atlantic waves, letting the heavy water pummel our backs like a free massage. After an hour we collapsed onto our towels, and against my desire to be technologically disconnected I checked my phone, likely because I was anticipating bad news and wanted it to hurry up and get there. I saw a missed call from yet another number I didn't recognize. New York area code. They'd left a voicemail. Here it comes, I thought, I'm ready. I listened. It was a woman named Betsy, editor in chief of a prestigious literary journal based out of Brooklyn that also sponsored a first-book prize. She was calling to tell me my collection of stories, *The Troop,* had won and was to be published in partnership with an esteemed independent publisher. This was strange, because I didn't remember submitting to a prize. When I tried to explain this to Annie, lounging beside me on her towel, steaming in the sun, she thoroughly flipped, screamed, jumped in excitement, saying that I had very much submitted to it, many months ago, soon after Christmas, that we'd done it together one night in the living room. "We were sitting on the couch after dinner," she reminded me. I could see it now: the contest's deadline was at midnight and I didn't want to send it because it didn't feel right, there was a bad omen afoot—the Mist was outside, moving across the windows, chewing up the streetlights. It was always there, a demon, a physical force as much as a spiritual one. That's how I initially tried to describe it to a therapist many years back, when I finally had access to a therapist through my art school. I said it sometimes feels like a sinister mist is slowly uncoiling out of some crack where my spine meets my brain, moving in strange tendrils that grip my gray matter, sliding between the folds, and it's like I can genuinely feel it, a grip tightening on my mind, saying awful things to me while pulling me into its fog, and now at times it's like I can see it outside of myself, that's how strong it has become. The first therapist said that while that was a fine description, it has a less mysterious name: major depressive disorder with suicidal ideation. Call it what you want, I said to the therapist, but it's a fucking mist. And a mist it's always been, haunting me at all times, and especially that night, when I submitted my manuscript.

"I don't want to do it," I'd said to Annie on the couch. "There's bad energy going on. It's in the air outside. I don't know how to describe it, but I can just tell. It's atmospheric." I never told her about the Mist exactly. I talked around it, as I was doing then, but never named it outright, and not necessarily because I thought she'd leave me or think me mad, but because I worried what kind of power I might give it by letting it into her life that way.

"You don't want to send to the contest because there's a bad atmosphere?"

"The atmosphere right now is bad, yes. Outside. I can feel it."

She looked at the windows, then me, then she stood up and began putting on her giant Ugg slippers, saying we were going to go out there so I could show her. "I want to see what you're talking about."

"Don't be ridiculous."

"Ridiculous? You're afraid to press a submit button because of the 'atmosphere.' This is what you do—you think you're going to be punished for submitting to a contest. And you can sense that because of the air? I want you to help me understand." She was at the door now, holding the knob.

Sometimes when Annie wears her hair pinned back in an uncommon style, as she was that night, a rogue strip of scalp will be revealed that is so pale and alien that it stops me when I notice it, as if some unknowable part of her has been made briefly visible. This makes me feel good. It makes me feel less guilty for what I choose not to explain. And it makes me trust her because, in perhaps seeing for a moment a visible expression of whatever there is of her I cannot know, I feel less alone in the knowledge of what she cannot know of me, while also more connected to her in our shared withholding. I saw one of these flashes then. That's why I agreed to go outside.

Together we walked downstairs and stood on the stoop, and sure enough I could see how the rain was falling on the snow, causing a mist to rise up, and while that was all fine and good and thermodynamically accurate, I still knew what I was seeing. I said some false apology about fearing rejection and projecting my emotions, I can't remember what, then tried to find relief in knowing that Annie saw it too, even if she didn't understand what it truly was, because it is not always visible to others. Back upstairs I pretended to feel relaxed, but I only felt worse—it was a clear omen out there. But we submitted the manuscript anyways.

Then there I was, on a beach in Amagansett, a place I had no business being, listening to Annie saying I was going to publish a book, a thing I had no business doing. And while at first I wanted to reject it, I finally conceded to Annie's excitement for my own life, which was so immense, so incalculable, that I couldn't argue against it, and allowed myself to feel excited too. That night we were two big grins who floated into town and ordered lobsters at a restaurant that seemed to be constructed entirely out of wainscoting. We drank many white Burgundies and later made love in the secluded dark of Jules's screened-in porch, faint rustle of the tall old oaks conducting our movements, and then after lay there half clothed and silent in a way that felt like we'd just crossed some new threshold of understanding what all this is about, and probably could've stayed there into sleep, but suddenly Annie jumped up swatting at herself and rushed inside. I followed her into the light and once my eyes adjusted I could see that where she'd been swatting there was indeed a tick, right where you wouldn't want to find one. I tweezed it off and put it in a jar in case we'd need to show it to a doctor. She scanned me next and found one on my backside. It joined the other in the jar.

Later, while drifting off in bed, I came awake feeling very aware of all my guts and veins because there was something moving through them, something cold and full of purpose, like Novocain through the jaw, and I tried to pretend like I didn't know what was happening, but I knew—I almost laughed at myself for not expecting it, for thinking the Mist wasn't going to show, that it hadn't shown itself already as those two jarred parasites whose bites, I was certain, were the start of the punishment that was destined to come and now was here as Lyme disease coursing through us both.

But it never came. Not the next day or the next week or when the book was announced or when the literary magazine ran one of my stories and a woman named Lisa wrote to say she'd be interested in representing me as my agent and I accepted, not even when Annie and I got into an argument while packing up our apartment, Annie finally snapping at me for being in a mood—I was being a real shit—and saying to me, "When are you going to accept that good things happen. They just happen and that's it," and I said something like "I'll accept it when I start seeing that to be the case," and she said, "What about me? Wasn't I a good thing? Aren't we a good thing? I think you're being a shit because you're afraid a bad thing is coming for us so you're trying to make it go ahead and happen now by pissing me off, but that's not going to work. I want to know, do you truly believe that *we* will end in some punishment?" and without hesitation, before I could even think, I said, "No, I don't believe that." "Well, if you don't believe that," she said, "maybe you can also start believing that these good things are simply that—*good things*." Her eyes did something then, their elegant irises, gray and faint, seemed to swell as much with tenderness as a kind of purpose—it was like they were looking not at me, but *for* me: Where was I beneath the blur of lies I told myself?

→

I'D SEEN THAT LOOK from her before. Only once. Six months prior, back in late February. Two weeks before my birthday when I was going to kill myself but instead took the call from LD about the fellowship.

We had planned on visiting Philadelphia for a weekend. Annie was already going for a tech conference and suggested I join, since the trip was mostly comped by her company. I'd only have to buy a train ticket, and together we'd split a nice dinner on Saturday night. A small getaway, she called it. Feeling like I was at my psychological nadir and desperate for a change of scenery, I eagerly agreed, even though I had nearly no money. I hadn't sold any work in years, my cards were close to maxed, and my art-handling income had dried up because of winter weather. And yet I knew that if I let on even a little about how bad my finances were, Annie would sense just how bad and ask me to be honest about it, and while I'd basically never lied to her, my financial situation was *so* bleak I feared I'd have no choice but to lie, something I very much did not want to do, so instead I crafted what felt like a temporary lie I could turn into a truth: I said that my best patron lived in Philly and he'd been begging to see new work but was so busy he couldn't get to the city, so I'd already been meaning to drive down canvases for him to consider. "We could ride in the van together," I suggested. "It'll almost certainly end in a sale."

My best patron—and only patron, I guess—was, in fact, in Philly: a guy named Clive who appeared about my age but acted somehow much older and much younger at the same time, a trick of being that seemed possible only because of his immense wealth. He'd inherited a family fortune that originated in regional coal and steel production across Pennsylvania. Now he grew his wealth by "playing the market." Though he never elaborated on it, he once claimed it was his connection to coal and steel that attracted him to my paintings, which were strange, semi-abstract, gestural, half-graffitied/half-landscapish images of Appalachia and its industry done primarily in severe orange paints that mimicked the hues of the region's waterways ruined by acid mine drainage. (Describing them now, I'm not as perplexed as to why they never caught on.) Whether he was for or against the environmental legacies of these industries remained unclear.

"We really can't take the train?" said Annie when I pitched the plan. "You can't bring the paintings down another time? Or maybe I could take the train and meet you?"

"I feel like you're not taking my work seriously," I said. My stomach turned.

"I think that's a very shitty thing to accuse me of, but fine. We'll drive."

Feeling like an actual bag of trash, I sent Clive an email saying I was going to be down in Philly in a few days, then lied and said I'd be meeting another collector, but would definitely show him work first if he was interested. He replied with an email that was clearly voice-dictated onto his phone, saying sure give him a call when I'm in town we could meet at his place sounds good talk to you then. I had to take what I could get.

Friday morning I loaded the paintings into my van along with our bags and we headed south, immediately hitting traffic that persisted the entire way. Things got tense in the van. Annie kept checking her phone and craning her neck out the window. Finally I broke: "Christ, I'm sorry, I can't control the traffic. The eastern corridor is a crapshoot. How could I have known?"

"I should have taken the train," said Annie. "My morning is fucked."

"Sorry I am such an inconvenience."

"Really? You're really going to say that? The paintings couldn't have waited? This is a work trip for me. And if this collector is so rich, couldn't he have just taken a private helicopter to the city for the afternoon?"

"He's a very busy person. You clearly don't understand how the art world works." I could feel a large part of me howling on the inside.

As we pulled up to the hotel, Annie told me I'd need to check us in; I was to meet her later in the evening at a cocktail bar once she was finished. She got out of the van, closed the door without saying goodbye, and headed in toward the convention.

At the front desk I gave the clerk Annie's last name for the reservation. He asked to see my ID. I showed it to him. He said he couldn't get me into the room because I wasn't on the reservation. I lied and said Annie was my wife, hoping it would make me seem like the type of person someone would marry. The clerk glanced at my ringless finger.

"This is ridiculous," I said. "She's here at the conference, right now."

"Then all she has to do is come up here and provide her ID," said the clerk.

I stepped aside and tried calling her, but it kept going straight to voicemail. I leaned over to the clerk. "My calls won't go through to her."

"Oh," he said, "that's probably because if she's down in the convention hall she's underground. There's zero service down there."

"So you're saying I've got to go down into the convention and find her and bring her up here?"

"Sir, I'm not saying you have to do anything. But yes."

I descended deep underground on a long zigzag of escalators, finally arriving at a bay of double doors leading into the convention hall, but when I tried to enter I was stopped by a guard with a thin mustache asking to see my lanyard. I said I didn't know what he was talking about. In a shockingly loud voice he said, "Sir, you need a lanyard with a name badge if you want into this convention. Without one, you are *not* going in." He pointed at a person wearing a teal-blue lanyard with a name tag, carrying a tote bag, and in an instant I saw that everyone was wearing a teal-blue lanyard and carrying a tote bag, except me. My scalp got hot. I was clenching my fists. I said "Fuck this" under my breath, went up to the street level, sent Annie a text asking her to call me when she could, and decided it'd be best to try to meet Clive. None of the day's bullshit would matter if I had a check in my pocket for a couple of thousand bucks with his signature on it.

I tried calling him, but he didn't answer. He'd call me back soon, I told myself. I had a vague sense of where he lived, so I drove to his neighborhood, went into a sports bar, ordered a cheap beer, and started waiting. Hours passed. I somehow consumed many more beers than I'd intended and became more than a little drunk, feeling increasingly sorry for myself, then filled with self-contempt. At around seven, as people began packing into the bar wearing bright orange Flyers jerseys, I realized with a sense of deep dread that there was going to be a hockey game.

Raised a Penguins fan by my father—by which I mean he watched the Penguins while I watched him watch—I was taught to despise the Flyers, and while they weren't even playing Pittsburgh, the very fact of having to witness them playing a game felt like another affront to my spirit. To deal with this, I ordered yet another beer, then sent a pitiful text to Clive, saying, "Hey, don't know if my call went through earlier but I'm here in town. Looking forward to meeting up!" Early in the game the Flyers scored two goals and I took this very personally. It wasn't even my team that was losing and yet I was that team—each loser getting trampled on the ice was an extension of me, which meant all the fans around me were cheering for my demise, which was just about the most twisted fucking thing, I thought, and then I got a text from Clive, saying, "Hey can't do it tonight big apologies but the market never sleeps," which I knew was bullshit because the market totally does sleep. It even has a bell to wake it up. I ordered another beer and was lifting it to my lips when a man beside me wearing a jersey bumped into my arm, causing a little beer to spill on my crotch. He turned and apologized. I told him to watch what he was doing. He stared at me.

"Go back to your stupid fucking team," I said.

He asked me what I'd said, and maybe it was the beer soaking through my lap, or the orange color of his Flyers jersey looking very much like the orange of my stupid acid mine paintings, or because my brain felt like it was simultaneously in a vise grip and coming undone, but I decided it was wise to reiterate that he should go back to watching his shit team that hadn't won a Cup in almost forty years, a detail that's representative of how his city is nothing but a second-rate Quaker backwater, and then a few minutes later I was standing alone on the frozen sidewalk, drunk, broke, with bar napkins stuffed up my nostrils to soak up my nose's freshly flowing blood. Vapors rose through a manhole cover, twirling in my direction.

I called Annie. Luckily she answered. I explained the issue with the check-in, hoping she wouldn't get too mad, since it wasn't technically my fault, except that we were late because of the traffic, which kind of was my fault, but I didn't mention this. She let out a long sigh. "I'm still at dinner," she said. "I'm working."

I feared anything I did would impact the situation in a negative way, so I said nothing.

"I guess I can meet you at the hotel when I'm done here," she said. "The cocktail bar is near there anyway. I'll check us in, then we'll walk over together."

"I love you," I said, but she'd hung up.

Too drunk to drive and too broke for a cab, I walked the long way back and took a seat in the expansive lobby. A bellman came over and asked if he could help me. I explained that I was waiting for my wife so we could check in because the stupid desk people wouldn't let me check in earlier. He smiled, shook his head, then gestured to a bathroom on the other side of the lobby, saying I might like to clean up my face. I'd forgotten about the blood. I was about to unleash a stream of expletives on him when Annie came through the revolving door.

She walked over, grabbed me by the arm, and pulled me into an alcove near the elevators. She clearly didn't want to be seen with me.

"What the fuck happened to you?" She was kind of seething.

"I tripped on a manhole cover," I lied.

"I don't understand."

"I fell."

"Over a manhole cover? And landed only on your nose?"

I said nothing.

"Where are our bags?"

I'd forgotten about our bags in the van. "Clive kept feeding me cocktails. I couldn't say no. It wasn't safe to drive back." The lights in the alcove seemed to flicker, then darken.

She turned, saying something to herself, and walked to the front desk. I wasn't sure where I belonged, so I stayed where I was. She came back with room keys and we took the elevator upstairs. In the room, before I could even make it to the bed or a chair to sit down, she stopped and turned and looked at me. She demanded to know what was going on.

I knew then that I could've gone to the edge of the bed and sat with my head hanging and hands out to my sides as if gripping the greasy synthetic duvet for support and that she would've sat beside me and placed one patient hand on top of mine while

I explained everything to her—I was broke, Clive stood me up, my brain was unraveling, and I very much wanted to be dead, so much so I basically got someone to punch me in the face—and though she would have been upset, she would have also seen that I was clearly not well and would've said as much. Honesty, vulnerability, self-confidence: these were the qualities she said she saw in me, way back at the start of our relationship, when I first told her about my depression, a conversation I was certain would end with her leaving me but instead brought us perhaps expectedly closer, as sometimes seems to be the purpose of confessions, she following mine with assurances that while my depression rightly scared her and made her sad she was not unused to it, for in fact her grandmother has suffered from it throughout her life, having even been hospitalized like I'd been once, but she was not about to let her own fear punish me for my situation and was hopeful that we'd get through it, which made me teary when she'd said it because I felt both intense love for her and very sad that she believed that what I suffered from was a thing through which one could get, as if it had an exit other than the one exit it had always planned for me, an exit through the self, which I did not share then because I did not want to share it, meaning that even in my honesty I'd also chosen dishonesty, whereas standing in that hotel room in Philly I *desperately* wanted to be honest and clear and say something like:

Sometimes, Annie, I imagine myself as a grenade going off very, very slowly. This is what the Mist does. This is what it's like when you know for years how you're going to die and what the circumstances of your death are going to do to people because you're the one that's going to make it happen. It's not a question, it needs no reason—it is a purpose. I am a grenade and as soon as you said yes to dinner with me years ago the pin was pulled. I knew it then. I've always known it. I will destroy you. That's what I should've said to you when you walked over to my table at the café when we met. I will destroy you. I do not want to, but I will. I will destroy you, and maybe not only you—maybe for maximum effect there'll be periods of hope long enough to convince us to have a family, their helpless minds destroyed by what they inherit from mine, their hearts from what I'll do to myself. I should have warned you, but I didn't because I was naïve enough—no, desperate enough—to think some true comprehensive lifelong love might be the medicine needed to turn my mind around. I knew that wasn't true, Annie, but that didn't stop me. Because I'm selfish. Because I am a virus. Which is why even when you say you love me, even when you make me feel good, even when we kiss or lean our shoulders into each other in the back of a dark cab or together can feel a shared future expanding before us like a warm and benevolent path, I feel worse for every second I feel good and now I feel more than ever the once-small fractures across my surface cracking open and the heartless entropic light of detonation coming through . . .

But I couldn't bring myself to say this, no matter how honest I wanted to be. My tongue was not my tongue. My mind not my mind. Instead, I repeated my stupid story. She kept asking for an explanation and I kept lying and saying I didn't know what to say.

"I don't understand what's going on with you," she said. She looked like she was going to cry. This made me feel even worse, which made a part of me very happy. "I can't deal with this right now. I'm not doing it. I don't want you coming with me tonight. And tomorrow I think it's best if you go home and we talk about this on Sunday."

"Okay," I said, not fighting. This seemed to hurt her too.

When she got home on Sunday she gave me a simple ultimatum. I clearly needed more therapy, plus I needed to talk to my doctor about going back on the medications that had barely helped me in the past—agree or we were over. I agreed. I didn't bother confessing that for over a year I hadn't been able to afford therapy. It didn't matter. I had already begun to plan out how I would die.

But when the time came two weeks later on my birthday, I didn't die—I answered the call from LD. And so when Annie looked at me, for *me,* in our apartment while we were packing for California and said, "Maybe you can also start believing that these good things are just that—*good things,*" I agreed with her, and beginning then I truly started to believe it, and kept believing it, more and more. I believed it for those last weeks in the city, and I believed it when Annie landed phone interviews for the position of design manager in the robust AI R & D division at a digital products company, interviews she nailed, leading to a full two days of in-person interviews scheduled for when we arrived in California, and I believed it at our going-away party, thrown by Jules on the roof-deck of his warehouse studio, and I believed it when we got in the truck and for the last time left the city, its saw blade of skyline turned up against the blue, framed in the rearview as we headed west, Annie driving first while I helped her prep for her interviews either by reading from *Discussing Design: Improving Communication and Collaboration Through Critique* or *Org Design for Design Orgs: Building and Managing In-House Design Teams*—both somehow industry standards even though the books, with their hideous covers, seemed entirely devoid of any quality design—or by asking her questions written on note cards, ranging from "What is design?" to "How do you conceptualize the components of design culture within an org?" and sometimes recording her answers on a phone and then playing them back so she could edit or memorize herself in real time, both her past and current voice in near-perfect tandem saying, "Now that everyone *wants* to lean into constraint and champion it as the design team's sixth man, especially in AI, there has arisen—in my opinion—the unintended consequence of designers acting like they're 'leaning into constraint' when really they're letting constraint become an excuse for unremarkable work. Part of my job as design manager is to implement a culture in which that does not happen, and that starts with clear values," the leatherbrown Susquehanna flowing wide beneath us as we crossed south through Pennsylvania, and I believed it when we made our first stop that evening at my father's house in West Virginia, the house where I grew up and lived when the Mist first appeared as a true mist, during the Great Monongahela River Chemical Spill of 1996, an event whose damage was still rippling out across my life, across the dynamic medium of spacetime itself—or so I imagine it after having read the work of the Physicist, though who knows if I've comprehended it correctly—awaiting me in my future in ways I couldn't have ever predicted, couldn't have even conceived of, when Annie and I pulled into the driveway and were greeted by my father standing on the front steps, smoking a cigarette he wasn't supposed to be smoking.

This image of my father smoking brings me to a thought about smoking I've sensed developing since I arrived in Italy but feel I can only now articulate: namely, that when I see older Italian men smoking at a café or on a street corner, men who look not unlike my dad, I feel a small sadness at how dignified they look, knowing that my father has likely never been perceived as "dignified" while smoking, least of all by me. I understand it's basically a cliché as an American to wax about how Europeans look so much more dignified while smoking—free as they are from all the American projections about class and place and health—but that doesn't make it any less true, and it certainly doesn't erase the fact that for my father, cigarettes are one of the few little rituals he can afford, not to mention one of the only ways he could steal away an extra break during a long day of labor, a break he paid for with his health. I've been no saint about this, I know—I spent a lot of my youth complaining about his smoking, only to go on and rip hundreds of cigs myself while *still* ragging on him for doing it, saying things like "You're slowly killing yourself," which might be literally true, but, as I'll continue to show, I'm the last person who should be judging any suicidal behavior, however extenuated. So before I say more about my father, some of which is deeply inelegant and upsetting, I first want to say that I've decided just now that when we arrive in Bologna I'm going to step out of the station during my brief layover and I'm going to smoke a cigarette for my dad, and if that's sentimental, well, I frankly do not give a shit. I'm going to do it and enjoy it for him the way I could tell he was enjoying his cigarette out on the front steps that night that Annie and I arrived from New York, which must have been why, in conjunction with what was my new, less fate-obsessed vibe at the time, I didn't let it frustrate me, and instead gave him a big hug and inhaled his Marlboro scent I'm supposed to hate but love, then stood back and watched him glow upon meeting Annie, as I'd hoped he would, and she met his glow with the glow of her own, a glow I would encounter during my treatment as the immense and unending peach-champagne aura of her very spirit, and for a moment as they embraced they became a single radiating body against the humid dusk of late summer. I could hear the TV playing loudly from the living room, but thankfully it wasn't on Fox News, an accommodating gesture I first attributed to my dad, until I realized of course that my brother, Ben, was home and had changed it himself. I could see him sitting in the living room, his large oxen frame spread across the same mustard-tartan couch I used to sit on as a kid.

Growing up, as I became more and more aware of the tasteful interiors of my friends' homes in the ritzier neighborhoods of

Lafayette Park and Cheat Lake, I learned to hate this house, with its modest ranch floor plan and dark, aged interior. Brown shag carpeting, brown wood-paneled walls, dark brown cabinets in the kitchen, linoleum on the bathroom floor with diamond pendants of brown. Chestnut, raw umber, taupe, burnt umber, cinnamon. Various shades of sand. But that evening, while sitting in the living room, running my hands over the couch's rough upholstery, I looked around and realized for the first time how the space, so obstinate to change—except for the large flat-screen TV—had survived finally into a state of postrecession hipness: the half-rustic/half-midcentury furniture, the wood-paneled walls, the faded family pictures on the walls beside paintings of mallards flying over cattails, and beside those a real mallard, stuffed and mounted in perpetual flight, and beside that a clock made from a tree stump carved into the shape of West Virginia, all of it under the watchful eyes of a stuffed buck mounted above the fireplace, an eight pointer frozen in the same posture of regality and calm regard as my grandfather, the man who'd killed it, making it less a decoration than his idol—it was customary to nod or point at the deer whenever my grandfather's memory was invoked and to turn your back to it during family disagreements. On the mantel: a service photo of my uncle Eugene—my dad's older brother—who died in Vietnam. The ashtrays were ceramic, logoed by Canadian Club. Bars in Bushwick not a year old looked like this and charged fifteen for Bombay with a twist.

I could tell Annie dug it because she walked around looking at everything saying, "I dig it," which made me happy in personal, romantic, and aesthetic ways. Ben was her docent, pointing out the pictures in which I look specifically tragic. I've always hated looking at those pictures, not out of embarrassment, but because I can see the exact shift from carefree child to child burdened by

the Mist. My smile fades from wide and wild to tense and appre-
hensive, as if I could see, just behind the camera, just behind the
awkward photographer's bald head, a small, sinister cloud beginning to gather.

But that night I didn't care. Instead I let Ben take Annie around
while my dad rummaged in the kitchen. And it felt good to see
Ben. Not that we were ever enemies, just that we'd drifted. After
I left West Virginia for art school, he doubled down on life in the
region and chose to skip college and go straight to the frack fields.
He always said it was for the fast cash, but I suspect it was out of a
desire to get lost among the deepest of the deep Appalachians, to
prove that he could make sense of them in a way that I never could
on canvas, which is to say I think he did it not because he craved
money, or because he wanted to work in the fields, or wanted
to stay in Appalachia, but because he wanted to understand our
father—which is to say he wanted to understand the world that
made our father. Whether or not it was working had yet to be
seen. My time away from West Virginia had in so many ways isolated me from it, and the paintings only isolated me further, and
as for my father, well—I'd basically become an alien to him. And
yet there I was, sitting in my childhood home, a truck full of my
possessions parked in the driveway, on my way to California, all
because of some stories I'd written about my time as a Boy Scout
in West Virginia.

Sitting on the couch, drinking a beer out of a glass mug engraved
with the image of the university's Mountaineer mascot, listening
to the cicada song that sounded so delightful, so psychotically full
and unending after years of city noise, I felt happy. I was enjoying
myself. But then I noticed the low bookcase that separated the living room area from the dining area had changed. Specifically, its

contents. Its books were missing—all twenty-nine volumes of the Time-Life Library of Art.

When my mother left us, never to be seen again, only heard from in occasional birthday or Christmas cards Ben and I stopped opening to stave off what they did to us—sometimes they weren't even signed—the only thing she left behind were these books. Twenty-nine volumes. *The World of Goya. The World of Manet. The World of Leonardo.* Each was bound in leather, with embossed gold lettering down the spine, and housed in a cardboard slipcase adorned with a print of one of the artist's works. My mom likely bought the set at a garage sale, likely drunk. They were all that was left of her after she was gone, so I became obsessed with them. I believed she left them for a reason; that they were a kind of code. To crack it, I'd need to read them all and find within the pages, within the images and words, an explanation of why she'd left and what I'd need to do to bring her back. At first it was nearly impossible for me to read them, primarily because I was young and the texts were exceptionally boring, but the images called to me, and right away I began to draw them. This was my earliest education in composition, form, movement. What began as visual echoes in a boyish hand evolved into clearer translations. For each significant image you could find a corresponding page in one of my notebooks. About some artists, and some images, I became a fanatic. I was so committed to Rembrandt's *The Syndics* that I traced it dozens of times until I'd memorized the composition and could draw it on demand. Of course what I was drawing wasn't the painting but a rendering of the print of the painting made even more flat and two-dimensional in graphite gray, but it didn't matter. I did the same with others: one of Lichtenstein's *Brushstroke* paintings, *Canoe in Rapids* by Winslow Homer. Eventually I outgrew the illusion that these books had anything to teach me about my mom, and I never did read them all the way through, even the ones about the artists I most admired were a struggle, but I began to appreciate them differently, perhaps more intensely, for what they provided me—besides a much-needed boost to my education—which was escape.

You would think then that I was growing angry about the missing books because of their connection to my mom or my life in art. And while both of these connections were true emotional links, they did not fully correspond to the anger simmering awake in me. After all, how many years had I been living as a working artist and not once brought them back with me to New York? But to that point I had an answer, an answer I'd held privately for years: I'd made the books into a kind of trophy. However irrational, I'd decided sometime in the months before I left for art school that if these twenty-nine volumes were the germ of my life, then it was only when I'd seen it through and made a career worthy of my own *The World of* that I would allow myself to keep them with me. I can still see them in the daydream, right in the center of my immaculate warehouse studio, all twenty-nine volumes snug in a simple bookcase beside the Eames lounger I'd lean back in while meditating on what to do with the big new canvas stretched by my assistants, a great blank plane glowing under northerly windows, the kind of scene a photographer might like to capture for a profile in *Art in America* or the *Times*: clean light, clean walls, clean floor, clean palette table, clean canvas, clean coveralls, clean haircut, an Eames chair. *And those books,* the journalist would ask, *what's the story with those?*

Those? I'd say almost sheepishly, first glancing back at them, then pausing, knowing that when I turned back the photographer would snap a candid portrait of me with my inelegant, second-hand, and triumphantly democratic origins arranged behind me in soft focus. *Those are where all of this began.*

Embarrassing to admit, perhaps, but posttreatment I don't really care. I understand it. I feel for the boy who thought this way. And anyways, by this point I'd let the fantasy go. If anything, I tried my hardest *not* to think of it because I'd come to believe my failure was partly a punishment for ever having had such a fantasy in the first place. Why then did I feel not only affronted by the books' disappearance but also desperate to solve it? A hot, panicky awakening in my pulse becoming panicky, sublingual thoughts. I can almost feel it again now, except—just as it felt when I revisited past moments during the treatment—there is a space between me and it, and through that space I can begin to make sense of what was happening that night while I was sitting on that mustard-tartan couch in the living room in which I grew up, and my conclusion is that I wanted to transform the totemic power of those books from a foundational catalyst for my painting into an explanation for *The Troop*. Wasn't it possible that these twenty-nine volumes that taught me how artists are products of their realities might have also taught me to see how people are products of their realities more generally? Sure, I barely glossed most of the texts, but eventually I learned to connect the dots. So couldn't *The Troop* have been a product of me doing a thing I'd learned to do years before, including during the years about which I was writing? Was it so different, being able to understand that young Pablo paints blue paintings because his friend Casagemas kills himself, and that thirteen-year-old Tenderfoot Roger Martinelli's speech impediment made him at once quiet, wounded, and capable of great compassion? These, I think, were the thoughts crawling out from under the back stairs of my mind while I sat fuming on the mustard-tartan couch. I needed those books—and maybe drove all the way to West Virginia to get them—because I was desperate for any sort of proof that the free-wheeling stories that became *The Troop* weren't happy accidents, because happy accidents didn't happen to me. "I don't know how I did it, they just kind of appeared" was not an acceptable explanation. No: these stories must be things whose origins could be traced down a clear line, cause and effect. Those Time-Life books would be the cause I desperately needed in order to justify to myself, however privately, that what I'd made was real, even if I didn't know how I did it, and that I was worthy of whatever good came of it. That's why I was so mad, I think.

And now, as the Frecciarossa cuts through the placid fields of Lazio at a smooth 256 kilometers per hour, leaving the last of Rome's outskirts behind, I sense the phantom of that anger receding as I consider for the first time that those books must have been such a colossal source of pain for my father. I blame the Mist and all its mechanisms for keeping me from understanding how hard it was for him to see, every day for decades, these tokens left behind by the love of his life who'd up and abandoned him, and to not only see them but see his one son obsesses over them to the point that I wouldn't even notice when my father was in the room until he performatively grunted or rustled the pages of his newspaper, so that even in my mother's absence it must have felt like she pulled more sway than his presence, a cruel taunt, and as I realize this now, alone in seat 19D, my heart hurts in a way I am grateful for, grateful for what it teaches me, for the way it makes me want to call my dad long distance and say thank you, though of course I can't, he wouldn't know what to do with what I was saying and would probably think I'm drugged, but I want to say it, so I'm saying it now: *Thank you for keeping the books there as long as you did. I am so sorry for how they must've made you feel.*

But that night I was not thinking like this. No, that night I was in a rage, not only for the reasons explained, but because they'd been replaced with shitty DVDs that looked like the bootlegs sold outside my neighborhood Key Food in Brooklyn, bootlegs primarily of Steven Seagal movies, in fact. I wasted no time walking into the kitchen and asking my dad where the hell my books were. He was biting a cigarette, wearing an apron, the sleeves of his Woolrich rolled up, stirring a pot of my Italian grandmother's Sunday gravy recipe. "They're in your room," he said calmly.

"Why are they in my room? You should've asked me before you touched them."

"I needed room for my DVDs."

"DVDs? Those are shit bootlegs, Dad. Who sold them to you?"

"I made them." He kept stirring.

I took a beer out of the fridge, refilled my mug, and went to my room—I hadn't gone in it since getting home, our bags still in the truck—to check on the books. They were all there, stacked neatly on my dresser, but that didn't change things. It still felt like a violation.

When I walked back into the living room my brother and Annie were sitting awkwardly on the couch. There was a kind of faux nonchalance to her posture that made me think she could indeed feel how she was likely the first feminine presence in that room in years and had to slowly make space for herself, even in the air around her. "Why don't you come relax," she said. I sat between them, sipped my beer, turned to Ben. "What's the deal with the DVDs? Did you know about this?"

"I guess I thought you knew. Dad learned how to work the burner on his computer and now he's been ordering movies from Netflix and copying them and collecting them and giving them to people as gifts. He buys the plastic cases too. Prints covers for them and everything. When was the last time you went downstairs?"

"What's downstairs?"

"You should probably go downstairs."

I STEPPED DOWN the raw-pine stairs into the dark basement. My whole life it had been half finished: some of the walls were bare studs, others were Sheetrocked but unpainted, the floor cold concrete. But that's not what my feet met when I reached the bottom; instead—the industrial knit of blue office carpet. I flicked the light switch, but the room stayed dark. My eyes strained to adjust. Bars of moonlight angled down from the thin ground-level windows. The room felt solemn, tomblike. Slowly I walked in and began to see that where there used to be an old couch and a TV on an island of scrap carpet, the place where Ben and I hung out with friends and learned to drink beer and roll joints and eventually felt the earliest thrills of our hands sliding under the elastic of girls' underwear, there were now tall white shelves lining the walls, with additional white shelves arranged like aisles across the floor. I could tell, even through the dark, that they were stocked with DVDs. Hundreds of them. Maybe thousands. I walked into the aisles, rolling my feet, like I was worried I might awake something. Blue-and-gold placards were mounted over different shelves: ACTION, COMEDY, FAMILY. The deeper I wandered between the shelves the more I could feel the present slipping away, each step leading me further into a place of pure nostalgia, an ominous shifting I could almost hear, like an old bell ringing from within. I did not ever want to feel like young me again, and yet that room, that chamber of the past, not only brought me back, it brought me back so furiously I could feel present-me getting slowly erased. I was certain the ghost of young Ben would soon come around the corner with a VHS in hand, and if there was one thing I wasn't prepared to deal with it was the ghost of young Ben, to look at him under his mess of thick hair, his smile oblivious to the suffering awaiting us when Mom would leave, when the Great Spill would happen, when Dad would unravel. I was whittled and light, like my marrow was drying up, and I was tapped into a frequency I can only describe as apocalyptic loneliness—the loneliness of those spirits preserved within the transported interior, but maybe more so the loneliness of my father's mind, the crack-up of which I was now standing within.

Reflecting on this moment now in seat 19D, knowing what I know from the reading I've done of the Physicist's writing, I can't help but think of a diagram in one of his books about time, showing how light cones could return to the same point in spacetime. I have no fucking clue how to articulate this properly—it's a complicated point, so complicated even the Physicist had to use a diagram to make it clear. All I can say is that since my treatment I understand this on a level that feels very—how should I say—*unnaturally natural,* meaning I'm not quite sure how I know it in the innate way that I do. And yet to question how I know it, let alone articulate it, brings forth a sense of disassociation and imposed metacognition and general dizziness I associate with learning grammar as a kid. The point is that this idea, about light cones returning to a point in spacetime, perhaps that's precisely what had happened then, in that room: I'd reentered a point in spacetime. I don't know . . . what I do know is that something splintered through me, I dropped my beer, and I fled back up the stairs on hands and feet, like I was a boy again, because I was.

Ben was staring expectantly at the basement door from the living room, waiting for me to resurface. So was Annie, except her eyes were begging me to come save her from the silent boys' club. I was too confused to be angry with Ben and my dad for not being more active hosts—they're great conversationalists when they want to be, but Annie's innate cosmopolitanism clearly made them insecure. I collapsed back on the couch between Ben and Annie. My dad was now sitting in his recliner, watching baseball, a beer in his hand resting on the shelf his belly made.

I tried to speak. "Are those shelves from—"

"From Blockbuster? Yes, yes, they are," said Ben. "He bought them. All of them. And the yellow-and-blue signs. He went to Blockbuster on the day they closed and bought their *used* carpet."

"That was a sad day for this town," said my dad, staring at the screen.

I asked him what the hell was going on and he acted incredulous, said he was making a collection. "Is there a movie you want? Name a movie and I'll get it for you."

"I don't own a DVD player," I said, trying to stay level. "I stream everything. Everyone streams everything. DVDs are dead technology. How did you afford all that? Are you blowing your disability checks on this? Those discs and cases aren't cheap. And you're printing labels, with the cost of the ink, how many have you made? How much money have you wasted?"

"It's not a waste. And I'm not sure how many I've made. I get ten movies at a time from Netflix through the mail, which is the maximum they allow—robbery considering what they charge. Then I go down to the public library and get more. They only let me take fifty at a time. Can you believe that? I pay my damn taxes. But that's the government."

I pretended for a moment like everything I was hearing was totally normal, and then I lost my cool, went off, started asking at a high volume what the fuck was going on. He got pissed, started yelling back, saying how he didn't expect me to understand, living in the world I live in, the bubble I chose, the elitist bullshit of New York, but one day I'd see, I'd understand what he understands, we've got to collect all the media we can now, before it's too late. "I want nothing to do with that streaming stuff," he said. "It's precisely the problem. You kids don't even realize what's going on. They've already got you in their grasp. No DVD player! Ha! Nope, not happening here, not in this house. Everything is through the Internet with your generation. That's exactly how they want it. That's how they're taking over all media. That's how they got your generation by the balls. Pretty soon you won't be able to find half these movies or shows. It's all getting wiped away, edited, reformatted for their liberal agendas. PC police. You stream a movie now and put it side by side with one of my DVDs, and you'll see, there are differences. Chilling differences. Things hidden in the scenes. Bits of talking. Characters going on about their love of the government. Other things are erased. It's what they want. They want to get everyone on streaming so they can control it. Then you'll only be able to see what they want you to see. But not me. I've got it here. This is a stockpile. And I'm not the only one. There're more out there like me. These are liberty libraries. What's America when you change its movies? I'll show you the clip where the guy explains it."

"No! I don't want to see any clips. I know who you're talking about and he's a nut!"

"He bought some of his protein powder," said Ben. "It upset his stomach."

"Goddamn it, Benjamin. You know damn well I already had stomach problems!"

I wanted to remind him that his "stomach problems" have been a long-debunked entry on his hypochondriacal rap sheet, but doing so would've likely caused him to tear the house down, so I refrained, breathed, picked a different battle. "You realize watching that quack online is streaming, right?"

"That's a misconception. That's digital TV, what he does. He's got to run his show through the Internet because mainstream media providers won't let him on the air, big shocker. 'Freedom of speech' my ass. But it's the same as being on the TV. Same technology. There's a whole segment that explains it. I'll pull it up if I have to."

He wasn't always this way. There was bitterness, sure, and cynicism, and distrust of the government, but that was part of being West Virginian. It was only after he got hurt and couldn't work and had to start accepting disability checks that things got strange. He stopped socializing, started obsessively watching the news, and replaced his sweat-stained Mountaineers baseball cap with a generically patriotic one he bought at the drugstore. It was like watching a teenager, the way he slid so obliviously into a uniformed social type while believing he'd never been freer from the fog of herd mind. Most teenlike of all, he began to relentlessly shit-talk and complain about abstract groups of people defined mainly by things he also did, especially "the takers." There is no self-hatred like that of the workingman who can't work, and there's nothing more dangerous than a self-hating workingman with an Internet connection.

As we drifted apart I tried to make sense of it all. What I've learned over time is that my father is a species of man who is defined by interaction. It's as if only through the countless interactions of his highly physical working life—with the other workers, the materials, the thousands of minor tasks that make up a massive project, the great machine of labor—that he existed, was articulated, was shown to be real, and that when these were taken away it was up to Ben and me to be the system with which he interacted, but because he was alone he lost his sense of shape and self, not unlike how "the electron is concrete only *in relation to* the other physical objects it is interacting with," and I want to make clear right now that that sentence is not mine, it's from one of the Physicist's books, and yet it just came through me as if I was quoting myself, and this keeps happening, and with concepts too, like with the light cones, they arrive in my mind not as associations but as deeply internalized pieces of knowledge, which they aren't, or shouldn't be, I can't explain it, and yet to resist them now would be a waste of a gift, because they're helping me see how my father's basement project wasn't driven by paranoia but desperation. We'd gone away, Ben and I, and so he was rapidly coming apart, and knew it. It's as if, in some last-ditch attempt to halt his disintegration, he tried to re-create a pocket of the past in which we were not only still there, we were everything, like when we were boys and every Friday he took us to Blockbuster and together we browsed the shelves, each selecting a dream to be shared, but I couldn't see this then in the living room. Instead I stopped interrupting him, stopped trying to argue, in part because I couldn't deal with how he looked back at me like I was the craziest, saddest person he'd ever seen. I excused myself to get our bags. Annie said she'd help and followed me out. Standing behind the cover of the truck, she asked if I was okay and I said sure, I was fine, except that my father was losing his mind. She asked if she could give me a hug, and while I didn't want to be touched, I said yes, and the hug was soothing while it lasted, but as soon as we unembraced I felt crummy again. "I think I need to shower," I said.

"I think that's a good idea."

"Could I ask a favor?"

"Of course."

"Would you go down to the basement at some point while I'm showering and look around and tell me if I was overreacting?"

She hesitated, then agreed.

While the bathroom filled with steam, I sat naked on the toilet and listened to a meditation app Annie had asked me to try—this was one of my earliest attempts at meditation; I've since been consumed by the practice. Thinking back to that moment, I can't help but laugh now, realizing for the first time that I'd fled into the bathroom only to fill it with steam, a kind of mist, because I didn't know how to feel frustrated or sad without it.

The meditation app I used was the voice of a man with a soft English accent who teaches you to breathe with such intention that eventually you can sit back and observe the traffic of your mind pass by without associating with it, but it wasn't working, so I set my phone aside and stepped under the water and let it scald me scalp to ankles, any sensation to supplant my urge to cry, which I did anyways, rejecting the Brit's advice by associating wholesale with my sadness and letting me and young me and all the other mes Russian-dolled inside me have a moment of release, a moment of mourning, as I accepted that my father's gradual decline as a generally sad but loving man of the Rust Belt had now nose-dived into angry paranoia, a schism of the mind, and should you have pulled back the plastic shower curtain then, you'd have seen me in an apish Malasana pose, rocking on my heels, the water burning me pink. As the tears slowed I made a bowl with my hands to catch the water streaming off my head. I told myself the bowl was my obsessive need to control my emotions, meaning the water was my emotions, meaning my emotions were overflowing and that was okay, because it was impossible to catch all the water, and it looked beautiful falling over my hands, rivering across the scuzzy bottom.

I surprised myself by how willingly I let these metaphors inhabit me. They had a mystical force so strong I was able to fall back into the breathing patterns suggested by the app, and for a moment my sense of time and place collapsed into the patter of rainfall, the aroma of my bodywash performing its billed therapy as I experienced a catharsis across time, something I didn't yet understand was possible, and wouldn't fully understand until years later during my treatment when, for example, I could feel my body healing in my bed in every bedroom I'd ever had, all at once, all those versions of myself in glowing, tranquil repair.

When I left the bathroom after my shower I caught Annie looking at me from the couch, her eyes charged with a singular message: *You have a Blockbuster in your basement.*

WHEN WE SAT DOWN for dinner, Annie took the seat at the head of the table opposite my dad, where my grandmother used to sit. I don't think anyone had sat there since she'd passed away. Seeing a woman there made us men pause for a moment, sit up a little straighter, but also relax a little more.

The dinner was a real treat. A classic Italian American spread. Sunday gravy, sausages, sliced meats, mozzarella—we were getting after it and it felt good; Annie too—she is a terrific eater. We were drinking table wine out of squat glasses, like how my grandmother used to do it, and my dad even put down her old tablecloth. He asked Annie about Chicago without mentioning Obama, which was impressive, and she responded with familiar anecdotes about "the most suburban suburb," before eventually getting onto the subject of her grandmother's jewelry studio, describing it how she'd first described it to me, and when she mentioned "the little foundry area" my dad really perked up, saying, "A foundry area?" and then she said, "That's right. For casting work mostly. It sounds more impressive than it is. Ninety percent of what went on was your standard bench work, classic smithing stuff. Forming, filing, polishing. And lots of soldering," which caused my dad to set his fork down and pull his napkin over his mouth and say, "You know how to solder?" "I haven't in forever," she said, "but I don't think you lose it," and at this my dad turned to me and said, "Do you know how to solder?" in a way that made me feel both jealous of Annie and like I pretty much hated him, and while I wanted to say, *No, I don't know how to solder because your ass never thought to teach me in the eighteen years you had the chance to,* I took a sip of wine instead and said, "Not yet, but I'm hoping she'll teach me," then shoved some bread in my mouth to hide my embarrassment as Ben started chiming in too, he of course knowing his way around metal from his work, and soon enough all three were going on about how "the forgiveness of copper is also what can make it tricky" and how "anvil work is all about your hammer, everyone thinks the metal is what's tough, but if you don't have the right hammer, then forget it," until eventually she'd ingratiated herself so deeply into the group that she'd hemmed me out of it in the process, however unintentionally, leaving me to sit on the perimeter and witness her experiencing a level of intrigue from my father I hadn't felt since I don't know when. It was a confusing moment. But again, as I'd tried to do all evening, I let it go, chewed in silence, and eventually the conversation shifted. We talked sports, we talked food, we talked about my grandmother, we talked about California, and the fellowship, the unexpectedness of it all, and it was then that Annie mentioned how exciting it was that the stories that got me there were going to be a book, and when she said this I could feel the eyes of my father and brother slowly turn on me—I hadn't told them about the book yet. Not on purpose. It simply wasn't something we did, sharing good news. It had to happen naturally, and that natural moment hadn't yet happened. In fact, I hadn't really told them about the stories either. In part because I wasn't sure they really knew what stories were, in the sense of a story being out there in the world in a magazine. Not because they're dumb, but because it isn't a part of their ecosystem. Both stick with nonfiction. "What do you mean a book? Like, a book book?" said my dad, and Annie jumped right in, just kind of ran with it, saying, "Yes, a book, like the ones you can buy at Barnes and Noble," and at first I could see them sort of shocked, then excited, then proud, but then, as she started describing *The Troop,* its structure and subject of interconnected stories about the members of a Boy Scout troop, based on the Boy Scout troop of which my brother and I were both Eagle Scout alums, and to which my father was still connected, I could see their faces drop with skepticism, then concern, then something like anger. "So these are fictional, huh?" said my brother. "These are fake stories."

"Well, yes," I said. "But they're inspired by experiences with our troop, obviously."

"But if they're fiction I don't have to worry about recognizing anything, do I?"

"Well, you might recognize some things, but it's fiction. I changed things. Why do you sound worried?"

"Maybe I don't want to show up in a book, that's all. How real is it?"

"What do you mean by 'real'?"

And then he asked the eternal question of the West Virginian. "I mean do we all look like a bunch of dumb hillbillies?"

"No, Ben. But I portrayed some stuff how it is, and to some people that might seem hillbillyish, and maybe some things are. That's how it goes."

"Well, who says you get to say how any of it is? Who says you get to use any of our stories?"

"It's fucking America, Ben." I couldn't believe I said that aloud. "It's fiction and it's America and I lived it all as much as you did."

"Oh, America. He's into America now, baby. Now that it got him the big fellowship he talks about America. Mr. Freedom of Speech over here."

"Oh, fuck off, Ben. Fuck off! You could've done it. You could've written it. It's not like I'm some fucking whiz or something. Write them yourself if you're so fucking worried, see if I care. All that would require is for you to stop pretending you're a roughneck for once. Big shocker why you're so worried about how you're portrayed. Don't worry, I'll give you an accent."

Many *fuck you*s began to fly. Ben backed up his chair like he was ready to pounce, so I backed up mine and moved a hand across Annie like we were stopping too fast at a red light, and while there was no music playing, it suddenly felt like there was music playing and it was playing very loudly, and finally my dad slammed his hand on the table.

"I have mesothelioma," he said.

Ben and I looked at each other, a mutual exhaustion suspended between us. I kindly asked my dad what the fuck he was talking about.

Again he said, "I have mesothelioma."

"Jesus Christ. When was this diagnosed?" I asked. "Why haven't you told us something was wrong."

"I didn't want you to worry."

"But when were you diagnosed?"

"Well, I haven't been yet, but I know it. I can feel it. I guess I've always known it was going to happen because of working on the basketball Coliseum." The Coliseum was the infamous arena where the university basketball team played. "The whole place was infested with asbestos."

"You didn't *work* on the Coliseum. You were on a cement crew in the nineties who did some repairs."

"But it hadn't been removed by then. I can feel it in my lungs. I've got the cough. I've got the pain in my lower back. The symptoms are there. I saw what it did to Jerry Yount and now it's like I'm living it too. He was gone in nine months, you know." He coughed and I couldn't tell if it was performative or because of the Marlboro he was smoking, its gray tendrils creeping low over the table.

"The work you did wouldn't have exposed you to asbestos," I said. "And Jerry Yount helped build the damn place. He suffered real exposure." My face was getting hot, my jaws tight like a stirred mutt. Something like a freight train was barreling forward from the back of my mind, a rant assembling about how my father has mesothelioma like he has Crohn's like he has early onset Alzheimer's like he has rheumatoid arthritis and it'd be better for everyone the sooner he accepts that he can't work anymore because he got hurt on the job and that's okay, no one judges him for it, he'd busted his ass his whole life and he doesn't have to latch on to diseases he doesn't have to assuage his shame, especially when he *does* have early stage COPD but chooses to ignore it, but instead I said, "Well, Dad, when you get diagnosed we'll figure out the treatment plan, and then we'll get you a lawyer, and he'll get you a will figured out, if you haven't done that yet. But until then, let's have some sambuca." I surprised myself at how I handled it, and I could tell Annie was surprised too.

I got the sambuca out of the liquor cabinet and my dad got out the glasses my grandmother had blown herself down at the glass factory where she'd worked, the very glass factory that brought her parents and her, as a baby, here from Venice, along with most all the other Italians around, to set up Little Murano on the banks of the Monongahela, and soon we were all at peace again, talking casually, and I was rolling the tablecloth's tatted ends between my fingers like I did as a child waiting to be excused from the table as the adults had their sambuca, just as I was having it then, and I began to feel how I felt all those Sundays ago when I was young and messy, always spilling Sunday gravy on my patch of tablecloth, and always my grandmother would laugh and say "Va bene" as she leaned over and wiped my face, a gesture so tender it compelled me, I think, to be even sloppier in hopes of her repeating it, and as I'd sit there, still waiting to be excused, I'd suppress my fidgety boredom by putting the stained ends of the tablecloth in my mouth to suck on the sauce patches, and I want to say that in that moment I was salivating out of nostalgia for that special flavor of ragù and detergent, but it could've been from the licorice flavor of the sambuca, the medicinal rinse of its alcohol, its punch of anise; one sip of the licorice flavor and the whole experience of the Great Monongahela River Chemical Spill of 1996 comes rushing back into the body—the licorice smell of the chemical that poisoned the river, then the water supply, then our bodies, our very cells, and how it made us all spit nonstop for weeks—but wait.

Okay. This is something . . . a very sudden and acute hot-flash-and-falling-gut combo has me gripping the end of my hard plastic armrest and leaning my face over the small AC vent inset below the window to catch its cooling updraft, for what's just overcome me is a fast, uneasy slippage of the body and mind as I realize I am unable to say for certain if that memory I just remembered remembering—the one about my grandmother leaning over and speaking to me in Italian and wiping my face—is in fact my memory and not a memory of the Physicist's relayed to me in one of his recordings that I transcribed into prose for his memoir.

AGAIN, THIS IS PART of the larger something that's been happening since the treatment—in part because of what happened during the treatment, which I'll explain eventually—but not always with such a wallop. What I mean is that at times it feels as if, having been the Physicist's ghostwriter over the past year, I spent so much time considering his memories, inhabiting them so that I could put them into proper prose, that they've become part of my own mind. They've become part of my own memory, not via replacement or overlap, but as natural fits, a feeling only amplified during certain moments of the treatment, which, again, I will explain soon enough. But what I wonder is if these memories have in fact become a part of me—what does that mean? "We are *histories* of ourselves, narratives . . . ," writes the Physicist about memory. "If all this disappeared, would I still exist?" I sat quietly and let my dad talk to Annie about my grandmother, describing her with great accuracy as the incredible woman she was, to whom I owe most of my qualities, I know, including the very little bit of Italian I've retained and have used while traveling here in Italy. After our drinks, Annie and I said goodbye to Ben and drove to the family storage locker to unload some of my paintings and art supplies, where I'd keep them while in California. The fellowship was only for two years and it was unclear what would happen after, so I figured it was best to store them there, where it was free. But I think it's more likely I put them there because I wasn't sure if I'd ever paint again and I wasn't sure if I'd ever go back to West Virginia, at least not anytime soon, and so this was a way of sort of dropping them into the middle of the sea.

On the way home from the storage unit I was suddenly overwhelmed with nostalgia for my hometown, a feeling that came rarely but, when it did, came with a fury, so I decided to drive Annie up to a secluded lookout point on a hill where I used to go in my car in high school to smoke weed. "Whoa," said Annie when we parked. I was surprised she was so impressed. "I'm not used to this," she said. "We didn't have lookouts where I grew up. It was so flat. All you could see were your neighbors or trees. I've never *seen* my hometown."

Hearing that, I reawakened to all of Morgantown stretched before us: the Monongahela River making its gentle crawl north to Pittsburgh, bending its way around downtown; the courthouse's redbrick spires rising proudly over the square; the vivid glow and strobe of neon red on High Street; the surrounding streets named for common trees and forgotten statesmen; buildings built of cream-colored brick and brick-colored brick, granite and bluestone; the humble city grid climbing the hillside, meshing with the university campus, the jewel of the state of West Virginia. From up there you could see university buildings in the Federalist style, the Second Empire style, Italianate columns and belvedere towers, the Second Empire Eclectic, pergolas and onion domes, iron finials and venetian windows, brutalism for hard sciences, Queen Anne for humanities—all these categories I never knew in the years I lived here but only learned about later in art history classes in art school—rows of dorms and fraternity houses give way to the rundown college houses of Little Murano in a patchwork of clapboard and shingle. Beyond the hills you could see the warmer radiant light of neighborhoods old and new, and beyond them the wisps of production steam trailing like miniature clouds from the exhaust stacks at the Alderwright Pharmaceuticals plant, the town's second-largest employer, and then beyond that the brighter sterile light from the research campus and satellite dorms, the hospital and medical school, the football stadium and basketball Coliseum, all of it nestled into dips between the rolling land, town to farm, field to forest, where the trees steamed in the evening air, steaming like the soft green farmlands we've begun to leave behind now on the Frecciarossa, pitching upward into the low hills, catching sight of the occasional villa once owned by a low-level landowner unseated only so many decades ago, and it's like I can feel, truly, the smooth, pleasant linking of fresh synapses in my mind as the past hardens with a new clarity, and I understand finally how all this recollection was toward this point: it was then, sitting there at the overlook looking over the city, that the seed was planted in my subconscious to write a novel about the Great Monongahela River Chemical Spill of 1996, to describe what happened to that glittering landscape of perpetual decay, an image I'd spend the next years in California, unbeknownst to me then, failing to portray, to make sense of, to untangle, to write a single word about, an artistic failure so immense that it put me here, on the Frecciarossa, hurtling into the north of Italy, Bologna to Modena, in search of a theoretical physicist who owes me his life's story so that maybe, just maybe, I'll have a chance at scratching my way out of the financial hell created when I cashed and spent the advance checks for the novel of a place I never had the means, or will, to tell.

I wish I'd known all this then.

No, that's not right.

Since the treatment I am at peace with what has happened, with the mess of things; I've learned, thanks to the treatment, that there is no benefit, none at all, in attempting to resist the sequence of what we call the past. I've learned that resistance is the root of so much frustration and pain. So perhaps what I am curious about is, how did I convince myself, when I signed the novel deal, that I *did* want to tell the story of the Great Spill? Posing that question makes me understand immediately that the money convinced me. The publisher—a New York mammoth different from the indie press behind *The Troop*—offered me a lot of money. More money than I'd ever imagined being offered. This was because *The Troop* did well. It got a lot of attention. More attention than I could have ever imagined, because I'd never imagined anything I'd written getting any attention because I'd never imagined myself as a writer, period.

WE LEFT WEST VIRGINIA the morning after our dinner with my father and Ben. The truck got on the interstate and ate up the road, climbing the hills, fat trees blurring past in a stream of greens and dark mountain shade, long slopes rising and dropping, leading us west toward where the dawn held on, still pregnant with the potential narratives of the day to come, the years to come, the sun at our backs as the hills leveled out into the rolling fields of Ohio, unambitious but honest, past dormant smokestacks and oil derricks abandoned in pastures, rusted and chipped, past Lake Erie country with its wide low sky and northern grays and around there is where I felt a pang of sadness and nostalgia for the world left behind, but it didn't matter as long as we stayed facing west, so we drove and kept driving past the fecal scent of Gary, Indiana, and the faint outline of Chicago shimmering in the night, and we took a motel somewhere in Iowa, a nonplace, a place where the facts of our life wouldn't mean anything to anyone, and by the time we got into the bed I was half dozed and my lower back was so sore it felt pumped full of napalm, but I was certain we were entering the new possible goodness, and though it felt like I was suddenly too tired to sleep I somehow woke up in the morning to Annie dressed and ready to drive, and I drank water poured straight from the faucet and told her all I wanted was to be in the truck so we got back in and bought drive-thru coffee and I quizzed her on interview questions while she led us fast into the plains where the road straightens out and the curvature of the earth bends faintly across the length of the windshield against which bugs died in small blips and explosive smacks of goo we'd occasionally stop to wipe off, then keep moving, and somewhere near Cheyenne we slept in a motel with a painting on the wall of two cowboys wrapped in horse blankets huddled around a fire, and in the middle of the night I woke and stood outside the room and smoked cigarettes and watched, I swear, a snowstorm in the middle of summer drag its way over the land, a fast wall of falling white that swallowed every sound and in the time it took me to smoke half a pack a few inches had sugared the parking lot, and the way the snow smelled and sparkled felt clean and brand-new and then when Annie woke it was gone, hot again and dry, and we drove on through the red earth country that felt Martian and soulless but also thrilling and kept on into the mountains so unlike my mountains, all sharp angles and stone, and then down into the sweeping grid of Salt Lake City with its double-wide boulevards and along the shores of the great dead water and back out into desert land, the wasteland, over into Nevada, and the truck kept moving, and I felt like I understood the secrets of the great wide-open expanse, the flat empty dust-strewn nothings, how they articulated a new emptiness in me, a serene emptiness, the calm left over after a natural disaster when the debris is dragged away and the trash is gone and the totaled houses are torn down, and though nothing's been fixed yet, it's quiet and things are going to get fixed, you can just tell, and somewhere out there in Nevada we slept again in another motel where the walls were painted the color of the earth and I slept there truly, a real sleep, a sleep I hadn't slept in years, and the TV stayed off, and when we woke up we drove again through dirty shimmering heat into the incandescent spasms of Reno light and then the almost fictional-looking Sierras with their snowcaps and slate grays and sharp pines and then we dropped into the Central Valley and around Sacramento, all flat and busy with big rigs groaning toward the continent's end, and then we rose again into low hills that trace the edge of San Pablo Bay, spitting us out into Richmond, then down along the edge of Berkeley, and to our right the waters became the San Francisco Bay and both of us stared wide eyed and childlike at its shining azure madness, and then the infinite Pacific framed in the Golden Gate, its grandness and its indifference to the world, and then we crossed the Bay Bridge and I counted the mammoth container ships crawling in and chugging out and I wondered when the last time was that I had a mind quiet enough to count tankers, and then we cruised into San Francisco and the streets cut up and down like they did back home in West Virginia and we both said that to each other, Annie and I, that the streets are like West Virginia's, the fast hills, the steep turns, and at the Golden Gate Bridge we got out and smelled the winds that had blown there all the way from Asia and watched the water shift from emerald to cobalt to slate to a green more brilliant than the emerald before, and I was crazy enough to think that's all it'd take—a quick drive across the country—to finally sever myself from my own private hell, when it turned out to be right there, waiting for us, with arms as open as the land.

→

A FEW DAYS AFTER our arrival Annie had her interviews: two full days of face-to-face meetings at the AI R & D offices in a newly converted auto-body-repair building in SoMa, a satellite to the company's larger Valley campus. She spent the night after the first interview day sitting on the floor of our Airbnb, typing up as many of her answers as she could remember, combing her performance for flaws, while also doing yoga stretches. Later I watched her practice for her presentation, including a PowerPoint she kept referring to as a "deck." I couldn't make much sense of its content, but her delivery was strong, if a little nervy. When I shared this feedback she said, "Right now I'm at thirty minutes of surging motivation, then thirty of nausea, then thirty of pure fatigue, but tomorrow it'll be more like half motivation, half fatigue, so the nerves won't be noticeable and I'll suppress the fatigue until they let me go to the bathroom and I can close my eyes in a stall for five minutes."

The next morning I thought I heard her crying in the bathroom where she was getting ready. I stuck my head in and asked if she was okay. I could see her wipe her eyes in the mirror. "I'm sorry," she said. "It's a lot of pressure. I've been waiting for this chance for a while and, with what it could mean for us, especially down the line, should we—"

"You can't worry about all that, not now. You'll drive yourself crazy. You said it yourself, you've been waiting for this. You've got it. Enjoy it, even. You're as prepared as you can be. No matter what happens we'll be fine."

Back alone in the hallway, I was overcome with shame that she felt responsible for us, like all I brought to the table was precariousness, uncertainty. At the edges of this shame were my old haunts—extreme self-criticism, self-hatred—but I had the good sense to know that now was not the time and pushed it all away.

That evening I met her around the corner from the offices when she was finally finished, and we walked to a quiet sushi counter. She was thoroughly fried, saying again and again without realizing it, "I've done all I could do," and "I think I did well, but you can never know for sure," while dipping the same piece of fish in soy sauce sometimes two or three times, the day's events replaying behind her eyes. I felt so proud of her.

We spent the next day, a Friday, walking Golden Gate Park. It was our last day in the city before we could move into our place in Oakland. Annie had no info on when we'd hear about her job. We'd scoured industry message boards for clues, but this was an awful idea—some people said if you don't hear anything before you leave the building you're basically fucked, while others claimed you shouldn't expect a call for a month, minimum. We tried to stay busy, taking in the park's diaphanous light, the Monterey cypresses held in their wind-tilted gestures, Annie doing whatever she could not to check and recheck her phone. By late afternoon we figured we wouldn't hear anything until the next week, relaxed, and decided to tour the botanical gardens. It was in there, while I took a photo of Annie standing in the riotous bloom of the Andean Cloud Forest, that she got the offer call. We shared a very emotional moment at the base of a wax palm. I had to wipe my nose on my hand, then my hand on the rough trunk. The sense of accomplishment Annie felt, the uncomplicated joy behind it all—I studied it. You could almost feel out in front of her all the swirling data points of possibility assembling at last into a plot, a plan made manifest, elegant and unthreatening. All I had to do was not fuck it up. I pretended like there wasn't a part of me waiting to feel a familiar scratching at the back of my brain, the first murmur of old worry, and did such a good job that eventually there wasn't.

The next day we moved to Oakland. We spent our first month there staring at the grapefruit tree outside our apartment, struggling to understand how free food was growing right there for the taking. We had grapefruit with everything—salad, tequila, in the vinaigrette on the salad, smoothies—so much grapefruit we both got canker sores from all the acid. Other times we'd just sit on the couch and watch the sunlight move through the room—it started when the sun came up and didn't stop until the sun went down—truly amazing.

Meanwhile my only obligation for the fellowship was to go to campus once a week for three hours to discuss my work with LD, the writer who'd selected me. LD has a ferocious but thoroughly intimate spirit, an immense mind, and an iconic body of work of mainly slim, piercing, often groundbreaking novels that have won essentially every literary award you can think of save the Nobel—she's one of our best. For these reasons, I had no business being there in her company, and yet we got along quite well. We spent that first year polishing *The Troop* before publication. She was very hard on my work, but it never shook me, likely because I still hadn't adopted the identity of "writer" into my ego, so there was nothing for her critiques to wound. She also loved to eat, like me, so over time our sessions spilled into evenings when we'd try the different Szechuan restaurants in the Bay Area, ordering a family's worth of dishes we'd then critique against the other restaurants while discussing books and art. Eventually Annie, who was a fan of LD's work, having studied some of her novels in college, began to join us, especially if we were eating in the city, where she could meet us easily after work. It was through this ritual that we grew comfortable with California as home, and through which I grew comfortable with the idea of writer as a part of who I was.

One of the restaurants we frequented in the Inner Richmond was known for hosting a *bian lian* performer on Sundays, a fact we'd forgotten—LD, Annie, and I—when we made a reservation to dine there one spring Sunday after attending a reading together. The *bian lian* performer—part of Szechuan opera, the menu explained—would appear in the middle of dinner service, clad in a large black-and-red silk cape and an elaborate headdress and mask. As speedy music blared through the speakers, the performer would march around the room, swiping his cape over his face in a swift gesture less than a second in length, but in which time his mask would change, always to the crowd's immense delight and awe. It was not that we disliked the performance, only that at this particular restaurant it would sometimes go on for upward of an hour, the entirety of which you felt socially obligated to stay engaged. Part of what made the performance awkward, beyond its length, was that nearly everyone in the restaurant acted incredulous about how the trick of the changing mask was managed, when it seemed pretty obvious that each mask was in fact a piece of fabric stretched tightly over many other fabric masks, and that some mechanism triggered by the performer would release one mask, allowing it to slide up into the headdress, revealing the new mask beneath it, the sliding motion hidden by his silk sleeves waved before his face. But on this evening, midway through the performance, the mask malfunctioned. The performer twirled his sleeve in front of his face, only to reveal the mask half transformed—the top half a somber green-and-purple design, the bottom a wicked red-and-black grin. The room lost its collective breath, but the performer didn't notice. He twirled his sleeve again, and again the mask malfunctioned, so that now it had dragged up into uneven thirds—green-and-purple eyes, a red-and-black flared nose, and a gold-and-red frown. "Now this is interesting," said LD. By now the floor manager had signaled to the performer what was wrong. The crowd, eager to dissolve the tension, began clapping and smiling even more incredulously than before. Annie, LD, myself—we all were. This made the performer perform even more dramatically, swinging his sleeves with immense flourish, but again the masks caught, another and another, until the face was a collage of color and emotion that looked altogether tortured. Still, the crowd clapped, smiled, some even began to cheer. The show could have ended then. The performer could've bowed and walked off, and it all would've seemed somehow more special, more intimate— it'd be remembered not for the malfunction but that we'd carried him through. Instead he tried to change the mask—or masks— yet again, but of course it failed. The crowd persisted, much of it clapping now, until suddenly he stopped in the middle of the floor, the music still blaring from above, and slowly lifted the large mask-and-headdress apparatus off his head. His face was young and sweaty, his black hair tied into a topknot. He looked down at the many-masked mask in his hands, then up to the ceiling, then back down to the mask. Someone had cut the music. His mouth tremored, then fell open, and a wail began to fill the room, like a man imitating the worst cries of a newborn or a newborn possessed with the most shameless cries of a man, or both, the work of two throats, a coming apart, and right when it felt like the very walls of the room and all of us inside it might explode, he ran out the door and was gone.

No one spoke much for the rest of the meal. The room felt flipped around, backward. Later, while getting ready for bed, Annie and I wondered together why he didn't bow and leave. The group had collectively decided to sustain the illusion, and yet it seemed as if this was precisely why he broke down, suggested Annie as she dabbed her eyes with cream. It was like, without there being any kind of real performative gesture, all our clapping and cheering, our collective incredulity, became cruel, even insulting, like we'd violated some contract and stripped the performer of all these layers of confidence and rationale and unselfconsciousness that make performing possible, and in the process some raw, almost nascent part of himself was revealed to the room. Maybe even to himself.

I dreamed of the performer that night and for many nights to come.

IF THAT FIRST YEAR in California had one definitive feature, it's that nothing happened. We were happy. We lived in a beautiful place. Annie got immersed in her work immediately and I worked on *The Troop* with LD while also doing all the extra work of preparing it for publication, work I had no idea existed. Annie and I made some friends. I learned to love salad, learned that I didn't mind yoga, learned that people go to the beach in their jeans just to hang out, and gradually grew convinced that the Mist was more or less over; I'd not only moved across the country, I'd entered an entirely new phase of my life, one that was defined by peace, fulfillment, and steadiness. Things just kind of worked. I would come to resent this time so deeply. I'd hate it. I would become certain that it had happened only to trick me into thinking I'd entered a new phase in life, free from the years of failure and psychological pain. Had it not been for that year, I was convinced, all the turmoil that followed wouldn't have happened. It's almost like I can still feel physically how I felt when I first got the call from Lisa, my agent, saying something big was in the works. I was on BART in the very early morning, riding down to SFO with Annie. We were headed to New York for the release party of *The Troop,* which was to be hosted yet again on the roof-deck of Jules's studio. When I asked Lisa what she'd meant, she said a film option, a phrase I didn't really understand, and that we'd talk about it over dinner when I arrived in the city. I apologized—I'd put it in my calendar that we were going to have dinner on Monday, I totally missed that we'd made dinner plans for that night. "We didn't make plans to dine tonight," she said, "but I think it's best now that we do. We should discuss this ASAP. I'll text an address and a time."

Annie asked what Lisa wanted.

"She said she wants to discuss my film options," I said.

"What are they?"

"I'm not really sure. But it must be important because she wants to have dinner tonight."

That Tuesday *The Troop* had been released. To my complete shock (and everyone else's, I assumed) it was met with big positive reviews in the places you want big positive reviews, a major coup for an indie press. I was gleeful, scared, grateful—I felt different from how I'd felt when I got the fellowship or learned that the book would be published. The difference was that I'd let my guard down. I'd accepted these positive reviews, these huge gifts, as part of how my life now functioned, a life free from the patterns of its previous decades. I'd escaped the world of failure. This must be how Jules feels, I remember thinking, sitting there on BART after hanging up with Lisa.

And so eight hours later, after landing in New York, I found myself cutting into a large fried sweetbread at a new old-school bistro in Tribeca as Lisa explained to me and Annie that a film producer had read *The Troop* and wanted to buy the rights to the story called "Tents," about the hostage crisis. He was specifically enticed by the parts of the story that talk about the Great Monongahela River Chemical Spill of 1996. "Tents" is set a few months after the event, but in the story there are brief mentions about the chaos, the anise scent of the chemical, being poisoned, the way it made everyone have to spit all the time, the riots and societal fallout. This, explained Lisa, was what he was most interested in. He wanted to know if I'd written anything more about it—he'd never even heard of the spill, but it sounded terrifying, perfect material for a film. Lisa went on to explain how we needed to use *The Troop*'s fresh momentum to strike another book deal now, while houses were interested and there was buzz; we could use the producer's interest to up the deal's value.

"Well, this works perfectly," I lied, disassociating as I spoke. "My plan for the next book is a big novel, an epic, really, about the Great Spill. I lived through it. I've been mulling over this book for years, and now I feel like I've got what it'll take to write it. The great West Virginia novel. We've got great New York novels and Chicago novels and Texas and California novels—why not the great West Virginia novel? I don't even think it would take me that long. It's like I can see the whole thing already." Lisa nodded enthusiastically as she washed down her black cod.

I couldn't, of course, but that didn't matter, because what I could see as I spoke was an opportunity to settle any doubt about whether *The Troop,* and the good it had brought me, were not an anomaly but something I could replicate, that I had the mental and creative chops to get it done; second, and more inspired: I could see a wedding for me and Annie, and then a luxurious honeymoon, and after that a Craftsman house in California that belonged to us and our child, whose image I'd never before imagined and yet was now so vivid in my mind, so arresting, that my body jolted at the table, like I'd experienced a visitation. And yet as I blathered I could also see Annie staring at me as she took a long sip of wine that I could tell was only a performative sip, tipping the liquid to her mouth but not drinking it, instead letting it pool there on the upper lip while using the glass and her hand holding it as cover for her long, unblinking gaze. She was clearly as shocked as I was by what I was saying.

"Do you have any pages?" asked Lisa. "Even a pitch? I could help with a pitch. Then I can get this guy to option the rights to the story and the novel. For the story you'd get a payment right away—it'd be smaller, of course, but as soon as you finish the book you'd get a healthier payment. Easy. And then we have the buzz from a film deal when we start pitching the book to publishers. They'll jump all over it. And you really think it wouldn't take long to write? I mean, that's great. This could be *very* positive for you."

"No pages," I said. "But I could do a pitch." I didn't know what a pitch was, but it didn't matter. I was drunk on possibility. I was also a little drunk. I remember looking around then as I chewed my sweetbread, sipped my Beaujolais, feeling dazzled, truly, by the burnt-orange leather of the booths and seat cushions, the warm radiance of the hardwood banquettes, their gold trim, the marble bar twice as long as my old studio, and feeling that after almost a decade living in this city, it was only then that I felt for the first time like I was the kind of person for whom this restaurant was designed, whatever the fuck that meant.

"And so all this happened, this spill? And you lived through it?" said Lisa.

"I did."

"And it was, like, really real?"

"Of course it was. You've honestly never heard of it?"

"I'm from Westchester." She sipped her wine.

"I DIDN'T KNOW you had a new book idea," said Annie later that evening, back at Jules's new apartment, where we were staying in the guest room. (He was up at the studio in Amagansett but was set to come back in the morning.) Annie sounded hurt, like I'd been hiding a second life from her. Of course I hadn't had a new idea for a book, but I didn't want her to worry about me agreeing to a huge project I'd given zero conscious thought to, and I didn't want to admit that I'd lied right there at the table to Lisa, though it felt more like a half lie because of the way the idea had arrived with such force that it seemed like maybe I *had* been considering it for a long time, but had only noticed it right then. (It turns out I had been thinking about it in some outer borough of my sub-conscious, because the seed of an idea had indeed been planted, only I wouldn't realize this fact, let alone pinpoint the moment of its planting, until, well, today, a little bit ago.) But instead of admitting all that, I doubled down and said something about how I'd been thinking of the book but wanted to wait to speak about it until I felt like I had the confidence to follow through with it, which wasn't until that moment, something like that, whatever I needed to say right then so she could relax and feel excited about the portrait of our future I'd just begun imagining.

Early the next morning we walked all the way from Jules's down to the promenade and watched together as Manhattan undimmed into a white-gold reflection, and though I couldn't see it I could sense Antony's parents' building on the East Side where we last saw him, a memory that summoned fast waves of nostalgia and regret and gloom I attempted to escape by suggesting we keep walking, only to end up at our old place in the Slope, and once there we stood under the green shade of plane trees as old as the Civil War and looked up at what used to be our bedroom win-dows. Annie said something about how it was in those rooms that our life began, and I agreed, but all I could think about was how it was up there that I'd planned my suicide.

That Monday, a year to the day that Annie and I had left New York, I went to Lisa's office, where together we wrote a pitch for a novel about the Great Monongahela River Chemical Spill of 1996. A big hulking novel. An exploration of ecopolitics, postindustrial America, Appalachia at the end of the twentieth century, small-town life, heartbreak, tragedy, the darkness of our country's underbelly. Lisa added stuff, like how it'd be the definitive book of a place in the style of McMurtry, Bellow, and Stegner, writers I'd never read. "When the houses get a sniff of this," said Lisa, "it's off to the races."

"I THINK this is a very dangerous idea," said LD a few days later, after we arrived back in California. A bidding war had begun on the book that didn't exist. The producer was basically waiting for a deal to be signed, then he was going to buy the option. "You do this," said LD, "and you're a debtor to an expectation. The freedom the money represents is real, I don't deny that, but that money will make you a prisoner to a promise. You haven't written a single word yet. Meditate on that fact." She stared at me carefully through the veil of steam rising off a trough of a thousand chili-boiled fish.

I flew back to New York, went through the meetings with Lisa, signed the papers. I didn't care about the money itself, though the deal was significant, as Lisa put it. I stared down at the numbers and watched them melt away like they used to do in math class, when I'd stop seeing "4" as a symbolic representation of value and instead would spiral into a rabbit hole wondering why *this* graphic specifically became that value's representation—why the swoop and angle of the four, why the infinity of the eight, etc. By signing those papers I felt I was signing closed my past. The first movement of my life—with all of its hell, its immense and omnipresent hell, was officially over.

When I confessed to LD that I hadn't followed her advice and had taken the deal, I could hear her disappointment, and it knocked me down in a way I hadn't anticipated. I guess I figured my days of disappointing people were over too. "Well, it's yours now," she said about the money. "But that doesn't mean you have to spend it. Put it away or invest it, use it as the carrot on the end of a stick. You've got a lot of work to do. I'm here, I'll help with early drafts and edits, but you've got to do it first." I agreed with her advice about saving the money; said I was ready for the work, excited even. And then I went out the next day and bought Annie a diamond engagement ring.

Just before the winter rains hit, I proposed. We started planning a small wedding. Later we planned the honeymoon—or, rather, *I* planned it—an expensive trip to Italy, a Rome-Sicily-Rome itinerary spent hopping between posh, swank, elegant hotels and villas, dining each evening at the most exciting trattorias and osterias and *ristoranti,* the honeymoon I'm on now, that is, and if there's one truly good thing about the most expensive hotels and restaurants, it's that they always give you a deal if you pay in full up front, which I did, so when I failed to deliver my novel most of the money was already gone to payments for the wedding and the honeymoon, which is why I currently have nothing but am still able to stay at the G-Rough hotel, where Annie is certainly awake by now, sipping an in-room espresso, reviewing yesterday's vocab notes, and practicing her pronunciation, possibly even recording herself for maximum accuracy, while also noting how the morning practice is going, including which words she retained through REM and which were lost, and hopefully she's read the note I wrote on the stationery, an image of which I have included here because I took a picture of it, which I did in case I began to question whether my memory of writing a note to my wife in a hotel in Rome was my memory or a memory of the Physicist's, in whose life it's much more likely, obviously, that he wrote a note to his wife on hotel stationery in Rome.

I SIGNED THE CONTRACTS on a Monday in late September. Starting then, I had two years to turn in the first draft of my big West Virginia novel about the Great Monongahela River Chemical Spill of 1996. The first six months of that time were a wash. I spent the whole of them traveling for *The Troop,* doing readings. First some big bookstores, well attended but unpaid, and then campus visits, paid but attended mandatorily, during which I'd sit in front of a room pretending I had any clue what the fuck I was doing when I wrote the stories, before I'd hop into a cab or a grad student's car and get shuttled back to the airport, have a tall, overpriced beer at the terminal bar decorated with regional flair, and fly somewhere else. An indie bookseller in one of the Manchesters would email an open invitation to read, "should I ever be passing through," and within the hour I'd write back—sometimes while sitting at an airport bar!—and lie and say it just so happened that I would be, then burn whatever money I'd recently made at a college visit scheduling the new trip. It was heavy lifting, this level of avoidance. And expensive. Still, I always brought a notebook and a laptop, certain I'd start taking notes or sketching out scenes or characters while in transit, but I never did, not once. I'd bring books I was certain would inspire me, only to go to the airport bookstore and buy a different book I was suddenly certain was *actually* the book I should've brought, but of course I never cracked the spine of either, or of any book, not for six months. Instead I watched every possible film the plane offered, especially the animated films, whose hyper-rendered figures, by virtue of not being human, even when the characters are representationally "human," are stripped bare of the complications and distractions of human actors—performative tics, the cloud of celebrity, career ambitions, the burden of suspended disbelief—and are instead hyperefficient conduits of emotion, legible for the child, devastating for the adult, and so I spent much of my time at thirty thousand feet with my head in my hands, wrecked over the fates of toys that can talk, cars that can talk, princesses from Scandinavia and Polynesia, superheroes, monsters, and a boy from Santa Cecilia, Mexico. Whole layovers in LAX, ORD, and DFW I don't remember. Sometimes I'd wake in one of those dark speeding tubes in the belly of the night and not know where I was going or where I'd been, the plane rumbling through another silver cloud, or the orange lights of anywhere gleaming clear below, and feel a terror purifying in my heart about what I'd agreed to do and what it'd mean were I to fail. And it was up there one night, while drifting in and out of sleep in my aisle seat, the back half of fuselage fishtailing too perceptibly for comfort as we tore through a range of nimbostratus, that I heard the voice I hadn't heard in almost eighteen months, the voice that isn't my voice but is. I turned in my seat, looked down the aisle toward the galley, pretending to myself that maybe in my dreams I'd mistaken the whispers of a flight attendant, that the voice was coming from anywhere but inside my head, where I knew it was coming from, telling me it was time again to kill myself. I clamped down my eyeshade and dreamed that I was dreaming.

$$\longrightarrow$$

AS "TOURING" TAPERED OFF, I began to panic at the prospect of not having an excuse to not write. After Annie headed off for BART in the mornings, I'd consult a list I'd made of every coffee shop in the East Bay, select one, then waste a few hours trying it out while sipping espresso and "working," which meant doing nothing and feeling anxious about doing nothing until the caffeine made the anxiousness so sharp I'd break into a minor sweat and have to go for a walk around the block. During one of these walks, in an area where I'd never spent much time, I came across an office supply store, a big-box chain I thought had long gone out of business, and felt called to it like a pilgrim to a chapel. I wandered the aisles, marveling at how useless the place felt. As I turned one corner I almost walked into a six-foot-tall display of legal pads on sale. The sight of this golden tower shot me through with an epiphany: I needed to buy legal pads because I needed to do research. Yes. It was so obvious, *so* obvious. I was embarrassed it took me six months to realize it. What a fool I was to think I could write a great novel about a historical event without doing even the slightest bit of research, as if my mind could spin it all together like so much silk. To go with my stack of legal pads I bought a few boxes of Pilot V7s and V5s in black and blue and red, Post-its, sticky tabs, a box of expensive pencils. I think I was the store's first customer in months because one cashier came and watched the other cashier ring me up.

From the office supply store I drove straight to the university's library—the first time I'd set foot in it after a year and a half at the school—and had a librarian named Kelly Greene (scout's honor) show me to a reserved carrel, then teach me about databases, microfilms, Boolean searches, interlibrary loan, the A/V library, Dewey decimal, court records, testimonies; for weeks I hoarded data, took notes, made time lines, read records, as if I needed all this material to tell me that beginning in the evening of January 18, 1996, an immense and still-unknown quantity of a coal-cleaning chemical called hexacyclanol-9 began leaking into the Monongahela River, poisoning not only the water supply of my hometown of Morgantown—though it suffered most acutely—but large swaths of the river's watershed all the way up to a few miles outside of Pittsburgh, Pennsylvania, where its levels finally diluted only miles from the confluence with the Allegheny. Had it reached Pittsburgh, the spill would've received the national attention it deserved, but it didn't, so it didn't; hardly a surprise to us in West Virginia. I spent actual time doing actual research of these actual facts I already knew like I knew my own birthday, like I knew—yet still researched—how the spill was caused, in part, by a meteorological event, a polar vortex, a large tumor of arctic air that flopped down out of Canada, across the Great Lakes, then sat on top of the region, plunging it into temperatures rarely seen outside the Yukon. The vortex had two movements. The first was an initial flash that lasted from approximately 4:00 p.m. on January 18 to 4:00 a.m. on January 19, dropping the region down to a record thirty-three below. It was during this initial plunge that nine out of fourteen immense steel chemical tanks filled with hexacyclanol-9, positioned on a concrete pad on the banks of the Monongahela, a mile upriver from Morgantown, cracked in the extreme cold, unleashing an estimated four-million-gallon torrent of the chemical into the water. The reason for the cracks was long disputed. The EPA argued that Freedom and Liberty Industries, Inc. (scout's honor), the company that owned the chemical tanks, constructed them out of cheap imported steel that couldn't properly withstand the elements. Liberty Industries' attorneys claimed that it was an accident caused by the meteorological anomaly; temperatures were drastically below even the worst lows on record, and because the chemical doesn't freeze, it became colder than the air itself, putting the steel under pressures that no code or plan could have ever predicted. Meanwhile, sometime after 4:00 a.m. on January 19, as my research shows—though I knew this already— the vortex temporarily pivoted west over Ohio, allowing our region's temperatures to rise rapidly back to the midthirties just long enough that it was safe outside for children to wait for buses and go to school. I was one of those children.

At approximately 6:45 a.m. on the morning of January 19, a Mrs. Shirley Ashdown, resident of the riverside neighborhood of Star City, called 911 to report what she thought was maybe a gas leak, even though what she smelled didn't have the signature odor of gas caused by the additive mercaptan—instead, she said, it smelled very heavily of black licorice. She'd first noticed it, she reported, when she took her dog for its morning walk two blocks down to the river while it was still warm enough to do so. This was the first recorded report of hexacyclanol-9, which later came to be colloquially called "the licorice." She also mentioned that she was spitting a lot. An EMT came to her house because 911 thought she might be having a stroke. By the time the EMTs were done checking out Mrs. Ashdown, the switchboard back at the 911 call center was at a full glow.

It was a surreal act, doing the research, seeing what I'd experienced translated into so much language, so many numbers and graphs and testimonies—and yet, for such a huge event, there was a shocking dearth of material. Still, what material there was gave me a kind of solace, confirming for me that I hadn't just dreamed the whole madness, as I'd often been made to feel after years of people telling me they didn't believe it happened because if it was as bad as I said it was, they'd have heard about it. But such is the life of the West Virginian—half the country doesn't even know you're there.

What I hadn't anticipated in my research was discovering myself in places I didn't realize I had been, as I thought had happened one day when I encountered the testimony of one of the men sent into the spill site to attempt to stop it, then clean it up. As I read his testimony, I began to envision his narrative in my mind with an almost disturbing level of precision, as if a high-def film was being projected against the inside of my skull, an experience at

first shocking and enthralling until I realized that what I was reading was one of my own intense visual memories. Everything the
man said had been in my mind for decades. I grew dizzy at my carrel, confused—it was as if I'd found a piece of my own mind right
there on paper, like my mind had been robbed, I felt this acutely,
that there was less of me. But then I remembered where I had witnessed this narrative: on the news on TV. A few days into the spill
a local station finally broke from the party line and ran footage that
was sent anonymously from a self-proclaimed environmental activist. The footage, time stamped January 19—day 1 of the spill—was
shot on a home video camera from the woods surrounding the spill
site. Somehow the activist snuck past a perimeter of state troopers
and company thugs and captured footage of the state's "cleanup"
efforts. Up until this footage aired, the state had reported that
the crack was small, isolated to one tank, and had been almost
entirely contained by midafternoon on January 19. What the footage showed was different: individual cracks had formed in nine of
the fourteen tanks. Big cracks. Cracks big enough to march, say, a
troop of Boy Scouts through them. And the cracks weren't leaking,
they were gushing like hydrants. You could see the chemical flowing everywhere across the concrete foundation pads, down to the
river. Chemical streams six feet wide. Members of a hazmat crew
would appear on-screen, always running, always in a state of panic.
At one point a hazmat man runs into the frame holding a squeegee
attached to a long wooden pole, then drops into a squat, pulls off
his orange hood, and vomits. No, he doesn't vomit—he purges.
His neck swells and writhes and his face flushes purple and his eyes
sort of quake, then roll back into his skull as his mouth grows and
grows, like he's trying to birth a second head out of his jaws. When
he's finally done he doesn't wipe the vomit from his lips, now pale,
or run a hand through his hair, he just stays there in a squat, staring

at the chemical roiling over the tops of his boots, a stare of intense personal concentration, as if he were reading a secret message in the ripples. It was this man's testimony that I was reading. I began to cry as I read it; a soft, pitiful cry that aroused only annoyance, and not an ounce of concern or sympathy, from the history PhD student in the neighboring carrel.

Over the years I'd lost sense of whether that memory of the hazmat man was real or imagined. This was in part because that image of the vomiting man was an image to which I'd attached myself—it became the visual representation of my own first experience with the licorice, when I ingested it through the water supply along with the rest of my class at the end of gym, after having worked up a good thirst playing dodgeball, when we lined up at the water fountain and guzzled. This was the first scene I tried to write, in fact. Why not begin at the beginning, I'd decided, big genius that I am. Every day for a month I sat down at my carrel or my desk at home or my kitchen table (I tried everywhere) but never once could I find the words to say what it was like when I started to vomit uncontrollably at my desk during a geography lesson. The sheer volume of the vomit. I was the first to retch, likely because I had been first in line at the water fountain. One after another we convulsed and sobbed as vomit hosed out of us. Eight hours a day for a month straight I tried to find the words to describe it, how the vomiting was so severe that I lost visual perception, went inward, downward, way down in the darkness toward some center, until I was only spasm and sound, and then only sound, sound was all that was left of me or the room or anyone in it, a cretinous sound so hell-bent on getting out of me I thought it might crack open my face; for weeks and weeks I tried to describe this, but I couldn't, I couldn't find the words to describe the exact sound all of us kids were making between purges, the wet half hiccup that croaks from the throat, the kind a baby makes between screams, that's what we sounded like, a room of croaking babies, and by the time most of us were through being sick we'd practically become babies, sobbing out of terror and confusion, our eyes red with burst vessels, our lips white, our bodies damp and cold with sweat, but the words to say this never came. It stayed in my mind, where it'd been since the day when I watched the news footage on TV of the vomiting hazmat man with Ben and my dad and knew that's exactly what I'd looked like, that he was me, and I became him.

The revelation wasn't enough to make the writing come. And it didn't come when I broke the research down into different categories arranged into wide-spined legal binders—though these binders, along with the dozens of scratched-up legal pads I'd brought home and stacked in a corner, did serve as a kind of material wall I could hide behind whenever Annie would press about my progress. And it didn't come when I convinced a chemistry professor on my campus to have lunch with me and tell me everything I needed to know about hexacyclanol-9 and its effects on both coal and the human body. It didn't come when I tracked down a roll of butcher paper and made a time line of the events on a single sheet that ran the length of my apartment. Slowly in wool socks I'd walk along the catastrophe unfolding, hoping the pacing of events would get translated up through my muscles to assist in the generation of a complex but elegant plot. It didn't work. I felt no plot within my muscles. Instead what I mostly felt was frustration, a turning over in my chest, not because of my lack of writing (though I was frustrated by that too), but because here I was seeing a visual representation of the disjunction between what happened during the spill and how the authorities reacted to it. I could see, for example, how by 11:00 a.m. on January 19 the authorities knew the spill had occurred, they knew hexacyclanol-9 was the chemical, they knew it had leaked at extremely high levels, they knew it was poisonous, and yet, because it was a coal-cleaning chemical, and therefore an extension of the coal industry, they froze. West Virginia is coal and coal is West Virginia, which meant any attack on the industry was political suicide, especially now that it was in the heart of a decades-long decline. In their frozen state, the authorities called the governor, who also froze. So instead of alerting crucial—and very dated—infrastructural systems like the water-treatment facilities so that they'd have enough time to act appropriately, they didn't, and every layer of the water system, including its backup carbon filters, the Alamo filters, was compromised; instead of alerting people to the spill so that they'd know not to use the water, the authorities let them keep on drinking and bathing and cooking and breathing without knowing what was happening. A spill wasn't even acknowledged until 2:00 p.m., but even then, they wouldn't name the chemical or say if it was dangerous. A "Do Not Use" order on the water wasn't put into effect until 5:00 p.m. that night. Severe nausea, rashes, dizziness, diarrhea, trouble breathing, memory loss, numbness—symptoms that weren't corroborated until 5:00 p.m., when the chemical was officially named. By then people had died, including an elderly teacher in my school. She'd vomited so hard she had a stroke. Luckily it didn't happen in front of any of the kids, but I saw her covered gurney rolled down the hallway, watched it bounce jaggedly down a small set of stairs, watched her left leg flop over the side—the EMTs were in such a rush they'd forgotten to strap it down. The sight of that limb made me shiver. So that's what dead bodies do, I remember thinking. They flop around. Only an hour before, the same EMTs had been checking on us kids in my classroom, not knowing what to do besides tell the teacher some kind of wild hell had opened up across town and it'd be best to call our parents and get us home. Hearing this, our teacher asked the EMTs if they could step out into the hall to speak. We could still hear everything they were saying from the other side of the door—they were so scared they didn't realize they were yelling. The teacher felt certain we needed to be taken to a hospital. "We could take them there right now," said the EMT, "but I radioed over there less than ten minutes ago and they basically told me to forget it. They said there are so many people you can't walk down the halls. It's not good. People are fighting. In my professional opinion, if I had a kid, I'd be going to get them right this second." It's estimated that all packaged water in the area was sold out before the official 5:00 p.m. "Do Not Use" order was even announced. One man shot another in the Walmart parking lot over two cases of Poland Spring. The morning of the spill my father was working an industrial painting job at a new building going up on the university campus. He listened to the early events unfold over the radio—people calling in to the morning talk stations complaining about the smell, then the water, calls that grew increasingly panicked, then terrifying. Finally a chemistry professor from the university called in, claiming with a high degree of certainty that the chemical was hexacyclanol-9 and that the city, if not the state, most certainly knew this by now and yet they weren't saying a word and should be ashamed of themselves but that, more important, everyone should stop using the water immediately. Not long after, all stations ran the public service announcement telling parents to go get their kids from school if they could. In a small stroke of genius, my father didn't try to go buy water. He knew it would be nearly impossible. Instead, on his way to get me and Ben from school, he first drove to a small keg distributor on the edge of the student neighborhood near where he was working and bought five ten-pound bags of ice, ice made from purified water frozen and bagged weeks before in a warehouse in Ohio. Melted, it yielded six gallons of fresh water. He said he could've gotten more, but the owner of the keg store caught on to what he was doing and decided right then that the price of ice had gone up one thousand percent.

I put this on the time line on my apartment floor, an estimate of when my dad would've bought the ice and when approximately he picked us up from school. Right beside the official facts I put as much as I could remember along with what I'd read in testimonies and what I'd heard. I wrote in when Ben had his first asthma attack from the polluted air; when we saw the first clouds of smoke from the university riot (the first of many riots); when the power grid failed, because of surges caused by everyone running their electric heating systems at max power, often along with supplemental space heaters, sometime around midnight on the first night. But as I filled in the time line, the structure of the line began to fail. The linearity felt like a lie, a sterilization of what I'd experienced, an implied order. And contemplating all this now, just as another train has screamed past so unexpectedly that I've jumped in seat 19D and feel faintly confused that all I witnessed was a roaring red blur that vanished before my mind could even make sense of it, its speed imperceptible except for the fact that it's identical to my own, a mirroring that makes my current velocity seem not only impossible but like something I'm maybe not meant to experience, at least not in any precise present sense, or maybe only as memory, I'm reminded in some sidelong way of a passage of the Physicist's in which he's discussing how our experience of time is connected to the second law of thermodynamics—I think—and that we experience the past as a state of lower entropy and the future as a state of ever-increasing entropy, but how that's not really true; we see the past as a lower entropic state because we view it through a frame of particularity, the occurrences take on order in our mind, and so it seems like a period of lower entropic force only because of us, the perceiving instrument—I think?—and then he writes, "We often say that causes precede effects and yet, in the elementary grammar of things, there is no distinction between 'cause' and 'effect.' There are regularities, represented by what we call physical laws, that link events of different times, but they are symmetric between future and past. In a microscopic description, there can be no sense in which the past is different from the future." It seems that on some level I understood this: the closer I zoomed in on the spill, filling up the time line with what I could remember, what I'd heard, and what was recorded, the more it seemed to fall apart under the weight of illusion. Eventually I cut the time line into chunks, bent some of them backward, and gradually had a kind of coiled snail shell in the center of my living room floor. The isolation of each event became impossible. What had happened was not ordered. It was chaos. To portray it as anything else would be a crime against those who lived through it. But how do you write chaos? I had no fucking idea.

As my grip on the project rapidly weakened, I attempted to counter the feeling by spending increasingly more money. First, I attempted to amp up the wedding, but Annie shut it down. From the start she'd wanted something minimal and intimate, in part because that's her style, but also because I was obviously not in the best way, so the idea of us having to go around glad-handing a horde of drunk people, which would mainly mean Annie getting nudged in the ribs over and over and asked when we're going to start making babies, seemed like a bad one.

The subject of kids, mind you, was always in the background. Especially when it came to blowing money on the wedding or honeymoon. More than once Annie would say, "Why spend this money when we could invest it, let it grow. It could be a great foundation for us," and in that "us" I knew she meant more than our current duo. We'd talked about kids, of course—we'd been together many years—and had since early on. Annie wanted a family and I'd said I did too in the most abstract sense, but in the specific sense of my life as I was living it, I did not. This was not about the standard male terror of responsibility and a loss of freedom. No, I was afraid of a family because of what I knew I'd do to it. I couldn't even project myself that far into the future—I always assumed I'd be dead within a few months, a year max. But I never expressed this clearly. I couldn't come out and say that I was terrified of what my illness would do to kids whose very existence was half my responsibility but whose suffering would be more like one hundred percent mine, because to open that line of thinking would open the concurrent problem of why I thought it was okay to be in a relationship with her at all, and expressing that might end with me losing her, which I couldn't stomach, which made me feel selfish, unethical— you get it. Mostly I'd just say something like "It's so scary, with my depression, I can't bring myself to think of it," and then she'd look down into her lap, her fingers resting interlaced, palms up, and say, "I know," a bit defeatedly, and then we wouldn't talk about it again for several months.

In fact, it was only during the dinner with Lisa, in which I sold myself on the lie of the novel, that I envisioned for the first time, however briefly, Annie and me with a kid. But I kept this to myself. Indeed, I tried to keep it *from* myself, pretending it hadn't happened. Even with things seeming like they were maybe getting better, imagining something like a family felt like a line I simply should not cross. A step too far. Though I couldn't grasp this at any conscious level, it seems clear now that I believed handling the money responsibly, with an eye toward the future, toward *us,* was equivalent to poking the beast. And the beast was very big.

Though I was unaware of my spending as a kind of karmic release valve, I was absolutely aware of the brief dopamine boost it provided and the way it made me feel like I had some control over myself: spending made failure not an option. So after Annie said no to wedding spending, I flipped my efforts to the honeymoon. Posh hotels, three-star restaurants, prix fixe, business class. Live like a success. Give Annie anything she could imagine, especially a dream trip to Italy—I'd seen the way she enviously scrolled through Jules's Instagram posts when he traveled around for the Biennale; I'd done it too.

Another perk of blowing cash: I could use my lax attitude about the cost of things to give Annie confidence in the success of my work, which she'd continued to question, since I hadn't shown her a word and had become increasingly defensive whenever she'd ask. I'd often point to the ever-rising citadel of paper I'd amassed and say something like "The whole book's right there—I know you haven't read a word, but I'm telling you, you're looking straight at it. It's all a mess of pieces until it isn't. But also I ask that you please not disturb any of it until I'm ready."

What must be noted is that Annie didn't ask for any of this. These extravagances were not familiar to her, not by a long shot— she was a thoroughly middle-class midwesterner—and while all these luxuries excited her as they'd excite practically anyone who is honest with themselves, she most often said I should reel it in, my expenses and her anxiety about them growing in tandem. But spending was the only tool I had against what felt like a crumbling projection ahead. *Do not* dare the universe by saving the money but *do* dare the universe to make all of this future joy fall apart. I'd lost control.

Soon after I'd exhausted the library research, I woke one morning in a panic and told Annie I was going for a walk. I moved at a fast clip through the morning streets, up into the Oakland hills, breathing deeply the air still cool with Pacific night, wandered into a patch of redwoods that made up a neighborhood park, and began to sob as I could feel a fog curling around my brain. I dry heaved a little. The voice in my head that isn't my voice but is my voice started telling me what to do: I began punching myself hard in the face and temples, a rush of punches . . . I woke up on the ground's soft mattress of redwood needles, damp with dew, my heartbeat thudding in my skull, the ancient red giants leaning over, judging me. It'd been just over a year since I'd signed the contract. I had exactly nothing written. I sat up, wiped my eyes. My vision was a little blurred, my ass a little wet. My ears filled with the drone of an old phone left off the hook. Then there came a tap-tap on my shoulder. I acted like I didn't feel it, but this only made it worse— more taps, harder taps. Real pain in them. It hurt so much I maybe even gasped. And then I heard—in my ears? in my head?—*It's me*. And my nerves went very cool. I was relieved. What I'd been waiting for had finally returned: the Mist stood tall and menacing behind me, its long shadow darkening the ground. I gave one last good dry heave over the dirt, got to my feet, and started down out of the hills, slouched and ticking like a bomb.

On College Avenue I went into a café and ordered a cortado I instantly regretted and couldn't bring myself to drink because it reminded me of first meeting Annie, which right then I wished had never happened, because now I knew what she was going to have to live through because of what I was going to have to do to myself, thoughts that felt like a chain cinching around my gut, a wicked sensation. I quickly exited the café on a northbound trajectory up the street, a few doors later encountering my favorite bookstore in Oakland, which I knew was there and yet in my current state hadn't expected to encounter, and decided to go in to punish myself in the company of all those books people actually had the intellect and talent and discipline to finish writing. The staff knew me from some readings I'd done there, so I tried to act cool, walked around without purpose. I picked up a travel guide for Italy, then individual travel guides for Rome and Sicily, where we'd be visiting. On my way to the checkout desk I passed a rack of staff-recommended nonfiction, and there I saw, radiating on the shelf, a copy of Michael Herr's classic Vietnam War memoir, *Dispatches*. I grabbed it without thinking, paid, and got in an Uber to take me home, holding the book the whole way, rubbing my fingers along its spine like how my grandmother thumbed her rosary.

→

I STARTED READING *Dispatches,* not knowing why until the next afternoon, when I'd finished it: chaos. Here was a book about chaos. How dumb I was, I thought (or thought I thought; it was not me, but the Mist doing the thinking again): I needed to study books about chaotic events to learn how to write my own. Obvious, painfully obvious, to someone who knew what the hell they were doing, which I very much did not. I went back to the store and bought *Voices from Chernobyl, Hiroshima,* books about Katrina, the Dust Bowl, the San Francisco earthquake, any printed-and-bound utterance from disaster was now in a stack on my coffee table. This was the second phase of the research, I lied to myself. I'd decided, while gathering all the books, that part of my mistake was attempting to write a big hulking novel without having had the intellectual exposure to the kind of writing I'd need to do, which is to say that at the root of things I simply wasn't smart enough yet and I needed to catch up. But even with all those books around me I could only concentrate on Herr's *Dispatches*. I read it a second time, then a third, annotating passages, then paragraphs, then basically entire sections until I'd scribbled under almost every line of text. I made up outlines of the book's sections on my computer, did collections of the best passages, organized passages according to theme, subject, detail, bought a second copy of the book because my original became so battered, only to do to the new one exactly what I'd done to the old, my obsession growing fiercer every day, the first thing I looked at when I got up, the last thing I saw before I went to sleep—I kept a copy under my pillow, perhaps in hopes of uploading some of its brilliance via osmosis.

It became a bit of a problem. Annie, thoroughly waxed after a long day at work and wanting only to spend some chill and vaguely mindless time together watching a show, instead got me sitting beside her on the couch only half watching while working through my paperback, pen in hand. "Please," she'd say, "I'm in the city all day and then I come home and all you do is look at that," then I'd apologize and set it on the coffee table and stare at it instead of the TV.

Once I met up with her and her work friend for happy hour in San Francisco, the two of them sitting at one of those high, round cocktail tables that wobble and are too small to fit more than maybe one and a half of the drinks for which they're named, and after greeting them I set my copy of *Dispatches* on the table, which I'd of course brought to read on the way over, and draped my jean jacket over my chair and went to the bar to get my drink and when I came back saw that Annie had put the book into the large side pocket of my jacket to make room on the small table, or so I'd assumed, until this happened more than a few times—Annie trying to keep people from seeing my severely marked-up, dog-eared, creased, and warped copy—and I realized she was embarrassed.

Another time I came out of the bathroom after a shower, still toweled and damp, and found Annie standing in the living room looking through one of my copies, the page edges tea brown from my hand oils. "What are you doing?" I said. "You're going to lose my place."

"Your place? Literally this whole book is underlined."

"No, it's not. Just sections. It's close reading."

"This is close reading?" She fanned open the book and even from across the room I could see all the pen ink, black and red and blue. "This is weird. First the papers and the binders, now this. What are you doing every day?"

"Process is messy. Sorry it isn't some elegant decision tree set in Helvetica. You saw my painting studio—they don't teach you to be clean in art school, they teach you to trust your process. I trust what I'm doing, but clearly you don't."

She set the book down. "You're acting weird and you know it."

The following Saturday afternoon Annie and I pulled into an In-N-Out and when I got out of the car she stayed behind. I waited for her for a moment, then got back in the car. "Are you okay?" I asked.

She looked down at the copy of *Dispatches* in my hand. "I'm not about to go sit in an In-N-Out and eat across from you in silence while you flip through that stupid book. I've had enough of it. If the book goes in, I stay here."

"You're right. I'm sorry." I put the book in the glove box.

"From now on, when we're together, it's off-limits."

I agreed.

At first I believed the book to be a gift, a kind of high-octane fuel that was filling up my mind, teaching me how to write the book I wanted to write. On every page I found sentences that vibrated with the frequency I'd dreamed of channeling in my own. The more I studied it, the more certain I became in what I needed to do and how to do it. But then, of course, the opposite happened: when I sat down to write, I could feel, within the first minutes, but even still in the days and weeks after, that any scene I wanted to write would never—*never*—eclipse the genius of what Herr had done, not in a million years. The book that I thought was a gift was in fact a curse—classic doings of the Mist. As I flipped through the heavily annotated passages at my writing desk, I learned that I'd made a taxonomy of all the writing I'd never be able to surpass, even simple lines like "the rotor-thud of a helicopter, the one sound I know that is both sharp and dull at the same time." I read that description and knew I could never describe my own experiences hearing the helicopters because that is the only right way to describe how they sounded when they descended on us, my dad and Ben and me, during the water buffalo riot. "Water buffalo" was the colloquial name for the large freshwater distribution tanks brought in by the National Guard. During the Great Spill they'd set them up across town at two points—the football stadium parking lot and the parking lot of the abandoned mall—on January 20, the morning after the spill began and the power grid had failed. My dad brought me and Ben along because it was said on the radio that each person could fill two two-gallon jugs, and as far as he was concerned, we were persons. Overnight the temperatures had plummeted to negative forty Fahrenheit, a new record low for the state, and even with the morning sun coming up, temperatures climbed only ten degrees to negative thirty. The cold wasn't enough to keep us away—my dad dressed us in all our best winter gear, and we went. When we got to the football stadium parking lot, we saw the cold wasn't enough to keep anyone else away either. The place was full with a queue of people cordoned off by the interlocking metal gates used for ticket lines on game days. Armed soldiers were set up on the perimeter. Barrel fires were burning along the edges of the lines in hopes of keeping the crowds warm. The water buffaloes were at the far end of the lot, illuminated under spotlights. The air was so cold that its moisture content had frozen into a mist floating no more than eight feet off the ground, an icy cloud with the faintest purple hue from the licorice vapor held within the suspended crystals, growing with the rising breaths of all those waiting in line, the sun and sky concealed beyond, every color drained to a neutral pastel, except for the barrel fires' flames. I can't really say how long we waited there, shivering, smelling the licorice, spitting. The cold was unbearable. Every part of us hurt from exposure or violent shivering. At first the line moved at a decent speed, but soon after we got there it slowed, then stopped altogether. People grew restless. The ice cloud thickened, until I couldn't see more than four or five bodies ahead. Reports started trickling back from the front—it had gotten too cold, people said; the National Guard was saying it was too dangerous for people to be outside; we'd passed into a threshold of almost instant frostbite. People started grumbling, shuffling, cursing. *Fuck this fuck this fuck this.* They've run out of water, that was the next message. They'd run out of water and were using the cold as an excuse to get us to disband. Finally a guardsman got on a bullhorn and confirmed that it was too cold for people to be outside and that they were shutting down distribution until temperatures returned to safer levels or they could set up heated tents. Everyone must disband, said the voice we couldn't see. The crowd broke into madness so quickly I couldn't process at first what was happening. I think my mind had slowed because of the cold. The bodies began to converge, falling forward, then back, in a wake of down jackets and frosted breath, the gathering roar of the crowd like some demented train call, and it almost seemed like a joke, or some kind of play or performance, as I watched my dad join some other men to lift up one of the sections of fence barricade and launch it away from the cordoned area, the masses then spilling out and rushing toward the tanker, my dad grabbing me and my brother by the necks like cubs and pulling us toward it. Parked near one of the tanks was a box truck, and some men had climbed up and thrown open its hatch and inside were a few pallets of bottled water. They started launching them into the crowd, and I can remember grabbing a single sixteen-ounce bottle of spring water that fell before me, stuffing it into my jacket like a baguette, though I never once tried to write about this, never even tried to say how soon after I'd lost track of my brother and my father in the flow of people, or how in the disorienting static of the violet mist the thrashing bodies of the crowd blurred together in a single, smudged gesture, like a charcoal sketch, blurring me away with it, so that I was lost in a vibration of human energy so dynamic my legs were shaking and I started laughing because I knew I didn't exist, none of this existed, not the people or the cold or the water tanks, and especially not the great ferocious thunking sound I started feeling in my chest, descending down out of the sky in the form of a light beam, the spotlight of a helicopter, the silhouette of its underbelly faintly visible above, like a whale swimming over, the song of its blades "both sharp and dull at the same time," and then a voice warning about tear gas, whatever that was, I didn't know and it didn't matter because none of this existed, including the canisters falling down out of the mist, spewing out mists of their own, and it was only when my dad's arm wrapped down around my torso and pulled me up against him, my feet half off the ground, that I came back, the touch of his body making my body real again, and he dragged me through the crowd, away from the riot's center, and I could tell by the force of struggle in his breath blasting down against my head that in his other arm was my brother, and in that way he carried us out of the riot just as the gas clouds haunted toward us, I could see them from inside my father's truck where the three of us sat catching our breath as the heaters blasted our faces, my father making sure we put our noses and fingers right up against the air grates to fight off any frostbite, and at one point he even put my brother's fingers in his mouth to warm them as the grates warmed, Ben at this moment also having another asthma attack, my father holding his inhaler in his free hand, Ben's back against my father's chest, my father telling him to breathe with the rhythm of his rising breast, the tear gas meanwhile moving ever closer, and finally when Ben could breathe again, just in time, we pulled away, and right then I heard what sounded like a great big piece of paper getting torn in half and my brother and I turned in our seats and watched out of the truck cab's back window as two bursts of cold, white, inhuman light screamed up into the sky, then exploded and hung there like weird, dripping angels, their light briefly burning away the mist's shroud, illuminating everything—the bodies, the copter, the overturned barrel fires, the men with their guns— in slurred underworld serenity—lights I wouldn't learn are called magnesium flares, illumination rounds, until all these years later while reading Herr—and while they were up there at their zenith I heard nothing, nothing at all, even as all around us pure insane noise kept unspooling from some invisible source, but it must have all been too much for my ears or mind to make sense of, because everything was off-line. It was silent. There were lights like fireworks in the sky. My snow pants were wet at the crotch. We sped down the empty street for home.

FOR ABOUT A YEAR after my mother left, my father fell asleep on the couch most nights, drinking Wild Turkey, not all that much really, but enough, and reading until his eyes finally gave up and he passed out. Almost every night I'd go out to him on the mustard-tartan couch and take whatever he was reading off his chest, often a paper or magazine, then drape a heavy, hand-knit afghan over his body. He was still solid then, when he'd snore or turn over you could feel it in the floors, and to touch him was to touch something that seemed of a single material, carved from a great slab. This confused me, because I knew he was hurting, but it didn't seem like there was anywhere for the hurt to go.

Decades later, while reading *Dispatches* late one evening, early in my affair with it, I was seized by a vision: a copy of the book tented on my father's chest, gently rising and falling with the rhythms of his sleep. There was the cover, with its white stencil font and fatigue-green background, vivid and clear in the shimmering darkness, except that on my father's chest the cover glowed, an orange glow, flickering, which I understood, the more I envisioned it, was because of the fireplace.

My dad always made a fire, as soon as the nights cooled into September almost all the way to June. He'd build one in the evening, even if he had to open the windows—it wasn't for the heat, it was something about the fire's presence, the way it's a living thing you can admire, tend to, that can warm you, that can light the room or chew up your whole house if you don't pay it mind. Those were not good times, when he slept on the couch; little surprise I hadn't immediately remembered this detail. I suppose I should say something about my mother here, but there isn't much to say. She drank a lot and then finally she left. About a year later my grandmother moved in with us for a few years. We likely made it through because of her. But that year with Dad sleeping on the couch—it was tough. He wasn't absent necessarily, just gone; even at our age we could see it. But the book on his chest, *Dispatches,* reflecting the fire's flicker in the odd hours—often I wanted to call him and ask, why that book, why then? But I couldn't do it for fear that he'd ask me what the hell I was talking about. And then, completely unexpectedly, I was returned to this time during my treatment in a way that maybe can only be understood by those who've experienced it. All I can say is I was *sent* back there, *completely*. This was not memory; this was visitation. And I was right: *Dispatches* was on his chest, that was true, and it was tented—I hadn't made that up. But what I'd missed in my remembrances was that he'd never read it. He'd opened it, but never got past the first pages. I reexperienced it so clearly, how each time I took the book from his chest it was only ever opened to its start.

"There was a map of Vietnam on the wall of my apartment in Saigon and some nights, coming back late to the city, I'd lie out on my bed and look at it, too tired to do anything more than just get my boots off." It must have been this sentence that reminded me that my father had a copy precisely because that sentence sounds like a description of my dad during that time—his exhaustion, pain, confusion. It's a mystery where his copy came from—the treatment didn't reveal that—but my best guess is someone either lent him one, thinking it might interest him in the generic way war interests seemingly all men of that generation, or more likely he picked it up randomly from the lending shelf at the bar some quiet afternoon when no one was around. But still, why try to read that book then? Why read a book about war when your life is falling apart? To this, the treatment did provide an answer: my uncle Eugene, my dad's brother who'd died in Vietnam. The war had made Eugene a hero and then it made him nothing. His name is on a bronze plaque mounted at the base of the flagpole outside my high school, listed along with all the other Vietnam dead.

In all the hours I'd read *Dispatches* I'd thought about him only briefly. He was a ghost to me, someone I'm only now, in this moment, wishing I knew more about (representative of how self-absorbed the Mist made me). What I do know is that my father idolized him and was devastated by his death, though he'd never say it—only my grandmother let on to this. What the treatment seemed to tell me was that my father woke up and found that his life had spiraled into a kind of hell, and while he couldn't call his brother and ask for support, his path had crossed with this book and he thought that if he couldn't talk to his brother, then maybe he could at least find him somewhere in that record of the hell that'd killed him, or at least find some of the psychological fortitude that helped his brother get through it for as long as he did. I think he wanted to hurt with his brother instead of hurting alone. Yes, he never read it, not because he couldn't understand it—though its literary edge isn't really his style—but because he was so tired. Holding the book was enough. Like it was a box of my uncle's ashes.

It's there now, back in front of me, behind my eyes, and it's almost as if the cover's glow is coming from within, not from the fire, and I can feel the glow on my skin, the lapping waves of heat, the lemon glow, though of course it's only the Italian sun flashing between plane trees lining the tracks of the Frecciarossa fast approaching the Apennines, and Bologna waiting on the other side. But through this sensation I'm taken back there, to the living room floor in front of the hearth where Ben and I slept during the spill while the grid was down, our dad above us on the couch, which is also how we spent most of the daytime hours of the Great Spill, always trying to stay warm, logs always burning.

Between surges continuing to overtax the grid, the old infrastructure failing in the severe elements, and cars skidding off the frozen roads into utility poles, the power would remain out for days, making our wood a top commodity, which was good for us, because by midday Saturday Ben's albuterol was down to a few final pulses, which made Ben anxious, which of course made him need it even more. The pharmacies were picked clean and getting into a hospital was essentially impossible, so my dad struck a deal with one of our neighbors, a single woman nurse at the county hospital, to smuggle out a couple of inhalers in exchange for a wheelbarrow and wagon full of seasoned, match-strike cherry she could use to finally heat her house. I went with my father to deliver it, only a block from us. He was pushing the wheelbarrow and I was pulling a red Radio Flyer wagon. Ben was at home by the fire with camphor on his chest. This was early in the morning on Sunday. Restaurants, bars, stores, gas stations, pharmacies—everything was closed indefinitely. No power. No end in sight. Riots had persisted through the night. I'd hardly slept. There'd be an explosion, then siren blare, then crowd noise, then the chuck-chuck of police birds cutting low over the houses. The temperature that morning was still in the negative forties, the frozen air so dense we couldn't see where our yard ended and the street began. A thick quilt of icy fog, slow moving, with a violet tinge. Bad static. I was scared to go out there and couldn't say why and even if I could've I wasn't about to admit it. And then finally we did, we stepped out, and straightaway I could feel the soup around my brain turning to gel. I had to constantly blink to keep the liquid in my eyes from crystallizing. My dad said the plan was to run over to the nurse's house, quickly unload the wood, then run back. We started down the slick street, a black river revealing itself only a few feet at a time. It was very quiet. The first steps were uneventful. Then it began—"figures appearing and disappearing in the mist around us, odd, floating presences," to quote Herr, words that, when I read them, caused a flush of anxious heat to bloom up through my face.

I remember the figures like watery strokes of India ink against the dead pallor of the atmosphere. The first figures kept their distance, but then one approached—it was almost as if he assembled out of the frost with a dreamy look on his face, tall in a rough gray trench coat with scraggly blond hair. He looked like he was having fun. "What's that you guys got there?" he asked. My father didn't speak, just kept walking, so I kept walking too, and so did the man, and I knew I shouldn't look over at him, but finally I couldn't help it and when I did look his eyes caught mine and then his head turned toward his shoulder exactly ninety degrees, *exactly ninety,* like a broken action figure's. "That's a nice wagon," he said. His smile was a strange slit in the air. My father stopped, picked up one of the thinner splits of wood, turned to the man, said it'd be best if we all parted ways. "Very nice wood," said the man as he backstepped into the mist, then pivoted and went running the way he came. We could hear him hollering something, but not what; whatever he said, it wasn't for us. By then my father had lifted me up onto the wheelbarrow and was pushing at a sprint toward the nurse's house. I kept yelling about the wagon, but he said he'd come back for it. When we got to the nurse's house he pushed the wheelbarrow around the back and dumped the wood on her concrete patio beside her covered furniture. My father knocked hard on the back door, waited, knocked again, waited, and then when the nurse finally answered he walked us past her into the house and took me into the living room and sat me on the couch and told me not to move, then asked to speak with the nurse in the kitchen. I could see her shake her head, look out the window, look at me, then take a brown paper bag out of the cupboard and give it to my dad. He walked back to me and told me he was going to get the wagon, he'd be right back. I protested, I didn't want him to leave, but he said it'd only be a minute, that I needed to stay inside and warm up, the nurse was going to sit with me, and then he was gone out the back door. I ran to the front window and saw him walking through the yard, but then he was swallowed by the frozen air. And then the nurse closed the curtains. All I remember of sitting there was staring at the nurse's cigarette pack on the coffee table, the same golden brand my grandmother smoked, but I couldn't smell the smoke over the licorice smell. She kept shaking her head, saying something to herself, spitting periodically into a mug. When my dad came back he had his deer-hunting rifle slung over his shoulder. He thanked the nurse and took me outside. He told me we were going to run home. His eyes were very still. I noticed he didn't have the wagon with him, but I knew better than to ask about it. I said okay. He took the gun off his shoulder, held it like one of the men at the water buffalo station, asked if I was ready. There were frozen snot beads on his mustache. I nodded yes, then we were gone.

When we got back my dad closed the blinds, locked the front door, pushed the bookcase in front of it, then hurriedly opened the back kitchen door that let out to our woodpile and started bringing the firewood inside, stacking it right there on the kitchen linoleum. I ran over to help, but he yelled for me to stay by my brother. When he finished, he stacked some especially big logs in front of the back door, locked it, then took the rifle and joined us in the living room.

Later that day I stood by the fire with my shirt off while my dad rubbed steroid cream on the rash that had bloomed on my back and left side. His big hands were swirling slowly around my shoulder blades when at once they stopped, held still. Outside, slow footsteps sounded over the yard, the frozen grass crunching like glass. A shadow floated past the window, then footsteps scraped on the stoop. My father picked up the rifle, slid across the carpet, stood up, leaned his ear against the door, listened for a moment, then moved the rifle close up against the door and engaged its bolt, reloading the chamber, allowing the glide and click of the mechanism to echo against the wood. No movement, no sound, and then the steps went down the stairs, down the walk, and away.

FOR SO MANY HOURS—endless hours, it seemed—I tried to translate this memory into a scene for the novel, but always failed. Something was off. There was a snag in my mind. I was so desperate. I was running out of time. I was lost. I needed something, anything to get me going. For weeks during the summer months I decided to take BART to San Francisco to walk through the fog in hopes of reimmersing myself in a similar experience—at the very least I could take notes on how the fog moved, how the shadows of pedestrians looked through the distance, how the colors of the traffic lights faded, but with each trip I grew increasingly confused, then started getting lost, until one evening I was found crying on a bench in Dolores Park with no memory of how I'd gotten there. What memory I did have, however, was one from the past, a correction:

I'd always remembered leaving the nurse's house, my father with his rifle raised, and getting onto the street. From there I thought my dad and I made it home, no problem, but this was wrong. Between the nurse's house and ours something happened: I saw a dog. Or I saw what I thought was a dog. I'd heard on the radio that people should bring all dogs and cats inside, even those that weren't their own, or else they'd freeze to death. Remembering this when I thought I saw the dog, I stopped and tried to locate it, only for a few seconds, but that was long enough to lose sight of my dad and my orientation—you must understand, by this point the air was a flat, blistering nothingness; if you stuck out your arm you couldn't see your hand, though I hadn't realized this when I started running in what must've been the wrong direction, because after a minute I didn't catch up with my dad and instead was in a separate yard I didn't recognize, turned arouhd again, and after only a few steps was once again lost in the blank. I yelled for my dad, but nothing happened. This is the point: *nothing* happened. There was only mist. This was where my memory stopped. And it didn't pick back up until my dad was squatting in front of me, looking me over in a panic, asking if I was okay between yelling at me angrily about not staying by his side, though clearly he was most of all grateful I was there to be yelled at.

Months after this correction of memory, while in the early stages of ghostwriting for the Physicist and reading his work, I encountered the following passage in a chapter about quantum mechanics written for a layman like myself: "[Werner] Heisenberg imagined that electrons do not *always* exist. They only exist when someone or something watches them, or better, when they are interacting with something else . . . an electron is a set of jumps from one interaction to another. When nothing disturbs it, it is not in any precise place. It is not in a 'place' at all." When I read this, I doubled back, read it again, then again, then set the book down, certain I was to make something of it, but unsure as to what. That is, until my treatment. But there's not enough time to explain that now, not with Bologna so close.

→

THE EPISODE in the fog in Dolores Park was near the end of my attempt at writing. By then I was in rapid decline. I lost weight, couldn't sleep, lost my hair—wisps of it falling past my face while I tried to work, enough that I could gather it into a pile after only an hour—would sometimes cry when I woke up, so depressed to be back in my reality.

What did all this do to Annie? I'll never know completely, even with what she's told me, even with what I experienced during the treatment. A private disease spreads private suffering. I didn't want to tell her what I wanted to do to myself and how badly I wanted to do it, and she didn't want to tell me what my severe state was doing to her. A problem of care; a disease that feeds on it. But there's only so much anyone can take—both the ill and their keeper. "I don't want to get into threatening anything, I don't want to get into that kind of language, that's not how I think, you know that, but it's like I'm backed into a corner here and I'm trying and I need you to try too, whatever it is, you've got to try something." She said this to me one bad morning on the couch. I couldn't keep focus, my head kind of drifting, the room full of fog. She was crying and I could hear it, but it sounded muffled and distant, almost subaqueous. I was trying to tell her she was right to talk of leaving because that's the safe thing to do, but I couldn't get the words out because a part of me was saying, *Please do not go*. Five days a week she helps design virtual beings whose main jobs are to honor your requests and answer your questions, but at home she was stuck with me, who couldn't explain very simply why he felt the way he did. Answers, links, the clean lines of thinking that follow back to a moment of origin, a true source, a single explanation—even then I'd spent enough time in Wikipedia holes to know that if you follow the branches far enough what you find at the end isn't some hard edge, but a space where things fray. It's one thing to understand that that space exists, but it's another thing to *be* that space. To be the limit of something. To be the limit of what someone's love can reach. "Why aren't you saying anything? This is doing something to me, I know you see that. I know I'm talking loudly and sound angry, but I can't help it. I've got to say it: What about me? What about how you hurting yourself will hurt me? I *know* you care about that. I know you do. I'm not saying that to make you feel guilty, I'm saying that because it's the truth. I don't care if it makes me selfish. We can both be selfish together, it doesn't matter." The room full of fog. Daylight filtered through droplets I couldn't see. And very quiet. She put a hand on my back. The timeless prelingual power of the gesture—it was awful. I had no back. I was the grenade. The very slowly detonating grenade whose body is no longer a body but is many metal fragments beginning their random flights on the waves of a bright exothermic madness expanding out in total disarray. *Imagine this going on forever. Imagine her going through this month after month, year after year. How you'll wear her down. How you'll burn up her best years. Letting her get sanded down by hope, then fatigue, and then eventual devastation? There's only one way this can end, so why not set her free?* The voice not my voice. The room full of fog. I said to her, *I love you very much, more than I'll ever articulate or maybe understand, but I am very confused and very helpless and also I've tried my best and I'm very sorry,* but it seemed she couldn't hear me.

"You agree to therapy immediately or I'm calling Jules. Or Ben. Both, I don't care. They'll come and I'll leave."

A PSYCHIATRIST had helped me get through a rough patch back in grad school, so I found one through my insurance. Dr. Champlain. I went for a consultation at her office in Berkeley. I was specifically interested in her because in her profile online she talked about how she's primarily focused on a blend of talk therapy and holistic treatments and is much less interested in pharmaceuticals as a solution, which gave me hope, because I'd taken pills in the past, lots of them, and while they kept me from offing myself, they also made it nearly impossible to remember the contents of any book I'd read or conversation I'd had, and with regards to painting I was essentially neutered. My first meeting with Dr. Champlain seemed positive. She asked for a rundown of my history to bring her up to speed, so I explained everything, my childhood, my failed art career, the Mist, the fluke months that became a fluke year, then the contract and the writing years in which I was then imprisoned. I explained how I felt really connected to her approach as explained in her profile online. We seemed to vibe, which of course made Annie very happy, but when I went back for a second appointment I could sense a strained energy. I sat down on the couch and she asked how I was doing and I explained how I spent most of my day thinking about killing myself. She shook her head, feigned concern, said something about how awful that is, how I definitely need a lot of help, a lot of work, *a lot,* and because of that, she said, she couldn't see me. I said I didn't understand and in a kind of shaky voice she explained that my condition was so severe, so dire, that it'd require far more time treating me than she had available, but she did think I should start taking medication immediately.

I said nothing. I began to feel incredibly stupid, then observed, then set up. I couldn't look at her, so I stared at a black-and-white photo of *Spiral Jetty* hanging on the wall. She asked me what I was feeling.

"I feel like you just said I'm so sick you can't be bothered to help me. Like, I said I want to kill myself and then you were like *I ain't got the time for that.*"

"Okay, okay, good," she said, fake-shaking her head again. "Let's follow the feelings further. Tell me more."

"No. You just told me you don't have time. I'm feeling very uncomfortable." I could sense, with the utmost distinction, that someone was laughing at me, whether or not they existed didn't matter. "I'm going to go now."

She checked her watch. "But you still have forty minutes of time."

I double-blinked. Slipping out of the points of her mouth were thin ribbons of smoke. I said, "I'm leaving."

"Wait—we need to decide what you want to do about billing."

"What the fuck are you talking about? You want to charge me for a meeting in which you told me you can't help me?"

"Well, do you feel you should be charged?" The Mist puffed out of her mouth with each syllable she spoke. I didn't respond. I got up and went for the door. "Hold on," she said. "Here is a list of people I think would be a great fit for you." She was holding out a Post-it note. I walked out of her office. "I worked really hard putting this together," she said to my back as I rushed down the hall. In my car I tried to slow my breathing, relax, but I couldn't. What went on in that office was undeniable; the universe was telling me it's time to accept that what I'd been feeling was not a feeling but a reality: I am not supposed to be here. Even when asking for help I repulsed those meant to reach toward me. I hit my head against the steering wheel many times, with force. Some drool fell out of my mouth. I had a text from Annie at work, asking me to let her know how the meeting goes. "Another positive session," I wrote. "In bathroom break right now." I drove home and read *Dispatches*.

This was the turning point. As I sat stunned on our couch, looking at the book I'd studied with the devotion of the faithful, a pressure began to loosen around my mind. I was reading the book's central chapter, "Khe Sanh," about the monumentally horrific, deadly, relentless, and most of all pointless battle that took place there. I'd become especially obsessed with this chapter for the way Herr captured the claustrophobic and paranoid nature of the men who were forced to live through seventy-seven days of endless shelling in the year 1968, all because LBJ said on TV that we wouldn't lose Khe Sanh, so we couldn't.

At first I thought *Dispatches* was a book about chaos. But as time wore on, as I got worse, I began to think *Dispatches* was, in some way, a book about Vietnam that just so happened to predict many details of the Great Spill, and that maybe those details had been sewn into the text like a code, a code for me to find. Or maybe that the Great Spill was simply an echo of a single force that repeats itself across the planet, across time, over and over, only in different forms, with different characters and costumes and reasons. Whatever it was, I'd decided *Dispatches* was a curse. The book hadn't been revealed to me to teach me how to write, but to show me what I'd never be able to write, ever. But then finally, while sitting on the couch that afternoon after getting dumped by Dr. Champlain, flipping through passages about Khe Sanh I'd read a thousand times, I landed on the chapter's final graph, its final sentence, when Khe Sanh goes from being the Alamo to nothing: "In early June engineers rolled up the airstrip and transported the salvaged tarmac back to Dong Ha. The bunkers were filled with high explosives and then blown up. The sandbagging and wire that remained were left to the jungle, which grew with a violence of energy now in the Highland summer, as though there was an impatience somewhere to conceal all traces of what had been left by the winter." And that was the end of it. Westmoreland called it a victory, but by then everyone knew Khe Sanh had been nothing short of hell brought to life right there on the surface of the earth, just to see what would happen.

Hubris. Hubris and failure. That, I finally understood, was why I'd become obsessed with *Dispatches*. Two hundred sixty pages about hubris and the failure that hubris unleashes, failure that will not end until the hubris is realized, accepted, submitted to, repented for. Two hundred sixty pages about pain. Two hundred sixty pages about lying to yourself. Two hundred sixty pages about trying to convince the world a kind of future exists when it doesn't. Two hundred sixty pages about being where you don't belong, doing what you have no business doing.

There were many reasons why I agreed to write the big West Virginia novel. Of course the money was a primary one: I wanted to take the life Annie and I were building and help usher it into a greater reality of comfort, relaxation, security, freedom. But an even bigger reason was that I was so grateful to be wanted at all, to be believed in, and I didn't want it to end. I wanted to make something great, which is what I'd always wanted, all the way back to when I first learned to draw and saw that people liked what I'd made. It didn't matter that I'd written *The Troop* and that it might be great—I believed that because I couldn't account for it, I didn't deserve it. That it wasn't even real. But *I* would write this new book. *I* would be the cause of its effect. And so as soon as I signed that contract I told myself it had begun: I was a writer. And I believed it. This was the greatest mistake.

What I realize now—and I mean *right now*—is that the reason I was able to write *The Troop* was because I wasn't a writer. I was nothing. Or, if I was anything, I was recklessness. I composed those stories from a position of such naïveté, so far from any intention, that I was free from any fear of being derivative, any anxiety about being literary enough or smart enough. There was no identity involved, no ego; I was like a kid with a crayon. The central quality people found in *The Troop,* the voice they kept mentioning in the reviews, its "unselfconsciousness" and "spiritual rawness," was all because they were experiencing a voice speaking before the mind to which it was attached could even hear it. Pure instinct, and I realize now that it was so freeing because it was this very sense of recklessness that I'd lost in my art practice so long before. All the years of study, of being around the art scene, of going to shows and having drunken debates with friends and contemporaries, of reading *Art in America,* all of it was in service of an ego as big as the Met, a default mode network around my artistic mind that made me believe that there was one goal—pure heroic originality, a body of work worthy of *The World of*—and yet the only way to get there was by adopting a mind and identity through which I could think my way into it.

What better fuel for the Mist? It was always there, in my every move, emanating off every brushstroke like a fume. I couldn't draw a single line without hearing how derivative I was, how everything I did was a weak copy of something I'd copied out of my Time-Life Library. And maybe it's true, maybe every skill I had was thanks to copying from books. But what the Mist kept me from seeing is that through that copying, deeper skills and senses and intuition can develop into a deeper making mind. What matters is what you do with it. "I don't know what I'm doing, so that's good!" Antony used to say. I thought I knew what he meant, but I didn't. It wasn't about knowledge, at least not in the way I thought. It was about him *knowing* that there were parts of himself, deeper parts and more intelligent parts, that knew things before he himself ever could; the Mist robbed me of believing I could ever be this way by constantly convincing me that I wasn't good enough, I deserved nothing, I was a fool, I was deficient. I shouldn't even be alive.

But *The Troop* was proof otherwise. Writing it, I was where Antony was, only I was so ill I couldn't see it. All I thought I was doing was wasting time. I felt like I was being reckless, and I was right! But I misunderstood what that meant. And then when the book deal came along, I went from recklessness to an identity. It was that identity, not me, not my smarter mind, that sat down every day trying to write that novel, trying to *be* a novelist, and that's precisely why it failed. LD tried to warn me away from this so many times. "Let go of yourself," she'd say, sipping a Tsingtao. "Get back to the mystery. Get back to the unknowing." But I didn't listen. Instead I took it as a challenge. I doubled down. I needed to find a way to write a book that proved I knew what I was doing. And so of course it failed. Of course every word I called up seemed stupid: the Mist was there to greet it. This is why I went looking into other books, trying to find a way out. Follow the trail of those who "knew what they were doing," but of course this only reawakened fears of influence, copying, unoriginality. Yet what's so criminal about those fears is that I knew as far back as my boyhood that if you leaned hard enough into any artist's *The World of,* you'd find a record of their own Time-Life Library too. Hell, you could line the spines up in such a way that they practically told a story of whose work bloomed from whose. Nothing comes out of thin air. Including *The Troop.* It isn't some invention, it's just another permutation of those afternoons spent in the woods, learning how to survive. Maybe all of this is simple and obvious to you. Maybe it's hard to believe I lived as long as I did, missing so much that was right in front of me. I guess you'd be right: it is hard to believe I lived as long as I did, as ill as I was.

And worst of all, I was trying to think and write about West Virginia. I was trying to hammer it down into all of its component ideas, textures, characters, everything needed to make it a Place. But in doing this I'd ignored the one lesson that every West Virginian is taught over and over and over again every time someone in this great Federation of States forgets that we exist: there is no West Virginia. The mountain that was there last year is gone this year. The forest which fed your family for a century? It's gone. The opera houses, the old hotels—they're empty. All the earth inside the hills? Gone. Your neighbor? He swallows medicine every morning and floats away in a cloud of bronze light. This is why it was impossible for me to capture the Great Spill, let alone the state: because there is nothing there but undulating, ever-changing space. "The best grammar for thinking about the world is that of change, not of permanence. Not of being, but becoming," writes the Physicist, and that might as well be the entire Wikipedia entry for the Mountain State. The Great Spill is not a story. It is interaction. Miss one part of it and you've missed the whole thing. If you don't have the past and future of every soul standing and shivering in the water buffalo lines, you missed the water lines and so you missed the thirst and so you missed it all. Miss mentioning every time someone had to spit because of the licorice, and you miss all the gallons, the millions of gallons, of spit that disappeared. It was an impossible task. Anything I wrote would've been both a gross understatement and, by virtue of applying a plot and structure, an elegant overstatement. There is no point exaggerating what is already horrific, said someone somewhere. The point stands. It makes me laugh now, here in seat 19D, car 8, on Frecciarossa train 9318, sliding almost to a halt, my fellow passengers around me standing, stretching, gathering their bags, it makes me laugh because I've known this all my life. It's right there, in the state's unofficial anthem, a song I've sung countless times, shouted it and crooned it and mumbled it while homesick on the subway or the Dumbarton Bridge, the song sung by thirty thousand fans at the end of every Mountaineer football game at Mountaineer Field, gathering together toward the chorus in a crescendo of rare earnestness, "Country roads, take me home / To the place I belong / West Virginia," go the thirty thousand fans, the anthem, the spirit of the Mountain State captured in a voice eternally singing because they're anywhere but there.

Welcome to Bologna.

THE SUBTERRANEAN LIGHT of the high-speed rail terminal of Bologna Centrale is all halogen and LED, cold blue modern alien light that makes it feel like it's always night, but it isn't, not yet. I'm in 12D of car 7 on Frecciarossa train 9601, actively departing for Roma Termini, heading back the way I came. The interior is identical to this morning's car: gray leather seats, hard plastic armrests, clean oblong windows, clean floors, small TVs above the aisle, accordion doors between the cars; but there's a difference. If the morning's smelled of disinfectant and humans freshly scrubbed and perfumed, it smells like that now, but in decay. The bitter dirt tinge of espresso and cigarette breath. Cologne spritzed directly onto the damp underarm fabric of an oxford shirt. Sweat in the air, yes, and exhaustion—I've already seen one person's head yo-yo in involuntary sleep. Someone, I'm pretty sure, is eating cured meats. Yet it still feels clean and elegant and even cheerful. The real difference is, I think, that whatever the day was going to do it's already gone ahead and done. An unwinding. And where this morning's train was starting its journey fresh, I'm joining this one halfway through its own. The car feels like a little village that has accepted me—small smiles curled up as I came aboard, found my seat—and together just now we've reemerged aboveground into an early evening possessed by light like hammered copper that has the whole ruddy city glowing as if someone plugged it in.

When I arrive in Roma Termini in time for dinner, I'll stroll for thirty minutes in the newfound lightness of my body over to SantoPalato—a newer trattoria in San Giovanni much praised for its commitment to rehabbing Roman classics, forgotten staples hardly eaten by the young, which is to say they've been praised for going backward—where I'll meet Annie and we can enjoy the last days of our honeymoon. I can see her now, in her black jeans and white linen shirt, her pointed orange loafer-slides with a fashion heel, elegant and big eyed, eager to eat, smiling at me with her imperfect smile, not that it isn't perfect in its beauty—it is—but dentally speaking it isn't uniform because her left central incisor, her left-front tooth, is angled slightly away from the crescent curve held by the rest of her top row, a "flaw" she hates but which I love precisely for its radical remove from the uniform impersonal smile obtained by everyone in our generation thanks to the explosion of the orthodontics industry, a "flaw" that conveys so much confidence—old-school European model/film-star confidence—that I've seen people, women *and* men, subconsciously slide their tongues under their teeth while talking to her, trying to nudge out their left central incisor like hers. We will embrace. She will smell like Chanel No. 5. She'll genuinely ask me to tell her everything. And what will I tell her? I'm still making sense of it myself.

EARLIER, when I arrived in Bologna, just before noon, I ascended via escalator from the Frecciarossa terminals up to the old, hot commuter rails, stepped out onto the plaza, and, just as I said I would, smoked a ceremonial cigarette for my dad before returning to the local platforms and hopping on regional train 11536 and riding the three stops to Modena, a trip so short I didn't even take a seat, and then . . . and then things got complicated. The strangeness that came after—I just want to get it right, I don't want to blurt it out like when I finally told Annie I'd failed to write the book: a Saturday, early September, a few weeks after the incident with Dr. Champlain, a few weeks before the book was due. We were lounging in the sun on the grassy banks along Lake Merritt, down the street from our apartment; it was Annie's idea (to get me out of the house, I think, hoping some vitamin D might perk me up). My head was in her lap. Above, the sky was a clear electric blue I stared into until it transformed first from sky to a flat azure plane before morphing again into a space of many depths, all perceptible. Flying geese appeared from my right, airliners from my left. Lounging there, looking up, for a moment I forgot I existed, that the absence I'd created by not writing the book existed, and I felt something: not happy, but not depressed. Only a sliver of a moment, but it was enough. The first moment of acceptance. "I failed," I said up to Annie. "I'm sure you've figured by now, but there is no book. I'm defaulting on my contract. I'm giving up. I can't do it. I haven't got a thing."

"I know," said Annie. She ran her hands through my hair.

"What about the money? I'll have to give it all back, but it's gone. I really fucked up. I don't think you understand—I haven't written a word."

"No, I get it. For a while I thought you were working, and maybe you were, but then these last few months, when I still hadn't seen any pages, no drafts at all, I knew it was bad. I was afraid to say anything, with how things have been. I reached out to LD and she said she shared my hunch. She told me about what to expect. It's over now. It sucks, of course. It sucks a lot. We'll get it sorted out. We'll make it work. That's our only choice. I've got my job, so it's not like we're out on the street. And everything that's already been paid for is, well, paid for. Whatever happens, we can't go on with you like this."

"I think Lisa is going to be pissed."

"Likely. Have you told LD?"

"No, but we're having dinner at Z and Y on Wednesday, so we'll have that to talk about. I think she might be happy to hear that it's all finally over with."

"Well, however she feels, we'll handle it. We'll handle all of it on Monday. Nothing to do until then. It's over now. I'm tired." She leaned back again, closed her eyes, let the golden hour do its thing.

I felt something vicious in me then. Not toward Annie, but toward the universe. The relief I felt after confessing defeat wasn't what I'd hoped for. It was there, sure, but I could tell that it was temporary. I thought giving up on the book would free me, but I knew, head in Annie's lap, a beam of Pacific light bleaching my hair, that it was only a pause, a chance to catch my breath before I descended further, and by the next morning I felt terrible again, and then Monday came and I called Lisa.

"I don't have a single page," I said to her. "It's over."

"*Over?* We'll get an extension—this happens all the time. Send me what you have, so I can give them a sense of your progress. But I'm going to be honest with you—this is not a good look. The timing is awful. Things have changed at the publisher. There's new leadership."

"I don't have any pages," I said again. "Not one."

"How do you not have any pages? What have you been doing?"

"Reading. I took some notes."

There was a pause. "Like I said, we'll get an extension. They're not going to be happy about it, but it's unheard of to cancel a novel because it misses one deadline. Even under the new regime, they wouldn't do that, I don't think. But they've advanced you a lot of money already and they're not going to have unlimited patience. Have you told anyone about this? We need to keep wind of this away from our friends in LA. There are a lot of moving parts here. It's all very fragile. Hang tight, and I'll make some calls."

"No," I interrupted. "You're not understanding me. I don't want time. I want it over with. I can't do it. It's killing me. I'm done."

"Don't be ridiculous. You think this is the first conversation like this I've had? Writers freak out. I get it. Like I said, send me your notes. Send me anything. You need to understand: you can't tell these people you're not going to do it. Not unless you haven't touched the money and can write them a check to pay it all back. They'll come after you. And then think about the Hollywood money you'll never see. Do you understand how much you stand to lose here? Fly out here, bring what you have; we'll look through it all and get you back on schedule. The second book is hard for everyone."

"I don't have anything, Lisa. It's over." Another pause. Then she pretended she needed to put me on hold for a moment, but she forgot to silence her speaker, so I sat there and listened as she proceeded to unleash a rant of expletives. I felt honored by it, truly— I didn't know I could evoke such passion in someone I wasn't romantically engaged with.

She picked back up. "Do you still have the money?"

"It's gone."

"And where did it go?"

This time I paused. "Did I tell you I'm getting married?" I began, but at that she'd hung up.

A week later, even after I'd insisted I'd written nothing and had no plans to write anything because I fundamentally couldn't, even after I asked Lisa to make it end, she still tried to buy me time.

But it didn't matter. Once the publisher's new regime got wise to the fact that they were short a significant chunk of change paid out by the previous regime for, of all things, a literary novel about a chemical spill in West Virginia, of all places, a novel that didn't exist because the author didn't have a word to show for it, they said enough was enough. They wanted to send a signal: the days of literary patronage were over. They were running a business, not a foundation. They were coming for their money.

Letters, cold emails, lawyers: a whole machine creeped awake. Nothing interesting about it; it was business. A book can be a totem of the best the human spirit has to offer, but up until the moment it exists it's nothing but another gathering of hypotheticals, contracts, futures. Going through it all only exacerbated my mental situation. And yet, at the same time, it was almost rewarding: finally I was seeing people treat me as the disappointing virus I knew myself to be. At last reality and my self-perception had fully aligned. No more in between, no more overlap. I finally *was* what I always knew I was. I'd be lying if I said it wasn't a little exhilarating. When Lisa told me about the publisher's plan to seek remittance, I almost smiled. And for the first time in years, for a brief spell, there was truly nothing in my head, no projections of how the world despised me because no projections were necessary: every angry phone call, argument, lawyer's meeting, memo—they were all real. Gloriously real. One day an old-timey attorney who looked like he was born wearing a Windsor knot actually said to me, from across his desk, "You really screwed the pooch on this one," and I let out the kind of laugh I imagine someone might laugh when they've had a joint popped back into place. I knew I'd be dead very soon.

A MONTH LATER I heard from Terry Strickland for the first time. I was in my bathroom in total darkness, meditating on killing myself. Sitting there on the toilet with the top seat down, I was certain I could feel Annie's pack of disposable razors vibrating under the sink, calling my name, telling me they'd set me free. This made me cry gently, and it was while I was crying, trying to pretend I couldn't see the elaborate images of my suicide as the Mist built them in my mind while also urging me to take the pack of razors from under the sink and hold them in my hands and grow acquainted with the tools that would ferry me away, that I realized the motion-activated exhaust fan installed in the ceiling was not activating in response to my motion, my pitiful shaking, and for a moment it felt like I was already gone, already a ghost, and this made me smile for the first time in weeks, a smile that made me open my eyes and see that my phone was illuminated on the sink. Someone was calling. I didn't recognize the number, so I let it ring, and then it pinged with a voicemail notification. Either it didn't occur to me then that responding to my phone while on the brink of suicide is what got me in this position in the first place, or it did occur to me and I didn't give a damn because the Mist worked in patterns and this is how things went. Regardless, I listened to the voicemail. It was from Terry. He said, in his big surfer's voice, that he ran the eponymous Strickland Agency and wanted to talk to me about a very real, and possibly very flush, opportunity, and that hopefully I'd get back to him and we could set up a meeting at his office in Santa Cruz. Santa Cruz? Weren't all the good agents in New York? I googled him and he seemed legit—very legit—so I called him back. He answered at the first ring, and before I could so much as introduce myself he started explaining that he ran a literary agency that specialized in representing esteemed individuals from STEM fields. "Big Idea people" is what he called them. "Peo-

ple whose ideas are so big," he said, "they're often too busy changing the world to sit down and write their autobiographies and
memoirs and pop-sci books. That's what makes us at the Strickland Agency so unique—we don't just represent these people; we
also provide a team of coaches and ghostwriters to help them write
their books. Sometimes we even pitch a book to them they didn't
know they wanted to write." He went on to explain that one of the
most esteemed individuals on their list had requested me, personally, to be his ghostwriter. He couldn't say much more over the
phone but would love to talk about it in person.

The thought of doing any sort of writing work sounded like the
worst thing ever, but he said the phrase "possibly very flush" more
than once, and I couldn't deny that it piqued my heart a little with
something like hope, hope that maybe this could help me claw out
of at least one of my many problems. After all, if it didn't work out,
I could always go back to shutting down the dance. He asked when
we could meet. We scheduled a time for the next day.

The offices of the Strickland Agency were in a large, exquisitely
maintained Craftsman home on a residential street overlooking
the Pacific. In the entryway I was met by a secretary at a large
wooden desk (everything was wood, actually: high redwood panel-
ing, redwood floors and doors and trim, redwood furniture). She
seemed to be in her early twenties and very into natural fibers and
not very much into being a secretary. She asked if I'd like a kombucha; I declined. I waited in a chair next to her in silence and tried
to look down the hall to see if the other rooms, all of which were
closed, were offices or maybe rooms in which Terry Strickland
lived when it wasn't business hours, but the doors never opened
and no one ever came down the hall. Incense was burning, somewhere. Finally, her desk phone rang, and she said I could go up to
see Terry.

The stairs led to a single closed door on a landing decorated with a handwoven rug, Mexican in pattern, or so I guessed, and a very large framed art photograph of a curling wave. I knocked on the wooden door and waited, then waited some more, then began to feel kind of skeeved, but then it opened and standing there was a man who looked more or less like the business portrait of Terry Strickland I'd seen on his website, except he was much, much bigger. Enormous, in fact. But not heavy. A body like a colt's. And he was wearing a very fine suit. I didn't know anything about suits at the time, and don't know much more now, but even then I knew that what I was looking at was a top-notch garment. In fact, the suit is very much like the suit worn by the two men seated beside me here on the Frecciarossa train 9601, zipping toward Rome. Twins, turns out. It's a little strange. They're both tall, with chestnut hair and identical trimmed beards, in identical olive-green suits—a suit I'd very much like to own—identical in every way it seems; at first I attempted to keep sense of who was who, but no sooner did the Frecciarossa start its placid wake out of Bologna than one went to the bathroom, then the other, then one got up to fetch something from a bag overhead, then the other went to throw something away, and it seemed that each time one moved the other moved too—had to move, in fact—if only to the opposite seat.

Terry shook my hand and welcomed me into his office, which seemed to be the entire top floor of the house converted into a single room, complete with a kitchen and living room and desk area and a sort of bay window section that looked to be, judging by the floor bed and woven cushions, for meditation or napping or both. He led me to his desk, a grand piece I was fairly certain had been carved straight from a section of redwood trunk. Behind him, wide picture windows framed the slate waves of the sea. Terry seemed in every way a totally straight shooter—gray hair trimmed

high and tight with a side part, nice watch, silk tie, good posture—
and yet the more I looked around the room, the more I began to
notice, in addition to the meditation area, lots, and I mean *lots*,
of very arresting, sometimes disturbing, universally strange paintings. These made it difficult for me to concentrate on Terry as he
began to speak. He first made some comments about *The Troop*,
which made me anxious; I wanted to forget the accidental book
had ever happened. He went on to talk a bit about being an Eagle
Scout himself, before finally saying that it was *The Troop* that likely
brought us together.

"How do you mean?"

"Well, the client didn't elaborate why, but he asked for you by
name, and so my only guess is he read some of your work, or maybe
the whole book, who knows."

"Who is the client?"

He named the Physicist. "Are you familiar with him?"

I was. He'd published two small hardbacks about physics that
explained even the most complex theories in distilled, simplistic
terms. One was about major theories, the other specifically about
time. They were modest books put out by an academic publisher,
but they'd become unexpected successes. I was always seeing copies stacked on display tables in the bookstores I visited for readings. He must have sold boatloads of copies. They've since been
published in dozens of languages. From what I knew, he'd written
them himself and even translated them himself into English (he
worked at a university in the UK). I said as much to Terry, asking
why I was here, if this man knew how to write.

"As [the Physicist] put it, 'Physics is one thing, life is another.' To
be honest, this memoir was my idea. This is what I do. I keep my
ear to the ground; I keep my eyes open. I pay attention to the people that are different than the rest of us. Big Idea people, as I think

I mentioned. It was obvious to me that after two books about his ideas, [the Physicist]'s audience was desperate to know more about the man who had produced them; I told him I thought a big New York publisher would pay seven figures for a memoir, and that he wouldn't even have to write it—almost none of my clients do. He hesitated, so I asked him if he'd do it if I got him seven figures. He said he would, so I went and rounded up seven figures from basically every publisher in New York. The high bidder was—" He named my publisher. "Except one hiccup has developed: [the Physicist] has requested that we get you as his ghostwriter."

"Yeah, this is all a mistake," I said. "Those people, they are currently very, very unhap—"

"I understand there's been a failure to deliver on your part. I was briefed. To tell you the truth, they aren't thrilled about this demand of his. But I've more or less got them by the cojones, if you know what I mean. There's lots of buzz saying this guy is going to win the Nobel soon, so they want to get this book done so it can be released in accordance with his award. To be frank, they pleaded with me to find someone similar to you—anyone, really—and the editor on the project, this guy named Richards, pretty openly said he doesn't want you near this and would rather have a subway rat work on it. I understand his hesitations. He's got a lot riding on this. If I'm being honest, I sort of held him over a barrel to get him to go as high as he did, so he really needs it to go well. I mean, they all do, really. I get it. So I asked everyone to breathe, then instead I suggested that I talk to you, Eagle Scout to Eagle Scout"—I couldn't tell if he was serious—"and maybe we could come up with a plan where everyone gets what they want."

"A plan?"

"That's correct," said Terry. He pulled open a drawer to his right to fetch what I thought would be documents outlining "the plan" but was instead a long cylinder wrapped in butcher paper. He dropped it on his desk, opened it: a twelve-inch Italian sub. The stink of cured pork perfumed the room. "I suggested," continued Terry after taking a mammoth bite, shredded lettuce hanging like confetti from his lip, "that I put you through a kind of tutorial on ghostwriting, a personal tutorial, if you will, to get you up to speed and to give the publisher some confidence. In addition, I suggested we operate under a conditional schedule. [The Physicist] will provide you and me with materials for sections, either written or recorded, and then you'll be expected to write those sections within a certain number of days. For each section you complete, from drafts to finished pages, you'll be paid an installment. By the time a final draft is turned in to the publisher, you'll have been paid half your fee. When the book is published, you'll be paid the second half. Now"—he paused briefly, closed his eyes, took a *very* deep breath, dry swallowed, then throated half the sub like a python, hardly chewing before the mass slid past his Adam's apple—"because, as I understand it, you're in the hole with the publisher, they've agreed to forgive your debt dollar for dollar if you help them complete this book."

"So would I make anything?"

He looked into the distance for a moment as he throated another hunk of sub. "Yes. Not much. But it'd get you back to zero and into their good graces. Then there'd be royalties if the book earns out, which, if this sells as much as they think it's going to sell, will likely happen, making this more than worth it for you in the long run." He wiped his hands and face with a white cloth napkin that came from somewhere on his person, then without comment he got up from his desk and moved to one of the seating areas across the room, arranged beside another window bay with a different angled view of the sea. I followed him over and sat on what I guessed was some kind of Moroccan stool or ottoman. Out the window I could see long patches of violet seaweed shrugging together and coming apart with the rhythms of the surf. It was unclear why we'd moved positions. Hanging over the couch where Terry was sitting was a very large painting of a man and woman holding each other, except they didn't have any skin, or their skin was see-through, so their veins and nerves and muscles were all visible and radiating an orange, astral light that emanated outward into mandalaesque patterns. I didn't particularly like the image, and yet I couldn't stop staring at it—it reminded me, for the first time in a long while, that I was once a painter. When I came to, Terry was also staring up at the painting, smiling. Then he looked at me and smiled. I expected him to say something about the painting, but instead he asked me if I wanted a beer and though I didn't I said sure and he pulled two craft bottles from a small Smeg fridge positioned beside the couch.

"You might get more out of this gig than money," he said, handing me the beer, a sour ale. "Working on something could help, of course, but getting to know [the Physicist], what he understands, what he's come to understand for all of us—it's thrilling stuff. It's part of why I love this work. He's going to disclose the story of his great realization, you know—what happened when he had his physics breakthrough. He's kept it *very* hush-hush. You could be one of the first to hear it. I get kind of tingly when I think about it. Do you know any Italian?"

"I'm half Italian. I know a few phrases from my grandmother. But, like, no—I don't *know* Italian. And what do you mean: help with what?"

"I'm going to tell the publisher you do. It'll make them feel more comfortable." Something like sea spray drifted past the window. "Do you surf?"

"Why do I need to know how to surf to be a ghostwriter?"

"You don't. But you seem very tense. It's tensing me up now actually. I can understand why, of course, because of your situation, but you're clearly doing nothing to relieve the negative energy building up in you. We'll meet every two weeks to go over your work and to make sure you're on track, then afterward I'll take you out to teach you how to surf."

I just kind of stared at him. He stared back, then reached into the inner chest pocket of his suit jacket and pulled out a golden Zippo. He opened a wooden box on the coffee table and took out—instead of the cigarettes and ashtray I was anticipating—a single black stick of incense and a hand-carved Mesoamerican bird I quickly figured out was the holder. He lit the incense with the Zippo, blew out the flame, watched the smoke begin to spiral off the tip, then again inhaled deeply, *very* deeply. I said nothing.

"Ojai," he said.

I had no clue what was going on. "I've never been," I said. "But I hear it's nice."

"No. The scent. It's called Ojai. You should take some. Please." He took some sticks from the box and extended them out to me. I thanked him. He checked his watch. "Well, it's not yet five in Manhattan. What do you say we call them up and let them know you're game?" I didn't know what to say or if I wanted to say anything. The painting behind him seemed to be undulating a little. He pulled out his phone and called the publisher, *my* publisher, and I watched as he told them I'd do it. Documents would be forthcoming.

After he hung up he talked for a while about himself, how he'd gotten here: raised in the Midwest, a stint in the military, college on the East Coast, had some "experiences" that sent him west, by accident ended up ghostwriting the best-selling autobiography of a biochemist I'd never heard of, parlayed this into a business, and here we are. I enjoyed talking to Terry. Something about the collision between his traditional sartorial presentation and the decidedly West Coast vibe of his immense office should've unsettled me, but instead they transmitted a sense of vision and confidence that gave me calm. Even the way he moved between different parts of the room—it wasn't out of antsiness, but more like he was following some current.

When it was time for me to leave we stood to shake hands and as our hands bounced up and down I noticed directly below them on the coffee table was a black book with a framed patch of sky on the cover, as if a hole had been cut in a black ceiling. It was a book by Michael Pollan, the journalist who'd written the article Antony had read to me years ago, back in Brooklyn. Clearly I was staring at it for longer than I realized, because Terry picked it up and handed it to me. "Take it," he said, "I've already read it in one way or another."

"Do you represent him?" I asked excitedly. "I love his books on food."

"Unfortunately, no. But I wish I did. That's a wave I'd definitely love to catch. Please," he said, "take the book. A gift to new beginnings." So I did.

ADMIRING A ROW OF CYPRESSES lining a low ridge, the late-day sun coaxing a dozen golds and ochers out of the fields, I can almost feel here, in seat 12D, how uneasy I felt on the drive home that afternoon from Santa Cruz, the light not unlike the light in this moment, and I remember now that it was on that drive that I was listening to a British podcast that once a week gathers top scholars in a given field to talk about an academic subject, that week's being futurism, and it was during this episode that one of the guests, an art historian, began describing in detail the bronze sculpture *Unique Forms of Continuity in Space* by Umberto Boccioni, calling the piece the apex of the futurist movement, and as he described the piece I was reminded suddenly, almost violently—not unlike how I'm reminded now—of an afternoon back in New York, not long before Annie and I moved west, when I found myself in Manhattan with time to burn before lunch with a friend and slipped into the MoMA, a place I usually despised because of the crowds, but which seemed almost forgotten about on this Friday afternoon. I rode the escalators all the way to the top and was working my way down when I encountered the Boccioni sculpture on a pedestal in the center of one of the galleries. I'd always admired the sculpture in art history classes and felt grateful to see it in person before leaving the city—it felt like a gift. For a brief while I was alone with the sculpture and was able to look at it how I pleased, circling it, getting close, then stepping back, forming a little cocoon of intimacy with the piece. But then my solitude was interrupted by a docent holding the hands of two boys wearing sunglasses. Something about their sunglasses made the boys seem unbearably hip, and I was certain they were the children of unreasonably rich Upper East Siders, kids who got escorted to famous art whenever they wanted, and I hated them for it. The docent stopped at the Boccioni sculpture and let go of the boys' hands. The boys did not move, nor did they look at each other or the docent as she squatted down between them. Their glasses were so black I couldn't tell what they were looking at. I thought they might be looking at me. Then the docent reached into the side pockets of her dark suit jacket and pulled out two matching pairs of white cotton gloves. I looked around to see if there were any other witnesses, but there was no one else, only a guard, and he was, I was pretty sure, sleeping with his eyes open. The docent gently helped one boy put on the gloves, then the other, neither taking their eyes off whatever it was they were looking at—the sculpture or me. With both boys gloved, the docent rose and led them by their hands up to the Boccioni sculpture. My heart began to thud. The docent whispered something to the boys, they nodded, and then at once she placed each of their hands on the sculpture and stepped back. Big grins splashed across their faces as the white gloves began caressing the sculpture's rippled, flamelike bronze, tender at first, but then with increasing purpose. My breathing turned rapid. Their smiles widened. The docent began talking to them quietly, saying something about the art, I assumed, and they shook their heads enthusiastically, boyishly—they were laughing now—and the scene grew blurry; I didn't realize my eyes were wet. They were blind, of course, how had I missed that, and for a moment I hated myself for hating them, but this faded swiftly, for I knew then that I was witnessing something like a miracle as they met futurism for the first time, Boccioni for the first time, *Unique Forms of Continuity in Space* for the first time, the sculpture building out in the consciousness of each, both as a form but also a text containing a whole movement of art, history, politics, and culture, and all the while neither cared (or seemed to care) that I might be there, watching them, and as I watched them transfixed I no longer cared if anyone was watching me, a grown man, crying, and I realized then in my car, pulled over on the shoulder of 880 a few miles north of San Jose, because once again I was crying, that that miraculous feeling I felt in the gallery is exactly how I'd felt only weeks before when Annie and I were finally married. I should've mentioned that: shortly after I announced that I wouldn't complete the novel, we had our ceremony at a glorious green garden in Marin County. The day was perfect. We said our vows between giant sculpted shrubs in the shade of a two-hundred-year-old oak. A small tent was erected inside a half-moon of Japanese mountain grass that breathed with the wind. Family and a few friends ate together at a long wooden table. We made promises to each other I wanted to keep so badly, *so badly,* and briefly I believed that making it to that moment would be enough, that as soon as we slid rings on our fingers the sky would part, the air would shift, and I would be free from my hell, and while it is true that our wedding day, that ceremony, those vows, our tears and memories, were perfect in every way, it took almost no time after it for things to settle back again, and then for me to feel even worse about what I knew I was going to do to myself, and yet here I was on the side of the road, crying, and I recognized that even if the ghostwriting project was just another ploy by the Mist to get me to hold on a little longer, only so that it, too, could go belly up, I felt committed to working my way out of debt as far as possible before it was over, so that when I did die, Annie wouldn't be left with the financial burden, which an attorney soon after confirmed would indeed happen. It was the same attorney from before, this time finalizing the stipulations of the ghostwriting deal instead of overseeing the dissolution of my book deal. He'd asked me if anything about my situation had changed. I mentioned I'd gotten married and he made the face a person makes when they've heard someone confess to having done a stupid thing, because apparently I had by marrying Annie. He explained, "California is a community property state. Were something to happen and the lawsuit were to begin again, any money or assets that your wife has made since being married is up for grabs in relation to damages. Does she work? We're talking garnished wages, things like that."

"Couldn't I declare bankruptcy?"

"Same rules apply. Could even be worse. Puts all your property under scrutiny."

I looked down into my lap. I didn't know how to ask what I wanted to ask, so I just said it. "What if I died?"

He stiffened at this. My voice, my phrasing—I'd revealed more than I'd meant to.

"Then your mess becomes her mess, and hers alone," he said sternly. And right then the Mist began to fill every memory of my wedding day. Just another pain I'd caused.

When I got home from Terry's, I told Annie all about the meeting, the offer. She was working on her laptop, deep in a project. Still typing, she said, "The clear path to debt erasure is obviously promising, but do we feel any reservations about the nature of the job? Basically I'm wondering about our ability to execute." Whenever she's in the thick of work she'll sometimes do this—talk to me like a colleague. I hated it.

"Our abilities?"

She looked up from the screen.

"Would you rather I start hanging pictures again? Maybe some desk job where they have padding on the walls and give me a pill when I get there so I don't do anything rash."

"This is an opportunity and you're right to take it. I was wrong to think backward. I apologize. I'm a little lost in the zone here. I think it's great. I really do." I both believed her and didn't believe her, which is likely how I would've felt no matter what she said.

IN THE EARLY DAYS of the ghostwriting job I went down to Santa Cruz once a week to learn about the craft from Terry. This mainly involved him showing me excerpts from successful books, then comparing the finished pages with the materials provided by the subject, which together we'd study to discuss how the ghostwriter transformed the raw material into "lucrative prose," as he called it. It was understood that after every session I'd go out to surf with Terry, as agreed. He'd lend me a board and a wet suit, both kept right there on the back deck of the office-house where there were multiple boards, multiple wet suits, and a shower. And so we "surfed," though all we ever did was paddle out, then sit on our boards in the dark water and stare inland at the Santa Cruz mountains, smell the brine, say very little, then paddle in and sip beers on the tailgate of his perfectly maintained 1962 Ford F-100 with a white-and-orange body, which he owned, it seemed, for the express purpose of hanging out on after surfing. I genuinely liked Terry and came to feel that we were something like friends. He was a total enigma, yet his kindness was genuine, his nature was gentle, he didn't seem to get stressed about anything, and he was generous with his time. I enjoyed these weeks, but even still I knew they too would eventually come crashing down, and so a terror circled under them like so many sharks.

Having been requested by name, I expected to receive some introductory message from the Physicist when our work began, perhaps explaining why he chose me of all people to be his ghost-writer, but no message ever came. Instead, the week of Thanksgiving I received an email from elaine@thestricklandagency.com explaining that she'd be the intermediary between me and the Physicist. He would send her audio recordings, then she, as the company's transcriber, would put them down into documents before sending both to me. She emphasized that the Physicist was very busy; all correspondences, no matter how small, were to go through her. I admit, this was a bit of a gut punch, learning that the Physicist had no interest in striking up a rapport with me. And yet, as the Mist quickly reminded me, how could it be any other way?

Shortly after this first email, a second arrived from elaine@ thestricklandagency.com with a link to a cloud drive containing multiple audio files, along with their corresponding transcriptions. I pressed PLAY on the first file, and a booming voice, speaking in near-perfect English, but with a mischievous Italian accent, said, "Hello. This is me. This is my life." What followed were hours of recordings of the Physicist recalling his life through a casual monologue, beginning with his birth at home at his family's estate outside of Modena, then some family background, then his earliest memories. I've still never met Elaine, never even seen her. I've long wondered if she works behind one of the closed doors on the office's first floor.

My process was to first listen to the recordings all the way through without any expectation—simply listen and learn the voice. To do this, I'd listen to them while taking long walks through Oakland. Gradually the Physicist's voice became familiar, like a friend's. Moreover, walking helped me develop a physical, spatial relationship to the material: I could remember that the German-measles scene happened around the time I reached the redwood park, whereas the early reading scene was around the time I'd made it to the top of Temescal; slowly this went on, his memories translated into a pedestrian map of the Town. Because I couldn't experience the Physicist's life, I superimposed it over an experience of my own creation.

After I established my general time line for each section, I'd sketch it out on paper. It felt good, sketching again, using lines, even in the service of words. Then I'd break the time line into smaller units, then break those units into possible scenes. From there I'd go back into the recording and isolate certain memories, playing them over and over, making notes and transcribing bits of statement, learning as much about his memory as his voice. Then I'd take the professional transcriptions and cross-reference them with my notes, and from there I'd begin to build out the narrative.

The work was demanding, but not challenging per se—I knew each day what I had to write, and while some scenes excited me more than others, I never found myself in the total darkness I'd been working in—or, more specifically, *failing* to work in—for two years. My job wasn't creation, but transformation.

I was very nervous when I turned in my earliest pages. I emailed them to Terry, then the next day drove down to Santa Cruz to go over them in person. On the way there I almost vomited out the window of my car. When I got to the offices, Terry was waiting for me on the porch in his wet suit. "Let's surf first," he said. I took this as a bad sign. I changed into a wet suit and met him at the truck. Oddly there were no boards in the bed. I got in anyways. When we got to the beach, Terry got out without speaking. I followed him down to the sand, then into the water, until we were up to our chests. We stood there for a while and let the waves lift us up, then set us back down. Finally he asked how I thought I did. "Honestly, I have no fucking idea," I said. "My guess is the pages are horrible. I don't know." I was shivering, even with the wet suit on.

"Do you think you belong in the water?" he asked.

Once again, I had no clue what was going on. We rose up with an especially large wave, maybe six feet up. "I mean, I like to swim. I like the water a lot, sure. I'm a Pisces."

"So you like the water. But do you think you belong in the water?"

"I—I don't know."

He dunked under for a moment, disappeared. I looked around, confused. Finally he resurfaced, slick and gleaming. "We're over fifty percent water," he said, lifting up a cupful in his hand. "This is us. But you knew that already."

"Sure," I said, "yeah, I know that." And I did know it in the way everyone knows that bit of trivia.

"And yet," he said, smiling, looking up at the sky. I kept tread-
ing, waiting for him to finish, but all he said was "and yet" again,
then turned and bodysurfed one of the waves toward shore. I
swam in after him and met him on the sand where he was sitting in the lotus position, his wet suit stripped down to his waist,
steam rising off his shoulders. I positioned myself beside him in the
exact same way—lotus position, suit half down—if only because
it felt like I had no other choice. We sat for a while in silence. He
was breathing softly, with intention. When he began to speak,
he didn't look at me, but instead sent his words straight out to the
waves: "The pages are very good. Little things here and there, but
it's strong work. [The Physicist] will be pleased, I'm certain of it.
This is going to go well." Now he turned to me, put a hand on my
shoulder. "I've got a gnarly craving for some kombucha," he said,
then rose and walked to the truck.

I went home from that day in Santa Cruz feeling prideful,
happy. Then the Mist began to creep out from under the computer, from out of the headphones I used to listen to the recordings. Soon enough, every hour I spent ghostwriting in the days to
follow became an increasingly acute and persistent reminder of my
failure, every word I ghostwrote a shadow of the words I should've
been writing over the past years. Even when I'd receive a positive
email from Terry saying the Physicist enthusiastically approved
my work, I'd feel nothing but terror, knowing the ghostwriting
project would eventually unravel. It *had* to. Five days a week, nine
to five, I'd work on the Physicist's book. I was consistent. I sat at
my desk, drank drip coffee from a mug, ate something like a lunch
at noon, did the work. I seemed to not be bad at it, maybe even
good, I was getting positive responses, my debt was slowly thin-
ning. Moreover, all that time spent with the Physicist's memories,
playing them over and over into my ears, meditating on them,

finding their connections, then inhabiting his voice, or at least what I imagined to be his literary voice, gave me a kind of relief. "We are *histories* of ourselves, narratives," writes the Physicist, and so it seems that those eight hours spent each day writing a life I did not live as if I was the one who lived it provided me, if only briefly, with a reprieve from my own torturous narrative, from myself, and when I was away from myself there was nothing there for the depression to cling to and manipulate. But always, as soon as I was done for the day, the Mist swept back in, and I was lost in its haze. It often felt worse than the day before. Correction: it felt stronger; I felt worse. My ability to sleep devolved. I withdrew from friends. I withdrew from Annie. I drafted a will on my computer without bothering to research if it had any legal standing. I couldn't even sit up straight. I was very actively learning to disappear. The Mist had all but consumed my brain and I could feel its presence as weight and pressure on my mind. My whole body hurt. I knew I was getting very close to doing something awful. Some nights I'd lie in bed beside Annie as she slept and rub her ear and apologize softly in the dark, her face sometimes relaxing into a state of peace I imagined was her default before the problem of my mind entered her life. But of course it was only the simple peace of dreaming, just as the green-suited twins beside me here on train 9601 are dozing pleasantly, identically, the tilt of one's head mirroring the tilt of the other.

And then one afternoon, a few days before my birthday, while floating on a longboard down at Manresa State Beach, Terry asked me if I'd read the book yet. I asked him which book and he said the one he'd given me the day we met, the one by Michael Pollan. I said I hadn't and apologized for sitting on it so long. "I'll bring it back next time."

"I don't want it. I think you should read it, is all," said Terry.

"And I think you better do it sooner than later. Sooner seems to be getting smaller and smaller." I looked at him. He didn't look back, just smiled toward the beach cliffs, green and crimson under a quilt of ice plant, then paddled in.

That night, after again failing to fall asleep, I went into the living room and found the book underneath a pile where it had been since Terry gave it to me. It was late, the last of the winter rains sounding like snare taps on the grapefruit tree outside. I opened a window and sparked a stick of Ojai, thought for a moment about Antony, that day in my studio listening to him read to me, his death, my death, my guilt about my death in light of his, then opened the book, *How to Change Your Mind.*

I didn't stop reading until the sun came up, and even then I only paused to brush my teeth and make coffee before Annie woke, and by the night's return I'd more or less finished the thing, setting the book down on the table and feeling for the first time in over twenty years like maybe there was hope for someone like me, someone with a Mist, that it didn't have to be a persistent part of my existence, not some psychological limp that would have me dead before I turned thirty-five.

Of course, this is precisely what Antony had tried to make me see that afternoon in Bushwick years before. There was no doubt. When I got to passages in the book that began years before as small paragraphs in the article I'd first heard read to me by Antony, his voice would appear suddenly in my mind, overriding my own inner reading voice, and I could hear him so clearly, as if he were right in front of me again, sitting on the milk crate, that I had to take a long pull of air through my nose and hold it and count to ten to keep from going weepy in the way I sometimes do, like when listening to choral music in private, and as I listened to Antony again in my mind while reading along I noticed inflections and emphases in his delivery that I'd completely missed the first time, even though they were so clearly directed *at me,* a story about my possible future. What had changed? Why could I hear them now? I guess I no longer had the health or time to be skeptical. I was as desperate as I'd ever been. And whereas before I found the neatness of a psychedelic treatment to be a disqualifier, I now saw how it only appeared neat in contrast to the absolute mess that is Western mental health, a system of pills and indifference. The only irrational move was not to try. Even if it was nothing more than one grand placebo event, who was I to care? If bullshit is good enough to ruin your life, why isn't it good enough to save it?

Thankfully, *How to Change Your Mind* was decidedly not four-hundred-plus pages of bullshit. Instead, what I'd read was a history of psychedelics, from their precolonial origins and origins in laboratories, to their integration into the Western world, through their early successes in psychology and medicine, then their damnation during the moral panic of the sixties, and now their rebirth as a highly exciting area of therapeutic possibility, especially in the treatment of depression, anxiety, addiction, OCD, PTSD, and other diseases driven by rumination. In the book I found descriptions of depression more accurate than any medical text I'd ever read, sharper than anything a doc had ever said to me. The chapter on neuroscience described something called the default mode network (or DMN), the network of the brain that goes into action when the mind isn't doing anything else, or is simply wandering, or is engaged in "theory of mind," the extension of one's self into the mind of others—feeling their feelings, understanding their desires, which, it turns out, is crucial for the work of imagining characters and events, which is to say writing fiction. The DMN is also responsible for the ego and rumination, two interconnected forces that, when they get out of hand, seem to cause depression.

And then I encountered this paragraph, from a section describing the work of Robin Carhart-Harris, a British neuroscientist on the forefront of psychedelic study:

> Carhart-Harris suggests that the psychological "disorders" at the low-entropy end of the spectrum are not the result of a lack of order in the brain but rather stem from an *excess* of order. When the grooves of self-reflective thinking deepen and harden, the ego becomes overbearing. This is perhaps most clearly evident in depression, when the ego turns on itself and uncontrollable introspection gradually shades out reality. Carhart-Harris cites research indicating that this debilitating state of mind (sometimes called heavy self-consciousness or depressive realism) may be the result of a hyperactive default mode network, which can trap us in repetitive and destructive loops of rumination that eventually close us off from the world outside ... Carhart-Harris believes that people suffering from a whole range of disorders characterized by excessively rigid patterns of thought—including addiction, obsessions, and eating disorders as well as depression—stand to benefit from "the ability of psychedelics to disrupt stereotyped patterns of thought and behavior by disintegrating the patterns of [neural] activity upon which they rest."

There, in a few sentences, was a perfect description of my psychological existence.

Most promising of all was the book's description of psychedelic guides—a large field of trained therapists and medical professionals who use psychedelics to treat patients suffering from the psychological afflictions mentioned above. Though "underground" because of the criminalization of psychedelic substances, they operate as a guild, sharing training, research, referrals, and a code of ethics. In fact, the treatment administered by NYU, the very treatment I'd tried to convince Antony to receive years before, is based on the work of these guides. Its success rate when treating depression: huge. A game changer. Best of all, it turned out that the vast majority of these guides lived and worked right where I was sitting, in the Bay Area of California, a place shaped by psychedelics in more ways than I could've imagined.

When I told Annie all about it, the book, the history, the treatment, how I wanted to find a guide, there was some trepidation—she'd never taken any psychedelics; she stuck to martinis and margaritas and wine. Anything more than a hit of weed sent her down some unsavory mental paths. But the more I explained, the more the wariness in her eyes transformed into interest, then hope. By the time I was finished, she gave me a look I didn't recognize or understand and wouldn't until after my treatment—she was catching a flicker of *me*.

Which—speaking of looks, speaking of eyes—reminds me of a morning a few weeks before my treatment when I felt so horrible I couldn't get out of bed. It was raining outside, and the room's drab light felt dense and alive. Annie was working from home and I could hear her in the other room testing an interactive voice bot her company was building for a smart stereo. On this morning she kept saying, "Erase my history," and the bot would say different things, like "History—don't know much about it" or "History—what history?" except the bot would only respond about half the time, staying silent the other half as Annie repeated, "Erase my history . . . erase my history . . . erase my history," with increasing frustration. I hid under the duvet.

Eventually Annie came in and lay beside me. She was wearing one of my old West Virginia sweatshirts. "How are you doing today?" she asked. "You feel so far away, like you've drifted really far. I'm scared." Too weak to hide it, I said, "I'm very ready to die." I felt full of shame, but also surrender.

Annie wiped her nose with her sleeve.

"I'm sorry," I said.

"Sometimes I feel like I'm keeping you here. I know it's not my fault, but still I feel it. It feels so fucked to say it out loud, but I have to. Like if it wasn't for me you could be free from this." She'd suggested this before, in so many words, but this time, the ache in her voice—it shot a pang through me that made me want to howl. I refused the idea, saying over and over that it wasn't true, but I knew nothing I said mattered. We were both about as low as we could get.

Then something happened. It sounds strange, but, without comment, Annie quietly repositioned herself on top of me so we were forehead to forehead, nose to nose, chest to chest, with eyes closed, finding our shared breath. I was unsure of what she was doing and thought maybe it was something very literal, like she was trying to use her body weight to hold me down, to keep me from vanishing, but just thinking of the desperation behind such a gesture was enough to make me shudder. Annie gently shushed me, and again I slipped into our shared breath, more fully this time. I can't say how long we stayed that way, but when I finally opened my eyes, all I saw were her eyes blurred together into a single gray iris looking back at me with such stability and serenity it was like something was being revealed to me, though what that something was I couldn't say. "I love you," she said finally, sitting up. I felt better.

Posttreatment, I wonder if that something might've been about the permeability of our bodies, that through that single eye there moved between us all our different waves and particles and frequencies of spirit, like a kind of music I could feel even then, way down at the bottom of my mind's well. A precursor to the experience that would soon change my life.

I've since asked Annie about this moment—if she remembers what compelled her to do what she did, what was going through her mind—but she says she can't remember it. Not at all. "I feel like I've blocked out whole stretches of that time," she said. "I'd rather not return to them."

The treatment taught me so many things, most especially how much Annie saved me, but also how much she's been hurt. I've asked her to tell me everything she's willing to tell, and she's told me some, but it takes time. Much of what she's shared so far has been painful to hear, but that pain is made manageable by the gratitude I feel for being alive to hear it and, more important, for having the chance to honor the unpayable debt of life I owe to her. The true debt behind all of this.

I DECIDED to tell LD about my plan for treatment over a plate of Famous Five Spice Hot and Spicy Pork Shoulder, a bone-in hunk of swine as big as a cantaloupe, glazed to the sheen and depth of Italian leather. I told her about Pollan's book, its contents, how I'd first learned of psychedelic therapy because of my late friend Antony, my positive experiences with psychedelics in the past, the neuroscience of depression and anxiety, the DMN; I quoted a later passage in the book in which Pollan quotes from *The Noonday Demon: An Atlas of Depression* by Andrew Solomon, in which Solomon quotes the expert George Brown, "'Depression is a response to past loss, and anxiety is a response to future loss,'" saying this was exactly it—the depression that blossomed somewhere in my far past was made ultrapowerful by the failure of the book, which I spent all day thinking about while I was working on the Physicist's book, anticipating its collapse, my next ruin, and so I was stuck oscillating between the past and the future—wait, no—I was being pulled toward both at the same time, I was getting ripped apart; that was it. I described how these psychedelic medicines could, in a sense, wipe the mental slate clean, on and on, I rambled, sounding I'm sure like a freshman explaining a theory he's just learned to an elder who has lived long enough to have witnessed the theory's inception, rise, celebration, acceptance, disproval, abandonment, and rediscovery more than once. By the time I was done with my blather, the pork shoulder had been reduced to a beige bone alone on some cabbage leaves, two Tsingtao bottles resting empty on each side of the table. The waiter brought us our check with two fortune cookies. We each picked one up, bit open the cellophane wrappers, pulled out the cookies. "You know I know him?" said LD. "Pollan. We're friends."

My pulse spiked. Everything in the room tilted. I tried to play it cool, apologized for not asking, then asked how they knew each other.

"Well, we've been living in the same town for almost thirty years. And we share an agent."

"Of course. I'm sorry, I should've asked."

"I read the book. My sister read it too when she was dying of cancer. She asked me to ask him to put her in contact with a guide, so I did, but he couldn't do it because of journalism ethics."

I laughed a wild, almost rabid laugh, but only on the inside. What a clear expression of the Mist's sinister ends! Get me within one degree of separation of the man who wrote the book that might save my life, only to learn there's nowhere to go once you're there. I also wanted to cry, but didn't, clinging to some dignity, an odd sensation—to want to cling to some dignity meant I wanted to persist, it seemed, meaning my hope for this treatment had grown stronger than I'd anticipated.

"But I think you should do it," said LD. "It seems like you must. I'd do it, but I can't, for medical reasons. I think it's the best chance you've got. I don't think Michael would've investigated it for as long as he did if there was nothing to it."

"I'm sorry I spent this whole meal telling you what you already knew."

"You seemed awake telling it. I haven't seen that from you in quite a while. I didn't want to interrupt." Her North Shore accent came on thicker as she said this, underplaying her words, which only emphasized their import. On her wrist: a bracelet of many tiny golden skulls. I'd never noticed it and said as much. "My sister made it," she said, extending her arm to give me a better look, I thought, but then I saw the cookie in her hand. "Read me my fortune," she said. "Then I'll read you yours."

After the meal, I went home to sleep but was awoken shortly after by a flash of feeling I couldn't articulate. I went out on the couch and tried to read a book of stories that wasn't very good. The stories were awful, actually, pedestrian and formulaic, yet they'd recently been heralded. Maybe I was missing something. But who was I to have any opinion about writing? I couldn't concentrate. I was still ringing with the cruel injustice of being so close to Pollan but it not making a bit of difference. I tried to sit in silence and breathe, but all I could hear, I was certain, was the crinkle of the plastic razor bag under the bathroom sink. I got on my laptop and began scouring Reddit pages devoted to psychedelics, hoping to find instructions on how to connect with a guide. Scrolling down the posts, I came upon an image that sent me back into the cushions—it was an image of the painting in Terry's office, the skinless, radiating, embraced couple. Of course, I thought, of course. I sent Terry an email asking if I could meet him ASAP and when I woke there was a reply saying come on down.

"Absolutely," said Terry when I asked him if he knew any guides. We were standing at the island in his office kitchen. He slid another bunch of kale into the juicer he was running, a vicious screeching stainless-steel machine that looked commercial grade. Out of a bottom spigot spewed a stream of highly verdant liquid into a pitcher. "I've been waiting for you to ask." Next went ginger with the skin on, then whole lemons. "You don't look so good, you know. I don't want to say too much but, well, I guess maybe all I'll say is that I think this is a very positive direction you're taking." All of this he shouted over the screaming blades. The sound felt concurrent with my excitement, like something was getting shredded apart, torn open. Finally the machine quieted. Terry poured me a glass of the green juice. I felt I had no choice but to drink it and was shocked by how much I liked it. The taste of health! "I'll shoot my guide an email now," said Terry. "You should hear from her soon. I'm sure you'll dig her. She's kind of a big deal. She's been involved with this medicine since forever, almost all the way back to Menlo Park when it was legal. A great spirit. Great style too. You know, sartorially." I wanted to say thank you, but instead all I could do was curl up my bottom lip and look up to the ceiling for a moment—I was getting emotional. Getting emotional was all I seemed to be able to do then. But this was good, what I was feeling. This was gratitude. Terry didn't embrace me or act awkward or say anything. Instead he stood across from me and smiled, finished his juice, then suggested we go surf a little.

One week passed without hearing anything from the guide. Fine, I thought. Then another passed, then another, until each day without word meant some hope was chipped away, leaving a spot the Mist filled in. I felt stupid for thinking things would work out.

I wanted to email Terry about it but worried, in my paranoid state, that such a disturbance would cause him to sever our friendship and business arrangement, leaving me with nothing. As a final insult, I got a letter in the mail from the DMV telling me my newly issued REAL ID had had its REAL ID status revoked because of a mistake in the paperwork process (their fault, not mine); I'd need to go to the nearest branch with a second proof of residency in order for my ID to remain valid.

It was there, of course, in the parking lot of the Oakland DMV on Claremont Ave, just as I was to go in for my appointment, that I got the call. Fuck the REAL, I thought. I held the phone to my ear, said hello, then heard a voice boom all around with the totality of God. I almost dropped my phone—I had forgotten it was synced to the car's Bluetooth speakers.

"This is Denise," said the great voice, gently. "Terry gave me your info. I think I might be able to help you out. I'm sorry for being slow getting to you. I've been away for a month in Baltimore at Johns Hopkins medical."

"Oh, I'm sorry," I said. "I hope you're all right."

"Oh, yes, I'm great! Very good. Exciting things are about to happen there, and they've asked me to be a part of it."

"Are you moving there? To Baltimore?"

"Jesus, no. Of course not. But I will go do some teaching once a year. What's more exciting is that I'll be joining in a very big study they're leading, though I'll be able to do my bit through my offices at [she named the Bay Area teaching hospital where she works]. Things are very exciting. They're going to open a whole institute for this type of medicine. I guess I shouldn't be saying that, but that's okay. You won't say anything. Terry said you read Pollan's book? It's quite something, isn't it? It's really cracked things open in the public conversation. I never thought it'd happen. But here we are. Anyway, as I was saying, I think I can help you. We'll do some meetings at my office first, but the treatment I do off-site at my weekend house in [a location I'll say is somewhere between Santa Cruz and Mendocino]."

I said that was fine, not a problem, I'd been busy myself. She asked if I would tell her about my situation—what issues was I dealing with, how did I learn about the treatment, had I had any past experiences with psychedelics? I told her everything as smoothly as I could. I tried my best to maintain composure. I've never wanted to be liked so badly. When I was finished, Denise said, "It sounds like you're really suffering. The good news is this is a very promising step." She went on to tell me about her history conducting the treatment, its immense potential, how consistently she's seen it work over the years. "My patients get more out of four hours than they do out of four years of talk therapy." But there was one issue: because of being away in Baltimore, she was very backed up at work, so the earliest she could treat me was the end of May— nearly two months away. My insides crumbled to dust.

"I'll make it until then," I said aloud, surprising myself.

But I nearly didn't. Or, rather, I wouldn't have made it if it wasn't for the Physicist (though he almost killed me too). Coincidentally—or perhaps *not* coincidentally (I'm no longer sure)—it was during this same week that the nature of my work with the Physicist changed.

ONE MORNING I got an email from Elaine, different from the usual message: she said that the Physicist said that because we were approaching the tail end of his adolescence and the beginnings of his advanced education, I'd need to read through his general book about physics, as well as his book about time, so I'd be fluent in the foundational language and concepts needed to write cogently about everything to come. Except not only did the Physicist expect me to read the books, explained Elaine, he also wanted me to write outlines of each chapter, along with breakdowns of certain core concepts, and submit them to her, who'd then submit them to him for his approval. Only then would he be comfortable moving forward.

Up to this point the work involved listening to a pleasant but disembodied voice roving through memories, one expanding from the next. But then suddenly, through a single email, it was like I was back in school—a school I had no fucking business being at. Even through the medium of Elaine's email I could feel the Physicist's voice shift into that professorial, first-day-of-class tenor reserved for the "I'm a nice guy and I hope you take this course but also you should probably drop it because this class is famous for its complexity, abstraction, and pencil-to-paper tedium that have left many freshman valedictorians and self-declared math kids weeping in the halls over a pile of psets" speech, all of which I'm of course projecting because, as you'll remember, I skipped most high-school math to brush goo on walls, never even took precalculus, then went to *art school*. I was good at geometry because of my visual mind, but besides that I was inept. Using the calculator on my smartphone to tally up a dinner's tip is the main reason I keep the device. I had no fucking business doing anything with physics. Yet now I was suddenly expected to understand the general theory of relativity, quantum mechanics, black holes, something called delta S. But what choice did I have? The email said copies of the books should arrive sometime that day, and by 1:00 p.m. they had.

Work that I thought would leave me feeling somehow way dumber than I already felt at the time turned out to do the opposite—I was exhilarated. Not only was the writing simple and exceptionally clear, the concepts were approachable and intuitive. General relativity, for example, was a breeze. Now I can't do much of anything without thinking about it. Right now I tilt a bottle of San Benedetto back and forth, the water's surface rolling in one cool wave between the glass, and know that from the distance of the very wealthy owner of the estate house on the hill looking down at the Frecciarossa, the wave is moving at 256 kilometers per hour, whereas from my vantage it's barely moving at all. Hardly news, but it was for me. I understood that the flow of heat from a hot body to a cold one is the only law at the fundamental level of the universe that suggests a passage of time, a movement from order to disorder, and yet even this perceived order, all of these memories I have recorded here, are nothing but "a collection of traces, an indirect product of the disordering of the world," a disordering that is itself only a phenomenon of our perspective as beings, beings "whose brains are made up essentially of memory and foresight . . . the source of our identity." Maybe this is all too deep, too fast, but that's how it is. I found an early freedom in these lessons, a freedom that also began when I'd read in the Pollan book about depression as a time disease. This freedom was like a cool spring issuing from a source whose immensity I couldn't have imagined. "Memory and foresight, memory and foresight," I repeat aloud now to myself like a mantra, only at a murmur, but enough to make the twins shift gently in their seats, first one, then the other, the tips of their matching loafers almost touching. Even their temples the same gray. The only difference I can detect is their watches—the bands are the same, but one's case is rectangular, the other's round.

Having never understood myself to be much of a brain, I found it gratifying to present the outlines of concepts in theoretical physics to the very physicist who theorized them, then wake the next morning to an email from Elaine relaying the Physicist's approval.

"He said you've passed the test," she said. I didn't feel smart then, but I also didn't feel dumb—dumb being how I'd always felt in one way or another, thanks to the Mist, but felt most especially at that time.

Still, something was happening. It was like the Mist could sense the approaching treatment date and kicked into overdrive. The nights grew stranger, my dreams demented. One night I was called out of bed to the darkness outside, walked onto our stoop in my underwear and a pair of Birkenstocks, looked up at the sky both black and luminous, and watched as hundreds of versions of myself fell to earth, a noose around each neck, the horrid whistling of each rope uncoiling from some no-place growing louder until all at once they plucked into a single note when the ropes went taut, the nooses tightened, my necks cracked, and I woke up in bed in my underwear and Birkenstocks, lost in a whole new depth of loneliness. After that the voice in my head that wasn't my voice but was my voice took on a new urgency, a force.

The worse things got, the harder I threw myself into the work. Once the crash course on physics was complete, I did a write-up of the Physicist's first few years of college, including memories of certain classes and professors, of learning certain concepts—many of which I'd recently learned myself—all of which built up to him taking a leave of absence and fleeing to the United States to hitchhike. Soon we were to start the hitchhiking section. "A most important period" is how he described it in a recording, clearly because it culminated in the much-famed but never-reported great realization, which, to this day, no one had heard. Whatever the great realization was, it was only now, with his career established, accolades in check, tenure secured, best-selling books published, a possible Nobel cooling in the forge, that the Physicist finally felt comfortable sharing it with the world. It was speculated that there was something in the story that would make most scientists uncomfortable, that it lacked the simple "aha" geniality of a Newtonian apple plopped on the dome. I must admit, I very much looked forward to working on this passage. It felt like a small victory: one day plugging in my earphones and being the first known person to hear the story of the great realization, straight from the mind that harnessed it, and then to be the one to write it, so that my voice of his voice would be the voice through which the story was transmitted to the world. I'd be the one telling the story everyone had been waiting to hear—what else could a writer hope for? I thought that to myself. I said the word in my head, "writer," and then I flinched, tried to pretend I hadn't said it, but of course I had.

And it was then that the Physicist vanished.

←

THE PHYSICIST had always been punctual—that is, his digital self, embodied through the correspondences from Elaine, always arrived in my in-box on time. When the schedule called for a new recording, it'd always be ready, along with the transcript and often a corresponding document that included place-names, character names, and pictures from his and his family's archives that would help me do physical descriptions of people, but also interiors, exteriors, and landscapes, especially necessary for me, since I hadn't yet been to Italy. But when it came time to write the great realization, no message arrived. No email, no recordings, no documents. He went silent. I grew anxious, certain that I'd done something wrong. But at my core I knew it couldn't be any other way—this is how the Mist works. Why did I refuse to accept this? I called Terry, blathered in an incoherent chain of worry. I couldn't afford to have the publisher think this was my fault. What if they penalized me, what if they kicked me off the project or reneged on the financial agreements? Terry assured me that I was *not* the reason for the Physicist's silence. He'd spoken with the publisher, and they couldn't get ahold of him either. No one could. And so a very uncomfortable silence began.

It was near the end of this first week of silence (only a few weeks ago, mind you), when I knew, deep down in the folds of my marrow, that he'd never reemerge, or if he did, he wouldn't want to work with me, that this job-as-final-life-raft had done its job, as organized by the Mist, which was to buoy me along long enough to find a great hope, to feel invested in the possibility of healing, a new way of being, all so it could pop like a big balloon. This was also the week when Annie was scheduled to go on a weekend retreat with her entire AI R & D division in Palm Springs. The company had rented out a whole wing of a resort. Early Friday morning I was driving her to the airport, halfway over the Bay Bridge in the early gray, the downy Marine Layer churning over the city, trying to talk, to ask her about the trip, but getting only flat answers.

"Aren't you excited?" I pressed. "I know it's still work but—"

"I'm very worried about leaving you alone."

I'd already intuited this, but that did nothing to dampen the flush of self-hatred that followed her saying it.

"I promise I'll be fine. I'm not going to do anything stupid. We're almost there. I don't want you spending any time worrying about that. Enjoy this. If I could go with you, I would. I'm jealous! I like the desert. I like that super-dry air."

When we got to the terminal, the way she looked at me before walking inside—how much she was holding back while also intentionally but unknowingly bulging her eyes out of her head, as if to widen her gaze and let each lens see more of me, worried it'd be the last time—it was awful.

Back home alone, I spiraled away inside the Mist, or maybe it's that the Mist was spiraling around me, swallowing everything within reach until I had no perception and my world ended at the tips of my outstretched hand. By Sunday it was time. While Annie was in the air on her way back from Palm Springs, I called my father and talked about nothing, all the while screaming in my head, desperate to tell him that I was in a pain I couldn't begin to describe, that I was at my end, that I loved him and hoped he would forgive me and that he should know it wasn't his fault, it wasn't anyone's fault, that I was going to be freeing everyone from myself, this was a good thing, but I couldn't bring myself to say any of it, not a word, so all I said instead was that I'd talk to him again soon, hung up, realized I didn't know where I was, there was only the cloud around me, and then I was in the bathroom in the dark with Annie's pack of disposable pink razors in my hand, sobbing, finally ready to do it, first by selecting one of the plastic razors, then freeing the blades from their pink plastic housing, both tasks I carefully completed, and then all I had to do was pull the razors up my forearms and across my throat. I pinched them between thumb and forefinger, pressed them to my neck, held my breath— but then I stopped.

The blades felt too small. No bigger than paper clips. I was going to get this right. I think I even said that aloud to myself. I went to the kitchen, found my Japanese paring knife, then returned to the bathroom. I lifted the blade to my neck. Much better. I held my breath. My world went very still.

But I didn't do it. Somehow, while caught on the fulcrum of a single second, I saw the razor's pink plastic and connected it back to Annie. I saw her leaning her head against the window up in the sky where—I now knew after my physics course—time was passing faster for her than it was for me down at sea level, and in her pocket was her phone, and on the phone her calendar, and on her calendar the month of May, the month we were in, and ten days from that day, in the month's third week, a Wednesday, May 22, eight months to the day since she'd wedded me, was an event marked for my treatment, scheduled for 9:30 a.m. A day as important for her as it was for me. "What we call 'time' is a complex collection of structures, of layers. Under increasing scrutiny, in ever greater depth, time has lost layers one after another, piece by piece," writes the Physicist. And yet these layers, these structures, these illusions through which I could count away the torment, it is them I have to thank for my life.

I wrapped the razors and broken plastic in toilet paper and took them outside to the trash, placed the rest of the razors back under the sink, returned the knife to its drawer, and drove to SFO to pick up my wife.

TEN DAYS LATER, on May 22, at 9:30 a.m., right on time, Annie and I held each other in Denise's driveway and cried. For a few minutes we stayed like that, and then Denise came down from her main house in a loose white linen jumpsuit, her thick gray hair twisted into a high bun, and introduced herself to Annie, assuring her I would be in good hands, which I could tell meant so much to her. I hugged Annie once more and told her I'd see her in a few hours. She got in the car, rolled down the window to give me one more kiss, then drove off to the nearest town to try to work at a coffee shop.

I followed Denise through the screen door into the treatment house, a small cabin overhanging a creek in a copse of redwoods, a couple of yards down from her actual house. It was airy and smelled of cedar incense. A band of windows, many of them opened, wrapped the structure like a glass ribbon. Golden light cut across the interior: a small kitchen area, a bathroom, and a seating area with a couch, a floor seat, and a large therapy bed in the center of the floor. The whole building wasn't much bigger than the living room of my Oakland apartment. Beside the bed was a stack of blankets ranging in heaviness from a thin sheet to a twenty-pound weighted blanket. Around the bed were different altars with materials from different spiritual practices—a Tibetan singing bowl, a dream catcher, a Catholic prayer candle, two icons I didn't recognize, a wooden bowl of cedar incense, feathers. Potted plants were arranged throughout, along with small black speakers.

Denise and I talked casually at first so I could relax and get a sense of where I was. Two days prior we'd done a preparatory treatment at her hospital office using a small lozenge of ketamine to help me get used to working with her experientially.

"Have you reflected any more about the other day's treatment?" asked Denise as she pulled a large freezer bag of dried psilocybin mushrooms out from a locked drawer, along with a scale.

I said that I'd found the temporary distance between myself and my depression to have very exciting potential, and that it was good to sort of "get back in the saddle," chemically speaking, having not had a serious chemical experience besides alcohol and cannabis in a long time.

"Well, today promises to be a much wider experience," she said, smiling as she stacked five grams of dried, gnarled mushrooms on the scale. Then she stopped and looked at me. "I always like to ask one last time: You feel ready for this treatment, its intensity?"

"I do," I said. "Don't worry. I know I'm not going to lose my mind."

"Oh, by all means—lose your mind. Just understand that you'll come back, and better than before." She smiled, gave me a pat on the shoulder. "Let's begin."

She slid off her black canvas espadrilles, rolled up the bottoms of her pant legs, and asked that we first meditate. I sat cross-legged on the center of the bed and she sat near its foot, cross-legged, elevated on a yoga cushion. We breathed and centered ourselves. She oriented us north, south, east, west, then asked me to say aloud my intentions, what did I hope the medicine would provide. I said I hoped it would heal me and free me from over twenty years of suffering. I wanted the depression gone. I wanted the unending urge toward suicide to end. Denise asked me how I was feeling and I began to sob, surprising myself, and explained aloud that I hadn't been sure I'd make it to this day. I explained how I'd gotten so close to the end, which is why I was so grateful to be there, then I said that for the first time in my life I felt like I had some agency over my mental health, over *healing,* and that I was ready for whatever was about to happen. The alternative was death.

Next Denise sparked some of the cedar incense and began smudging—first passing the smoke around herself, then around me, using a feather to fan and drag the white smoke across my head and limbs and torso, blessing the space as a space of healing. She went to the counter and returned with the mushrooms on a wooden plate, on which there was also a small bowl of honey and a few cocoa beans. She explained how, in the religious ceremonies of the Mazatec—with whom she'd studied, and to whom we owed thanks—this sacrament, the mushrooms, "the little children," as they're called, are served with honey and cocoa. Honey to help you eat them, cocoa to help with digestion. "Take your time eating them," said Denise. "Meditate on what you're doing, why you're here, and understand them as the sacred medicine they are. Taste the medicine. I'm going to step away now for a little bit, go up to the house to use the bathroom and make some tea. I'll be down soon." She encouraged me to step outside when done, should I feel like it.

Alone in the small house, I took a deep breath, then began eating. The mushrooms weren't as acrid as I'd anticipated or remembered. They were dry, bland, vaguely bitter. I licked dollops of the honey off my finger between bites. Finished, I nibbled the cocoa seeds, skin and all. Though I ate with intention, I did it quickly, so there was no turning back. Looking down at the empty plate, sitting cross-legged as I was, just as I'd been while listening to Antony read to me years before, I thanked him in my mind, then apologized for wasting as much time as I had in getting to that moment. Still, I'd made it. My stomach, now gurgling, was proof.

I walked outside to pee between the trees and take some time to center myself. Through a break in the canopy I could see a cloudless patch of electric blue. A turkey vulture flew over. Suddenly thoughts like "what the fuck are you doing" boiled up in me, but there was nothing to be done. "The only irrational thing is not to try," I whispered to myself, then breathed, stretched, shook out my limbs, and walked aimlessly through grand trunks and sunbeams until Denise returned from the house and suggested we go inside.

She encouraged me to pick a blanket if I'd like one. I lay down on the bed and asked for the weighted blanket, which she draped over me. She reminded me that no matter what I needed, she would be there. If I wanted the blanket gone, she'd get rid of it. If I needed a muscle massaged, all I had to do was say so. And if there were things I wanted to express, I should express them without worry. If there were things I wanted written down, she would do that too; she'd also keep notes. Finally, I selected my blindfold—a large black one made of foam, with sizable domes cut for the eyes to have room to open. I lay my head back against the pillow, slipped on the blindfold, and it began.

Immense waves of emotion overwhelmed me. Waves with mass. Waves that gave shape to many versions of the same devious mustachioed cartoon face flashing in and out, combining into a pulsing, interconnected pattern, like a wallpaper print. These would be the only faces I'd see. They were deeply frightening.

I was crying harder than I ever had, so hard it felt like my mouth was stretching very wide, and then I realized that was because my face was splitting in half, and as this sensation intensified the cartoon faces dissolved and everything began to vibrate, shake, then rumble with terrific force. Now all of me was coming apart, particle by particle. I felt pure terror at letting go, but also a larger freedom waiting beyond it. Space and time collapsed. A great bright something roared around me, louder, brighter, every particle ripping apart, apart, apart—and then I died.

I died many times that day. Many times. Maybe hundreds of times. And I experienced many things, most of which are beyond language, but some of which are not, and when it was done— I will share it all soon, we are almost there, I can feel the distances shortening—I awoke from what felt like a thousand-year sleep. My depression gone. Anxiety not even a memory. No more rumination. My body as light as dust. You don't have to believe it, but you might want to ask what you'd lose if you did. And anyways, it's true—I am exhilarated in my being here alive. It is a gift. I smell the twinned spice of cigarettes and body odor wafting off a fellow passenger in carriage 7, and I breathe only more deeply. I breathe and breathe and breathe and begin to believe for a moment I can smell the steam swirling around the bathroom of the G-Rough hotel, where Annie, back after spending the day visiting an old boutique jewelry shop that for years carried her grandmother's work, is likely washing now in the marvelous walk-in shower, the walls of which are done up with mirrored subway tiles so that hundreds of Annies are fractaling across the walls, reflections of her reflection reflecting back on the tiles' beveled edges and corner pieces as she pulls grapefruit-scented Malin+Goetz shampoo and conditioner through her hair, glides a pink razor over her shins, rinses, dries, then dons one of the bamboo fiber robes as thick and heavy as a grizzly skin, pours a glass of local white, and walks up the spiral stairs out onto the room's private terrace, night seeping fast into the persimmon sky wild with starlings and LED-lit whirly toys launched spinning and flashing over the rooftops by the hawkers in Piazza Navona, only yards away, as somewhere a bell peals over the streets of the Eternal City, a paradise I stayed alive long enough to see for the first time ten days ago, when we arrived from San Francisco at our honeymoon's beginning.

AFTER OUR FLIGHT LANDED in the early evening we had a lovely dinner in the cellar of a *salumeria*, then slept until morning—our plan was to stay in the city for two full days before flying to Sicily, where we'd stay for five nights before returning to Rome. On our first full day we walked Rome and, in an attempt to fight jet lag, guzzled many oversize bottles of water it seems you can only buy outside the States. After lunch Annie decided to head back to our swank hotel to nap—a different hotel than the G-Rough, of course. I wandered over to Bar San Calisto, a neighborhood spot in Trastevere I'd come to follow on Instagram but which I couldn't remember how I'd learned about.

I'd brought three books for the trip: *The Leopard* by Giuseppe di

Lampedusa, which I had every intention of reading while in Sicily; LD's first book, *The Mermaid,* a novel-in-stories I'd snatched off my shelf on impulse, as if called to reread it; and *Out of Sheer Rage* by Geoff Dyer, which was gifted to me by LD a few days before leaving for Italy. We'd met for a meal so she could hear about my treatment—a meeting that felt redemptive from my previous blather, but also humbling when I saw how much she cared, how happy she was for me. Before we parted, she handed me a copy of Dyer's book, somewhat mischievously, saying she hoped it wouldn't offend me; instead she hoped I might find it especially funny. I asked what she meant, and she said it was a book about not writing a book. I laughed. I laughed at my laughing. How brilliant, I thought. A warm, unfamiliar energy umbrellaed in my chest. I promised her I'd read it and report back.

This was the book I had with me in my backpack when I sat down outside the San Calisto with a tall brown bottle of Peroni at a tiny wooden table printed with the Peroni logo. I knew nothing about the book but learned within the first pages that it's a nonfiction account of the author, Geoff Dyer, not writing a book about D. H. Lawrence, an author I knew essentially nothing about. For years I'd owned a copy of *Sons and Lovers,* but every time I read it my mind revolted—the prose was like sandpaper against my cortices. My ignorance about Lawrence and his work made me all the more interested, but what I was especially curious to read were his accounts of not writing what he was supposed to be writing, which is to say I wanted to know if Dyer's experience had any similarities with the two years I'd burned. I began reading. It felt good to read. Reading was different since my treatment—I could focus so easily, and it was like the language wrapped around my mind *and* moved through it. The sun was bright and hot, even under the bar's sunshade, and the young Romans spoke loudly and smoked continually, much like young New Yorkers, and I felt generally at home. On the second page I read:

> I even built up an impressive stack of notes with Lawrence vaguely in mind but these notes, it is obvious to me now, actually served not to prepare for and facilitate the writing of a book about Lawrence but to defer and postpone doing so. There is nothing unusual about this. All over the world people are taking notes as a way of postponing, putting off and standing in for.

I almost spilled my beer from laughing. There I was, both in description and as one of the many that make up the plural noun in the last sentence. It made me miss LD. Only a few pages later, Dyer mentions that he's decided to move to Rome to write his book. How cool, I thought, to be in Rome for the first time and encounter an Anglophone's record of moving here in the first few pages I've read in the country. Then, a few pages later, on pages 16 and 17 to be exact, Dyer sets up a meeting with a man who's brought him a book he's left in Paris, then says, "We met at the San Calisto, I bought him a coffee and he handed over the book." A chill uncoiled down my spine. I looked around, as if I was being watched, half expecting to find a cameraman in the partition shrubs. Only a coincidence, but something about it—perhaps the afterglow of my treatment—made it feel cosmically charged. I sipped my Peroni, pouring small amounts from the bottle into a squat tumbler for no reason except that that's what the Italians did, and it made the whole endeavor feel especially dignified, then I sparked a cigarette—I didn't usually smoke but made an exception in Europe because, again, it's somehow dignified—and read on. My mind moved easier as Dyer quickly leaves Rome for Greece. The pages blurred by, the language slid easily through and around my mind. But then, moments later, the following sentences made me start in my plastic seat:

> In the evenings we limped to . . . our local bar, the San Calisto, where Fabrizio, the barman, had elevated surliness to the level of a comprehensive world view. With an unrelenting scowl, he abused everything he touched, yanking the lids off the *gelato,* gouging out the *gelato,* dumping it in glasses, thumping the glasses on the counter.

I'd read this description of Fabrizio as Fabrizio himself, the very barman who'd just sold me a Peroni, was behind me performing the very actions Dyer described, in perfect synchronicity—"yanking the lids off the *gelato,*" I read as I heard in real time the metal clank of the aluminum gelato lid clanging against the others. Each action in the book echoed out into temporality. Or was it that temporality was writing the book? I experienced something like what I want to call the opposite of vertigo—it was as if my senses were no longer senses, no longer translations and approximations of mass streams of data, but facts. This synthesis between the moment and the narration, the voice in my head that wasn't my voice but the voice of Dyer read in my voice articulating by the second every bit of future unraveling exactly as it happened, had managed, in a way, to obliterate me. I felt not dizzy but so precisely in place, so absolutely at the crushed point between past and future, that I was gone, I was nothing, like how I was during the treatment, when I died, and an immense peace pulsed through me. Was I experiencing anything at all? What voice was I hearing? Was I reading the same book LD had read or a new book, written in the quanta of my experience? Whatever it was, it was too much to make sense of there at the San Calisto, so I returned the book to my bag, breathed with purpose, admired with deep love the shadows cast by the Calisto chapel, from which the bar gets its name, how they slid over the cobblestones I walked down on my trek back to the hotel, where I crawled into the air-conditioned luxury bed beside Annie and took a nap, my silenced phone flashing beside my sleeping head as I received no fewer than three emails and one voicemail from Richards, another thread of his various anxieties and terrors about what would happen when the project fell apart, all of it a general repeat of previous threads and calls, the writing more like mutating thoughts than messages, each an addendum to the one sent before, until finally he decided it was best to try to call me.

I went down to the lobby bar while Annie answered some emails before dinner, took an outdoor table facing the street, ordered a Negroni, and listened to Richards's voicemail. There was nothing special to it, but I could hardly listen. It wasn't that he was annoying, which he was, or that he was always reminding me of my future plight while describing his own, which he was, but that he sounded so desperate, so lost. It was as if within his voice I could hear traces of my own, from before the treatment. Not my real voice, but the voice in my head, the voice of the Mist. To be clear, it wasn't like some visitation or haunting. It wasn't calling me, trying to get back in. All that's over for me. But encountering it so intimately, still thriving within someone else—there is no need to say it any other way: it broke my heart a little. When you're desperate to get free from a hell, you never anticipate what it might be like to see that hell from the outside. And what you especially don't anticipate is how small it looks. Small and pitiful and unreal. Nothing but a dumb rut of thinking. Listening to Richards, I could understand why people would sometimes say to me some equivalent of "Snap out of it." It truly seems that simple, which is of course so much of its power. I even caught myself thinking that way while I listened, if only for a moment, and it'd only been weeks that I'd lived outside of it. It didn't matter that Richards had essentially never been nice to me, or that his attempts at foxhole camaraderie were bullshit. Behind it all was suffering. But what could I do besides send back a fast email saying how sorry I was that he was feeling so stressed, that I was worried too, hopefully something would change. Then I emailed Terry, pleading that he try again to make some kind of contact with the Physicist, seeing as his office is the one that'd been in communication with him, not me, and could he also please kindly reach out to Richards and explain to him again that there's truly nothing I can do, so he should stop contacting me multiple times a day. "He really doesn't want me to forget how bad all this is," I typed.

TWO DAYS LATER, while standing in line to board a morning flight to Catania, Annie said she wasn't feeling well.

"How do you mean?" I asked.

"I'm burning up. Aren't you burning up?"

She was noticeably sweating. It was true, it was hot outside, but the terminal was air-conditioned.

"And now my stomach hurts," she said. "Like, it's cramping or something."

She seemed pale too, now that I was looking. Pale and damp. I was worried. The flight to Catania would be brief, less than an hour. I asked if she would be okay to board and she said she thought so, yes.

The whole flight Annie sat with her face strained toward the seat's small overhead air valve while at the same time fanning herself with the seat-back safety card. I could actually see the sweat emerging out of her brow. "Feeling any better, or the same?" I whispered. "Worse," she whispered back, and then the plane tilted into its downward trajectory. She squeezed my hand, not in fear, but in pain and restraint, each adjustment of the aircraft flushing nausea through her body.

At Catania's airport we were met by a driver scheduled to take us to our beach hotel in Taormina. Luckily every private driver in Sicily appears to drive a black Mercedes-Benz with incredibly plush back seats and strong AC, necessary against the island's six months of relentless heat. I was nervous about the drive for Annie—Sicily's roads were notoriously treacherous, with many windy bends and blind spots and sudden bridges cutting around steep coastal cliffs, a situation made only worse by the Italian driving style being, generally speaking, more jazz than classical. Annie balled up in the back seat, mumbling thanks for the reprieve of the AC, her eyes pinched tight to resist any motion sickness. I sat back and watched the landscape and was struck immediately by the character of the light, how it seemed to fall straight down. How it was golden. No, almost sepia. Yes, sepia toned. It was exactly like the burnished hue that lights the opening scene of *The Godfather: Part II,* when the funeral procession for Vito Andolini's—not yet Vito Corleone's—father is marching through a barren rocky valley and suddenly shots are fired, an ambush by Mafia men, and his brother is discovered dead, a body in black garments sprawled over stones beneath the same sepia light falling through the next scene, when young Vito and his mother go to the *palazzina* of the Mafia boss, who has by now killed the father and the brother, the mother begging for mercy that he spare Vito's life, the result of which is her murder, right then, which Vito witnesses before fleeing for his life back down the entry path, past the bright bougainvillea and gardenias and mums I could also see, from inside the Mercedes, growing from nearly every balcony and cliffside, yes, it was this identical light, a light so arresting I remember seeing it for the first time on the couch beside my father, watching the film one Christmas night. A channel played both *The Godfather: Part I* and *Part II* back-to-back all day, and late after dinner we caught *Godfather II* right at the beginning, and my father was adamant we watch it, that I watch it, "Talk about a work of art," he'd said, perhaps a throwaway statement, but even the mention of "art" in relation to me felt like him acknowledging who I was becoming in a way he never had before, and that he was not only acknowledging me, he was trying to support me by making sure I saw this film, his own humble offering, so of course I watched beside him in a state of sustained exhilaration, and when I noticed the colored light I asked if everything in the past looked that way, and he told me no, it was an effect the director used to make things feel old, like how old photographs look, but now in Sicily I could see it was no effect, not at all, it was the true light of the island, a capital *A* "Ancient" light, the light of what is already over, and right then in the Mercedes I wanted to call my father and tell him this, tell him about the light, but I knew it would be a useless call he'd misconstrue as me saying something odd only to prove to him how smart I was, which isn't what I'd mean at all, of course, or all he'd say is that he's got both movies on DVD and could send me a copy—and yet this no longer fills me with sadness, not since my treatment, I get it now, I get it. Instead I noted this all in my journal, sat back into the ride, and admired paradise on our way to the hotel, a luxury beachfront property in a quiet cove below Taormina. Originally a private palatial summer getaway for a British family, the property was later bought and expanded by a British hotelier in conjunction with a sister hotel atop the mountain in the village proper, where we'd be dining the following evening. We were shown to our room—a bright, cool space of white marble and white linens and white walls and a balcony overlooking the water—where Annie rushed into the bathroom. Sounds of strain came from within. I did my best not to listen. When she emerged, she asked if I was certain I wasn't feeling anything. I told her nothing, a little guiltily. "Maybe you had a bad bite of something?" I suggested.

"It must've been. But what happened in there seemed to help. I think I'd like to try to take a nap out by the water."

The beach was set up in the traditional Italian style, with umbrellas and loungers already arranged in clean rows. A waiter showed us to our preferred spot, laying out the towels and apologizing for the unseasonably strong breeze. Annie lay down and closed her eyes. Excited by the sheer cosmic beauty of the place, I couldn't sit still, not even to read, but it was too cold with the breeze to swim in the sea, so I leaned over to Annie and told her I was going to walk over to the pool, a temperature-controlled infinity pool that jutted out over the water, right on the other side of some shore rocks.

I had the pool to myself—a still slab of sapphire. Slowly I walked into the water, trying my best not to disturb the surface as I made my way to the infinity edge and looked out over the cove—the high hills of yellowed grass behind the resorts, cliff faces thick with bougainvillea and agave, heirloom boats twirling on the blue currents below—and I felt immense gratitude for being alive to see it all, including Annie over on the beach, curled up on the lounger, which is not to say I was grateful for her discomfort, of course— I hated it—but at least I had the privilege to try to be there for her then, and hopefully share some fine days together once whatever she was dealing with had passed.

The breeze grew stronger, dragging waves over the water. The longer I floated, the more I felt as if, in some way, I'd gone out of my body. My senses became huge, beyond the borders of myself, and a fast chill came over me that sent me back to the pool's edge to look down at Annie, and even from that distance I could see she was curled up tighter than before. I got out, collected some towels from a stand to bring to her for blankets, then walked back over the wooden walkway to the beach.

Annie was holding herself, her eyes still closed. The wind was making a scene.

"How are you feeling? I brought you some towels for blankets, but maybe we should go up. You're shivering."

"I'm worse. Everything is spinning and my stomach really hurts. I don't want to open my eyes. I tried googling 'food poisoning,' but it made me sick to look at my phone. You still don't feel anything?"

I was trying to think of what to do when, as I was crouched beside her, an immense gust of wind blew into the cove and lifted the top half of our umbrella off its anchored bottom pole, the top half's pole then spearing into the top of Annie's lounger. Before I could think I'd grabbed it in place and, in shock, both Annie and I stared at where it had landed: directly above her head. Had she been sitting up, it would have gone right between her eyes, almost certainly killing her.

The two beach attendants ran over, shouting in Italian, and lifted the umbrella from my grip. Other guests were sitting up, staring and whispering to one another. Annie later said that some-one had shrieked, but I didn't hear it. I yelled at the attendants, ranting about how it could've killed her. They stared at me. I hated being there. I didn't want to be angry, but I didn't want to not be angry either. "Well?" I said to them. They looked at each other, then stared back.

"I need to go," said Annie, tugging at my arm. "I need to go *now*. It's an emergency." Doubled over, she got up from the lounger and rushed for the main building. When we made it back to the room, Annie once again rushed into the bathroom, this time vomiting violently. I rubbed her back as tears welled in my eyes. She kept apologizing between movements, and I told her that was ridiculous, there was nothing to apologize for.

Seeing her in such discomfort, feeling helpless in the way I did, I was overcome with guilt and sadness thinking how Annie must have felt that way for years, but on a monumental scale—it almost made me need to sit down—and then through this it occurred to me that I was experiencing the first true spat of sadness since my treatment, and yet it was totally unlike any sadness I could remember. This was different, almost like a signal I was catching in the air, a certain frequency I was temporarily tapped into, whereas before my treatment it was like a tremor from within, or not a tremor but a whole chord thrumming deep down in my nuclei in a way that seemed so foundational it was as if gloom was the original force that made up whoever I was, meaning that everything else, from joy to hunger to boredom, was nothing but static, useless signals that had gathered and distracted me from the truth. And though I was still sad about Annie being sick, I was also now getting misty with elation about this new sadness—lesser, unimportant, to simply be experiencing a thing that happens, but is not me.

I understand this all might sound obvious and even potentially a bit stupid or even narcissistic, but I don't know how else to explain it except to say that it felt like I was learning how to parse a new reality: if each moment used to feel like an occasion of loss contributing to a greater, singular loss, each moment now felt like an opening in one greater, continual opening. And while I get how that description might've only worsened the potential stupidity or obviousness of what I'm trying to say, so much so that upon hearing it the average soul might want to say, *Who the fuck is this guy?* that's okay. All I ask is that you ask yourself, *Why does this one person's description of life postdepression cause me to jerk back in repulsion?* Might I add: Is it even you that's jerked you back, or has something pulled you? Maybe if you stretch your jaws you'll realize all along they've been snapped stiff around a bit whose reins lead back to that most attractive, manipulative, and ultimately successful of babysitters—our girl Cynicism. She gets paid by the hour and lets you think you're freer and older and wiser than you are.

Someone knocked at the door. Likely a maid, I thought. They'll come back. I wasn't about to leave Annie's side. But the knocking persisted. I shouted for them to come back later. There was a pause, but then the knocking resumed, this time with a different rhythm meant to suggest, I assumed, that it was someone who felt it absolutely necessary to speak to one of us right away. Finally out loud I said, "Fuck it," told Annie I was going to get rid of them, stormed over to the door, and opened it enough to see a butler holding a silver tray on which rested a bottle of champagne in a silver wine chiller, along with two coupe glasses and a letter. I wanted to grab the tray and get back to Annie, but when I reached for it the butler pulled back. "Sir, please, please—allow me."

"It's fine," I said, "really, I can put it down." I reached again and he recoiled, almost in disgust. Annie erupted in a particularly audible retch. The butler and I blinked at each other. "Please," I said.

"Please," repeated the butler, smiling, almost childlike. I thought I could smell the stomach acid in the air. I began to understand that he was worried that if he himself did not complete the task that it may somehow get him in trouble, as if I'd take the tray, then call the front desk to say he did not place the tray but made me do it myself. Annie retched again, and we both pretended we couldn't hear it. Finally I conceded and let him into the room just enough so that he could place the tray on a bedside table, before I more or less shouldered his body into the hall. I ran back to Annie. Now she was sitting up, leaning against the marble tub. "That fucking quiche with the savory *zabaione,*" she said. "You didn't have any, did you? You had the mortadella sandwich thingy, but I had the quiche with the *zabaione.* At breakfast. The one cook came over and spooned some on my plate, right out of the little copper saucepan, remember? Maybe it was that. It's got raw egg in it, I'm pretty sure. Can you look it up? I think it's one of those raw-egg situations. The eggs here, they're different."

She was right: according to the Internet, *zabaione* is indeed a raw-egg situation, and I'd eaten none of it that morning at the very swank breakfast at our posh Roman hotel; I'd had the mortadella sandwich thingy. "I feel much better now," she said, before breaking into a laugh. "All this because of a sauce. Who the hell was at the door?"

"Some butler-waiter guy."

"What did he want?"

"He brought a tray of champagne."

"What for?"

"I have no idea."

Annie rose, washed her face and mouth at the sink, and together we inspected the tray. The letter was from the head concierge apologizing profusely in perfect cursive for the umbrella incident, hoping we'd accept the champagne as an apology.

That night we decided it'd be best to have dinner at the hotel's terrace restaurant beside the water so that Annie wouldn't be far from the room, to be safe. I took a quick shower and went out to the terrace cocktail bar to wait for Annie. At the bar I took a seat next to a large bald man wearing what looked like very expensive clothes made of cotton that seemed somehow different from all other cotton. I ordered a Negroni and sipped it as I once again admired the cove, still entranced by how the light fell like a sheen of sepia over everything. It was as if the light itself was a kind of gossamer, a mist almost, a thought that made me smile. Just saying the word in my head, "mist," how remarkable. It had no power anymore. It felt so stupid, so far away, while I felt lighter, less encumbered by the past, more fully free to the sensations of the moment. I'm so excited for Annie to see this, I thought, which then made me think of her being sick earlier from the quiche with the *zabaione*, yes, the *zabaione*, a thought about the *zabaione* was forming just as I checked my watch, and when I saw its face I almost choked on my drink. The hands were stuck. Or not stuck so much as trembling in place. And while I knew that this "proper time," as the Physicist calls it in his books, represented here by this watch, is nothing but a projection on our temporal experience, and not some law of the universe, I hardly expected to see it coming apart right before my eyes.

"Your battery is dying," said a voice behind me in an accent I thought might be German. It was the bald man. "When the hands do that, it is to tell you the battery is dying. Soon it will tick again, but the second hand will skip many seconds at a time."

"Oh, of course," I said, pretending I had a clue. "So you're sure it isn't broken."

"No, of course it isn't. That is very standard. Trust me. I am Swiss." He smiled.

I was embarrassed. Clearly my shock showed on my face. I had no idea; I'd never owned a watch before this one—a Christmas gift from Annie. I thanked the man before he walked off with his martini into the terrace garden. Soon after, Annie came out for dinner, taking her time down the same garden path the man had taken away. I thought so many things while watching her, all bright thoughts except one. It was about the quiche with the *zabaione*. I had had some of it. A couple of bites off Annie's plate. I was certain. So why hadn't I gotten sick too? I decided not to mention this to her in case it'd make her worried that what she thought was the cause of her stomach problem wasn't in fact the cause, meaning it might potentially be something more serious, which might make her feel sort of lonely or anxious in a way I very much wanted to avoid, and besides I hoped it would pass within twenty-four hours.

Still, the next morning Annie's stomach was sensitive again. We returned to the beach anyways. The breeze and sea were calm. She relaxed into a lounger and ordered a tea. I went straight for a swim out to a tall hunk of marble rising out of the surf in the cove's center. Someone very long ago had carved steps into its side, and rusted nubs stuck out of the rock where a handrail used to be, the steps themselves worn by the sea like the steps of the Vatican made concave by the feet of believers. I lay atop the rock and looked around for a while, admiring the light, how it moved in sheets over the cove, how it played off the cliffs, the cypress and lemon trees and bougainvillea spilling from crags like violet beards, the writhing agave like Medusa heads. Bergamot wafting down from the hotel terraces. Everywhere this blooming, this perfume, the profusion of life, and yet I began to feel death was everywhere. Not unpleasantly. That was what the light suggested. That's why the black casket of Vito's father, abandoned on the rocks when the guns begin firing, radiates like a space of absolute blackness on the screen, as if someone has cut a rectangle right out of the TV. There is a peace, a resignation, an unwillingness to rage against change. This is what I understood after these first twenty-four hours on the island, after driving through Catania, then the villages, then around the hills and cliffs and over the ruddy earth, so many times already I'd noticed when the sky was invisible behind the brilliance of the burnished light, as if centuries of humans staring up at it had worn away its blue, even as the sea below radiated deeper blues than I'd ever seen, as if maybe the sky itself had fallen into the sea, giving it a planetary blue that almost stays in your hands when you cup the water, Etna meanwhile steaming her head off behind us, the same as she did when the first souls walked gingerly over the beach rocks, and right then it seemed inconceivable that any structure here was ever new, as if the bricks crumbled and the stucco cracked moments after their installation, as if this island was the center of the engine of entropy, the wide, thrashing, expanding probability we call the future. The water around me exploded in fractals, in quantized sparkle, its sapphire blue so radiant each bend in its surface was like a cut in a gemstone, but then it evolved, grew more liquid, changing its movement in relation to the tall hunk of marble upon which I sat, its swirl and bend and rise—my visual plane ceased to be my visual plane, which is to say I ceased to be a subject and as I watched the water I knew I was witnessing the curvature of spacetime, I understood it clearly, the principle first articulated to the world by Einstein, the gravitational field, time itself as a material moving around a body, it was all so clear. I laughed, rose, jumped in.

Back on the beach lounger I called for a waiter by pressing a button installed on the umbrella's table, ordered a Peroni, then took out *Out of Sheer Rage,* which I hadn't cracked since the Calisto incident back in Rome. The waiter brought me the bottle of beer with a glass and said, "You must drink quickly. In Sicily, the sun finds its way even in the shade." The second law of thermodynamics, of course, the only suggestion of the flow of time, right before me—I took a long drink and felt lucky to be alive. I began reading, sipping my Peroni as instructed, sitting lotus, witnessing out of the corners of my eyes the seawater drying to salt on my arms. To my right I noticed Annie sneaking a picture of me on her phone, something that I used to hate, having my photo taken, but now I didn't seem to mind and instead let it happen while I kept reading, my attention split between Annie sneaking the shots and the words on the page, until the words on the page started saying right then "a photograph of a writer is not really a photograph of a person but an emblem—a colophon—of the works published," which should've uncoiled a minor spell of gooseflesh but instead caused me to relax more deeply. I actually found myself agreeing with the claim. I'd experienced it firsthand, back when I had author photos taken for *The Troop*. It started with my agent, Lisa, and I sitting together, deciding which one to use. She eventually admitted that she didn't like any of the shots. She said I looked like "someone who fishes."

"But I do fish," I said. "I fly-fish."

"Yes, yes, of course, but that *look* isn't good anymore. Not these days. You look too much like a guy. People don't want a guy. Why don't we use the picture you've been using?" It was an older picture Annie took early in our relationship. "You look less like a guy in that one."

"So I look, what—feminine?"

"No. You just don't look—never mind."

I chose one of the professional shots anyways.

As I toured for *The Troop,* I noticed on more than one occasion that either a host or a student or a reader in a signing line would mention that I'm gentler than they expected. Each time I'd laugh awkwardly and say, I'm happy to hear that, then ask if they'd maybe explain what it was that made them anticipate a lack of gentility—was it the writing? No, it was never the writing. They always said it was my picture. You seem much older in your photo, they'd say, in one way or another, you look like you know something. "I tried to warn you," my agent said when I relayed this to her over a dinner. "They go to the book cover, then the author photo, then *maybe* the writing. Maybe. That's how they build you in their heads. The writing, fuck, who even knows anymore. Finish that new book so we can get a new picture in circulation."

Like any honest living person, I was bummed about this. But I wasn't surprised. I'd seen what people were seeing. I'd seen it most of my life. Looking back through old photos, all the way back to when I was a boy, time and again a facial tic appears: a furrowed brow, furrowed even as a baby, as if even then I was trying to contain something happening within, to control it, dampen it, take it apart. It's always been hard for me to look at those photos because of what they record but also because it's simply always been hard for me to look at myself. Why shouldn't this be the case? When the singular and oppressive focus of your mind is the destruction of an organism and you also happen to be that organism, then any sight you catch of yourself is going to be unpleasant. And how couldn't a disease of twenty years, a Mist thrashing within my skull, not also alter my appearance? And yet, after my treatment, when Annie picked me up from Denise's, the first thing she said after we hugged and cried was how different I looked. "I don't know what I expected," she said, "but you look like a boy. You're glowing. And your hair—it shines!" The same happened when I saw LD, the same night she lent me the Dyer book—"You look so different"—which is also what Denise said when I saw her a week later for my integration session. In truth, I'd noticed it too, as early as a few hours after my treatment while walking down a street on the way to a bistro with Annie. I caught my reflection in a storefront window and, for the first time in twenty years, liked what I saw because I was not seeing the image of a dying man. The same was true then on the beach when I asked Annie to show me the picture she'd snuck: my hair was wild with dried brine and, all around, the ancient light suffused the picture with an air of nostalgia while also turning my red beard a fierier orange, like Lawrence's was purported to look, so I learned, returning to *Rage*.

Yes, I was not dying anymore. It was all gone and in its place was a new energy I could feel down in my elbows and in the relaxed muscles of my face, could feel it in my whole being on a beach in Taormina, broke but in luxury, beside saintly Annie, reading a book about D. H. Lawrence in which, only a few pages later, Dyer says he is going to go to Taormina—where Lawrence lived for three years, it turns out—to take some pictures. This made me laugh again. I took a moment to stare at the sea, and I said to Annie how blue it was, only to return to the book and turn to page 48 and see Dyer describing the sea in near-identical terms. I paused to sip my beer and I mentioned to Annie how the waiter was right, the beer was getting warm quickly, it was almost like the tall beer was too big to be had outside because it warms too quickly in the Sicilian heat, only for Dyer to explain on page 53, "The trouble with *grandi* beers, though, was that we couldn't drink them fast enough: after a few minutes they were as warm as tea." I laughed because it freed me to experience how nothing I was experiencing or noticing or even *thinking* was original; it was as if I was reading my experience in real time, in the time of my temporal reality, an amplification of the present that isn't, and in this state I devoured the book, reading in Taormina about Dyer in Taormina tracking down the ghost of Lawrence in Taormina, on and on I read until, in a passage describing Lawrence's parsimoniousness—if not outright money-grubbing nature—Dyer quotes a sentence from a letter Lawrence wrote to Robert Mountsier about what he feels to be the exorbitant cost of a train ticket. Robert Mountsier. I stopped, went back over the name once, then again—Robert Mountsier. Mountsier.

This is not a real name, *Mountsier*. It's the Anglicization of "monsieur." An Anglicization of a rank adopted as a new surname by a family of Huguenots who'd fled persecution to London and were eager to sever ties with their Gallic past, a family that eventually came to the New World. It's a rare name because it's made up, and because it's made up, those who carry it are basically all from the same family, and I know all this because Annie is from that family. Mountsier is her last name.

I set the book down and asked Annie, "Do you have a relative named Robert Mountsier who happened to be D. H. Lawrence's agent?"

"Oh yeah. He's my great-great-uncle, I think? My grandmother told me about him."

"How come you never told me this? You know this book I'm reading is about Lawrence? Look, your uncle, he's right here." I showed her the page.

"Very cool."

"It is very cool! I can't believe you wouldn't have mentioned that."

"Why would I have mentioned that? It's not like I knew him. How come you haven't told me about your great-uncles?"

"I don't know if I have any. Certainly none that were D. H. Lawrence's agent."

"Would've been better if he *was* D. H. Lawrence. But you know, now that I think of it, I'm pretty sure I did tell you, like way, way back. Very early. When your stories started."

While I'm certain she was right, I have no memory of this. Likely because I didn't really dig Lawrence at the time, but also because, as I've said, I didn't consider myself a writer in any way—to my mind I was still a painter, albeit a failed one—so the literary association, while impressive, mustn't have clung to me, whereas had she mentioned that she was the niece of someone like Joan Mitchell I'd have flipped. And yet the reason Annie claims she ever even mentioned her great-great-uncle way back when was because of the little narratives I was scribbling down during the hours when I should've been painting but couldn't because I felt totally stalled out in failure, narratives that of course became the stories that in one way or another led to me and Annie—great-grandniece of Robert Mountsier, American agent to D. H. Lawrence—sitting there on a beach in Taormina, where I was reading a book about a man failing to write a book about D. H. Lawrence, who lived in Taormina, and whose agent was now a relative of mine, Great-Great-Uncle Robert, RIP, wherever you are—and so what to make of all this, what to do besides laugh, which I'd already done. I couldn't help but feel, sitting there on the lounger, and I feel it right now too, that this tension between coincidence and order seems to build on the central paradox I experienced within my treatment, the tension between at once no longer existing and existing precisely, but far beyond any terms of existence we can truly comprehend, especially linguistically. In one sense, all these details seemed to amplify the *fact* of my reality, while at the same time making me feel as if I didn't exist at all, that I was nothing more than a reverb of an energy already expelled, every observation and experience already documented. And likewise, the pole incident that could have almost killed Annie, great-grandniece of the American agent of D. H. Lawrence, the writer who lived for three years right there in Taormina—was it a coincidence that she fell ill? Ill in such a way that she was curled up on the lower half of the lounger, which maybe saved her life? It seemed that everything was happening exactly as it needed to, while at the same time I was experiencing how *I* didn't really exist at all—that my utterances were echoes— "there are only events and relations," writes the Physicist.

That night, over dinner, Annie was still struggling to eat. She said she felt hungry when we'd ordered, even suggesting, perhaps too ambitiously, that we split a plate of local raw fish, but when it came she managed only one bite of a small prawn, red as a raspberry, before setting down her fork. She looked frustrated.

"We can order something simpler," I suggested. "This is obviously very rich. Maybe we got ahead of ourselves. Why not some pasta?"

"I really hate this. It's heavy in the morning and then it feels like it fades off by the evening, in time for dinner, but when I try to eat it comes right back."

Her description gave me pause. "Should we see about a doctor? I'm sure a hotel like ours has doctors they like to use. At least I hope they do, for what they charge."

"It's only been twenty-four hours. I know my body. It'll pass. It's already better than it was yesterday."

"Are you sure, because I'm sure it wouldn't be a trouble, and maybe they could give you something to get you through it faster."

"I don't want to see a doctor on my honeymoon," she said, giving me a dark stare. "I said I'll be fine. I can soldier through."

I let it drop.

As we ate, I shared with her my vision from earlier in the day, out on the marble rock, when I stared at the water and suddenly understood on a deeply intuitive level everything about the gravitational field, the physicality of spacetime, its elegance and simplicity.

"Well, that's partly true," said Annie, not even looking up from her food.

"How do you mean?"

"Well, I don't doubt that you experienced that, but that's [the Physicist]'s memory, from when he was in college and went to the beach, no? Didn't you have me proof that passage? He's on a beach reading and then he looks up at the water and suddenly understands Einstein's theories? But you did also say during your treatment that you witnessed the universe being rebuilt, with the field and all, so maybe this was playing off that. Isn't it in your treatment report?"

I set down my fork and took a sip of Etna Bianco, salty and angular. She was right. What I'd envisioned on the rock while looking at the water was an early breakthrough moment for the Physicist. I'd written out the memory myself. I'd chosen the adjectives and verbs and syntax to amplify the physicality central to the experience. Sapphire, that's the color I chose for the water, before I'd ever even seen a drop of the Mediterranean in person. "Sparkle," I'd written, "radiance," "fractal."

"Are you okay?" said Annie. I'd drifted off in thought.

"Perfect. It's strange, is all. It was so real, the epiphany. I guess I'm sad to lose it."

"Is it that you've lost it?"

"Well, it wasn't mine. It was [the Physicist]'s memory. So it seems it wasn't really mine."

"But that reminds me of something else he's said [the Physicist], something that you said that you understood after your treatment, about how 'nothing is: things happen.'"

"That's right."

"So if you *aren't,* then you can't lose something, right? There is no need to feel the loss. And anyway, it still happened, yeah?"

The way we're almost hovering over the rails now because of our speed, it's like it pulls all the friction out of the mind, which in turn has allowed this memory of a memory not my own to reveal to me with complete ease that this is also how I'd ended up at the San Calisto—I've just pulled up the file and scanned back and sure enough, in an early passage of the Physicist's youthful days, describing his first free, bohemianesque trip with college friends from Bologna to Rome, how it was on that trip that they wandered into Trastevere and drank and smoked and debated and tried to pick up girls at the Bar San Calisto, a place he described with such tenderness—or that I described with such tenderness—that I'd convinced myself to go there without realizing it.

After dinner we walked down the alleys until we found a cannoli shop, ordered two, and ate them sitting on a set of stone stairs beneath a lemon-tree bower before heading back to the hotel. Someone somewhere was playing music. A real person with a real guitar. The air smelled rinsed clean. I was very glad I was not dead.

Though death was still on my mind. Or, more precisely, death-as-change, because of the sepia light. I told Annie as much the next night. We were waiting to have dinner at the restaurant attached to our sister hotel, up in Taormina proper, and were sipping Negronis out on the Literary Terrace, named, I now understood, for Mr. Lawrence, as well as Truman Capote (who rented the same home as Lawrence), and before them Oscar Wilde, Goethe, and Nietzsche, who is said to have written *Thus Spoke Zarathustra* in Taormina. I wondered for a moment how I would've felt sitting there on the Literary Terrace as a failed writer if I'd *not* had my treatment, assuming I'd even lived that long. It would've felt cruel, no doubt. The drinks would've burned like bleach, like insult. And how would it have felt had I not failed, had I finished the book—I'm inclined to think no different. I'm beginning to think that had I finished the book I would've still felt like nothing more than an interloper, an impostor, someone waiting for the shoe to drop, for the Mist to swallow me whole. I'd almost certainly have sat there, sipping my Negroni, looking at Etna, so close with her hoary head of steam braiding up into the darkening sky, and thought, There it is, there is *my* Mist, look at how it's found me here, on a cliff at the edge of the world, a terrace I had no business being on but had managed to get to through the fluke fortune of being rewarded financially for writing things down, for thinking I had anything to say at all, for having allowed myself those years ago in my studio—my room dedicated to my other illusion: that I had artistic vision—to set the brush down and start writing, to turn away from the canvas, the last canvas I ever began, a painting I never finished, a painting I realized for the first time, while sitting on the terrace, was of bright, almost neon bodies celebrating below a volcano, a fact that would've filled me with a sinking feeling, deep and pitiless. Instead, I was asking Annie about the sepia light, if she noticed it too, if she remembered the opening scene of *Godfather II,* or any of the Sicily scenes, for that matter, like when Michael walks along the hills in the first film and meets Apollonia, and she did remember, said Annie, "and then the marriage, of course, and then that horrible car bombing, and then the retribution killing by De Niro in part two," she said as the waiter set down two fresh Negronis in heavy-bottomed rocks glasses cut with geometric patterns.

"De Niro," said the waiter, smiling. "My father waited on him many times when he was here. They stay here, you know, when they film the movie. The whole cast."

"Here at the hotel?"

"Well, actually at the villa, the sister property down by the sea"—where we were staying—"they wanted to be by the water of course, after shooting those scenes in black coats all day." The coincidence did not move me; it seemed inevitable that he would say that. I could tell Annie could sense it too—she'd also been noticing the coincidences blossoming around us, the change of energy. We thanked the waiter for telling us, saying kindly how fascinating that was to hear, then enjoyed our drinks and went to dinner.

That night we were scheduled for an elaborate tasting menu I'd already paid for in advance, much like every other very expensive thing. On the walk there, I tried to assure Annie that she didn't need to put herself through this meal just because it was already paid for. If she didn't feel good, she didn't feel good. I didn't care.

"This morning wasn't so great, but I feel better than yesterday and I really do have an appetite," she said. "I am bloated, though, which sucks. I'm surprised you can't tell. I feel like I look like I'm going to burst." She stopped and turned in profile.

Annie ate the entirety of the first course, then the second, but by the third her bites were becoming infrequent. I didn't want to press, so I said nothing and instead brought back up the subject of the sepia light, and elaborated on how I believed this light to be an expression of an omnipresent feeling in Sicily about death, specifically that the island radiated death, which is to say that part of the island's beauty and mystery was that it felt as if something was always ending.

"Couldn't that mean that things are also always beginning," matched Annie, "especially with all the flowers, and the volcano right there, this big churning mountain that could literally make new earth," and this was true, I said, this is the way of the universe, of course, the cones of light flared forward and back, but here, in the temporal reality of human Sicily, I suggested, one seems to always *feel* the end, for that seems to be the vibration, the death of one empire for the beginning of another, which begins its death, just like us, just like everything, the moment it begins. "Do you feel like death now?" asked Annie, unfolding and refolding her napkin. "No," I said, "but that's only because I have recently died hundreds of times, and while death will come for both of us, I can't even be bothered to think about that anymore because I'm so grateful to be here with you, and I feel very, very lucky," and to that she smiled in a way that I know I will never forget, or at least I have not yet forgotten, which is to say it is memory, which is to say it is part of who I am, right now, in this moment on the Frecciarossa, heading for my wife.

THE NEXT MORNING I woke to an acute sense of dread about the debt situation, thanks in part to another thread of anxious emails from Richards asking if I'd heard anything. I scrolled past these before even turning over to see if Annie was awake, the room still dark, but when I finally did she wasn't there. She was gone. The dread grew.

I got up, checked the bathroom, then noticed a note on the desk: she'd woken up feeling the best she'd felt in days and was desperate for some exercise, so she went for a morning walk before it was too hot. She'd gone out to a network of old goat paths that ran along the cliffs around and above the hotel; we'd seen people hiking them from our chairs on the beach. Some exercise would do me good, I decided. I got up, put on my sneakers, filled a water bottle, and left a corresponding note for Annie telling her I'd gone walking too in hopes of catching up with her, but if I missed her, I'd see her down at the beach.

Even in the early dawn the trails were scorched bright. There was little shade, only scrub and baking rocks and a different little lizard every twenty feet who would bolt away from his perch along the path. Still, it felt good to sweat, to be able to see my heartbeat through my chest, blood thudding through me. I followed the trails as high as they seemed to go, up to a cliff point on the side of the cove that afforded a view of the open waters to my right, the beach to my left. I could see Annie walking out to one of the loungers, the first one out. With no reason to rush, I decided to meditate, which also felt good. But when I opened my eyes and looked back down onto the beach, Annie was no longer alone. Her lounger was set up along the wooden path over the sand, and on the other side of it, on the opposite lounger, was a figure sitting up and facing her, as if talking, a male figure, large and pale and round. He looked like a peeled potato. Except for his head, which, even from my vantage, I could see was blocky, flat on top, *profoundly rectangular.*

I was running back down the trails before I realized I was running. Meanwhile in my mind I was practice-ranting all the things I would say to Richards when I got down there. He's lost it. He's mad. And how has he found us here? Who does he think he is, to come here and harass Annie! I was running so fast I accidentally dropped my water bottle and watched it bounce over a cliff's edge, then disappear. It didn't matter; I didn't stop. I kept on to the beach. By the time I got there, he was gone.

Annie sat up when she noticed me coming close. I was heavy with sweat. Her face changed as she saw mine. "What's the matter?" she asked.

"I was up there," I said between breaths, pointing at the distant cliff point, "it looked like someone was talking to you. A man."

"Oh, yeah. Some older Russian guy kind of came over. He was definitely pervy. I couldn't understand anything he was saying. One of the chair guys noticed though and sort of shooed him away."

"A Russian?"

"I think so. You know that Russian vibe. I don't know. What's going on?"

The way she looked at me then, as I was sitting on the foot of the lounger, breathing heavily, I knew she knew something had leaked into my mind. It wasn't only the absurd fear of Richards that bothered me, or the pressure of the debt, it was that for a full moment it felt like my mind had slipped backward, like maybe it was relapsing into my old psyche, and as I was witnessing it happening I was powerless to stop it.

"I got confused. And then I kind of panicked. I—for a second it felt like I might be how I used to be, like I was relapsing. I don't want to go back," I said. "I can't go back."

She placed a hand on mine. "It's not going to happen. I'm guessing the idea alone made you feel like you were going backward, but you weren't. I understand, though. It's scary. But you're not going back. I promise. Maybe you had too much wine last night? We're still getting used to this. It's okay." And as she said this my pulse slid back into its normal click. I caught my breath. I wiped the thin lines of tears off the bottoms of my eyes. "Go put your trunks on and meet me back out here," she said. "I'll order you some coffee. What about a water? Did you not bring a bottle with you? I told you, you've got to stay hydrated in this heat."

That aimless day we swam, lounged about, had sex. Sex—this too is so profoundly different since my treatment. How couldn't it be? My desire for her felt the most charged it'd ever felt, but that was not the only difference. The physical experience had completely changed. Where before her touch was a signal I had to translate into the *fact* of her desire for me—and like any translation, had the potential to be mistaken or mistrusted—her touch was now the fact itself. Her body was the fact. Not a surface, only a total truth. I'd experienced this before, of course, but not like this. Sometimes I'd catch a flash of melancholy about how much time I'd wasted in the past questioning her, questioning everything, but it passed. It all passes. I don't know how else to describe it but to say that through her touch I became very pleasantly invisible to myself.

We also ate and sipped drinks and, when we weren't doing anything else, I read. I paused the Dyer because I wanted to make sure I read all of *The Leopard* while on the island, as had been my plan, so I did and found it to be a blast, especially near the novel's end, when the protagonist Don Fabrizio is explaining to a visiting member of the new national Italian government why he, like most Sicilians, wants nothing to do with government, and goes on to say:

"Sleep, my dear Chevalley, sleep, that is what Sicilians want, and they will always hate anyone who tries to wake them . . . All Sicilian expression, even the most violent, is really wish-fulfillment: our sensuality is a hankering for oblivion, our shooting and knifing a hankering for death; our laziness, our spiced and drugged sherbets, a hankering for voluptuous immobility, that is, for death again; our meditative air is that of a void . . ."

And so it seemed even that perception of mine was nothing more than a long-present understanding I gradually intuited, a perception so apparent that it was ensconced in the sociopolitical climax of the greatest Sicilian novel, and while the old me would've felt saddened by losing ownership over an utterance, I instead only laughed as I'd been laughing the whole trip, and felt grateful again for the reminder that, at least when it came to me, there is no original thought, nothing original at all, there is only this composite, this system of experiences and memories, of which this ancient, death-seeped island is now a part, and I a part of it.

The next morning, on our last full day, Annie woke up feeling unwell again. "I clearly pushed it too far yesterday," she said. "The run, all the sun, then white wine, some richer food. I should've eased back in." I wanted to pick up the phone and call the front desk about a doctor, but I also knew that wasn't my call to make, so I said nothing. But by dinner, her appetite hadn't returned. We were at a small trattoria at the end of a stone footpath, a plate of olives between us.

"Could I ask you a question?" I said.

"Of course?"

"Well, it's partly a question but also first I should confess that the quiche with the *zabaione*—I had some, a few bites off your plate. I should've mentioned this, but I hoped what you had was maybe a quick bug and I didn't want you to worry or anything. But obviously you're still sick and because you're still sick I'm wondering why I'm not also feeling sick, which leads me to my question, which is: if I'm not also sick from eating the same thing, maybe it isn't food poisoning you're dealing with, well, maybe it still is just a bug, but going off how it seems to behave, showing up strongest early in the day, is there any concern, like—have you thought at all about it being morning sickness. I know the 'morning' part can be a misnomer, but."

"It's not that."

"Are you sure, though? With the way you describe it, the timing of some of the heaviest waves of nausea . . ."

"May I ask you a question?"

"Sure."

"Did it occur to you just now that you're asking a woman if she's ever considered whether or not her nausea might be because of pregnancy? Like, that maybe you'd noticed something about her body that maybe she didn't notice herself?"

"Hearing you put it like that—I guess because you hadn't said anything about it—"

"I love you, and I love that the treatment worked for you, but I don't think it uploaded *Women's Wisdom* into your brain. You've got to remember that part of what you're experiencing at times as a fresh sense of intuition is maybe sometimes just you seeing the world with a clarity or attention that you couldn't before because your head was shut down. Obviously that doesn't apply to everything and I don't mean that to be mean, but anyway the point is that of course I have considered that. I didn't say anything because, well, to be frank, I'm not sure how to say something about it."

"Why couldn't you say something about it?"

She looked away for a moment, tugging at her ears, smoothing her hair. "This might be hurtful to say, which is not my intention, but it was only a little bit ago that something like me being pregnant wasn't on the table for discussion. That would have been very bad. Very bad. Obviously I want kids and have wanted them, but you got really ill. Then one day I drop you at Denise's, and when I picked you up, there you were, looking brand-new, and practically the first thing you said to me was 'I want to be a father.' I'd never heard you say that before. Not in any real way. Just hearing that made me deeply happy. But also, it's not like you can expect me to hear that and suddenly be game for kids right away, or even feel like I can believe it. At the same time, I also wasn't about to look at you right there in Denise's driveway and tell you that I'm glad you want to be a dad, but I don't know if what you're saying is real or not. It's just been a lot. I see that you feel different now—I feel the difference too, I really do—and I'm not saying I doubt this change in any way, but it is going to take me time to get used to it. It wasn't that long ago I was in Palm Springs wondering if I was going to be flying home to a dead husband. I don't say that to be cruel, it's just the facts."

"I'm sorry, Annie. For this conversation, for everything before. Especially you having to be afraid."

"It's okay. We're here now."

"Have you thought at all about getting a test? I don't know if I'm allowed to ask that."

"Today is the only day when I've considered it. I think to get one you've got to walk up to the pharmacist's counter and ask for one aloud. I just wasn't up for that today. Tomorrow is going to be a wash because of traveling, and at this point it's like what's the rush. If I feel better again tomorrow, then maybe I'm fine. If not, I'll pick one up when we're back in Rome or see a doctor or something."

A bit nervously, I said, "Maybe now isn't the time and if it isn't I'm sorry but I feel like I should say—and I know I already mentioned some of this because of what went on during the treatment and all—and that all still feels completely true, by the way, like deep down in my bones epiphany true—but I feel like I need to say just clearly and honestly that were it to be the case right now that you were, or are, you know, pregnant, I'd feel really lucky about that. And even if that's not the case right now I hope someday that could be the case."

"I like hearing that," she said, then spit out a violet olive pit.

We were due at Catania for our flight the next morning, so I woke before sunup and walked alone to the beach for a final swim. The air was cool and the water shadowless and the day was just emerging as a glare on the sky's rim. I sat on one of the loungers to wait for the light and finished reading *Out of Sheer Rage*. Unsurprisingly, the book culminates in a meditation about depression (caused for Dyer by not writing his book). How could it have gone any other way?

Once you are depressed there is almost nothing you can do about it. It is useless trying to snap out of it or buck up because it is impossible to see the point of doing anything. You cannot think of a single thing to do, or place to go, or book to read. In his periods of "huge stagnation" Pessoa's Bernardo Soares compared his condition to that of "a prisoner deprived of normal freedom of action in an infinite cell."

"An infinite cell." That's what it was, ultimately, the years failing to write the book, but also all the years before that, going back to when I was a boy. Meditating on the passage, I grew curious about it, looked up its source in the back of *Rage*, learned it was from *The Book of Disquiet*, a book I'd seen on countless bookstore tables but knew nothing about. Using my phone, I googled *The Book of Disquiet* and began reading, right there on the beach, translator Richard Zenith's introduction to the Penguin Classics edition. In it I learned that Pessoa spent his days in Lisbon writing under dozens of names, the most important of which he called "heteronyms," including Bernardo Soares, the speaker of the phrase "an infinite cell," whom Pessoa called specifically a "semi-heteronym," and to whom he attributed *The Book of Disquiet*. Except even that wasn't so simple, as Zenith explains: " 'Fernando Pessoa, strictly speaking, doesn't exist.' So claimed Álvaro de Campos, one of the characters invented by Pessoa to spare himself the trouble of living real life. And to spare himself the trouble of organizing and publishing the richest part of his prose, Pessoa invented *The Book of Disquiet*, which never existed, strictly speaking, and can never exist." And so it seemed the quote I so admired, first read in a book about a book that didn't exist, came from *The Book of Disquiet*, a book that, "strictly speaking," didn't exist, yet was attributed to Soares— a man who didn't exist, strictly speaking—by his inventor, Pessoa, who himself is said not to exist, albeit by de Campos, another of his inventions. "There is almost nothing you can do about it," says Dyer about depression, "almost" being the key word. It seemed to me then, and still to me now, that the human being in Lisbon, whoever it was, who wrote so sharply of depression, was very close to understanding (or perhaps already knew) the one thing it seems you *can* do against depression, against the *infinite cell*: blow up the foundation upon which it rests.

"An infinite cell," repeated no one on a beach that isn't there before closing the book about a book that was never written, rising, and walking into the cool blue bend of spacetime.

SIPPING A CAPPUCCINO at the Catania airport, waiting to board our flight back to Rome for the final leg of our honeymoon, I checked my email for the first time in days. After scrolling past half a dozen messages from Richards that I chose to ignore, I came upon a message from Terry, which was a bit of a surprise, seeing as the last few times I'd tried calling him I'd gotten his secretary, who'd each time said something to the effect of "Terry wanted me to tell you that there is some epic swell at Steamer Lane so he's taking some personal days out of the office but knows you'll understand."

His email said that they'd finally heard from the Physicist's department at his university in the UK, but their response was that it's the university's policy not to report on the whereabouts of its employees, so even if they knew where he was, they weren't going to tell us. The good news was that they did confirm that he was still answering some emails, which meant he wasn't dead. Yet his whereabouts were still unknown.

I finished the cappuccino and boarded the plane with Annie. Soon after sitting down I slowed my breath and slipped into a semi-meditative state, encouraged further by holding Annie's hand and rubbing the meaty pressure point between her thumb and finger in a circle to aid with her flying anxiety and light nausea—it was there again—and it was in that state that I began thinking of how else I might contact the Physicist and communicate to him how important it was that I finish this project, but nothing was coming to mind. There was a blockage. I could feel it in the head. A familiar feeling. A feeling that, in the past, I'd dealt with by doing what people talk about doing in novels and films and old-world existences where distraction is never the solution to a problem: I'd retreat to the country, to my family's estate. This is what I remembered as we ascended off the island, coiling upward on our brief trajectory to Rome—I should go to my family's country estate, just like I used to do, and have a real good think. Yes. Why hadn't I thought of that sooner? I need to head to the country and give my mind and bones the kind of detoxifying shiatsu that only abundant square footage, human absence, and all-around dirt and chlorophyll can provide.

Except of course I have no family estate in the country, because this was not my memory but the Physicist's. And it was not even a memory, just a blip of his speech, something he'd said offhandedly on one of his recordings very early on in the project while describing his family's country estate where he was born and for a time grew up—"It is still there I retreat to sometimes when I need to think."

I came awake in my aisle seat.

Some of the earliest files I received from the Physicist via Elaine were recordings describing the family's country estate, including its landscape and the history of how his ancestors had become comfortable landowners through successful alfalfa farming. In the file, along with these recordings, was a folder of photos of the property, old black and whites. I'd asked Elaine if she could ask him if he happened to have any up-to-date photos, mainly to see the colors of the place, and he replied to Elaine who replied to me saying he was surprised to learn he hadn't taken any photos of the house, at least not that he could remember, a weird realization, though not so weird, he supposed, for how often do you walk outside your home and take a photo? I found this funny, something I'd never myself considered, which caused me to look through my phone and discover I'd never once taken a photo of our home in California and had only once taken a photo of our brownstone in Brooklyn, on the day we moved. But it was while I was scrolling through my phone, looking for pictures that weren't, that it occurred to me that I'd only ever seen photos of my building in Oakland via a renters' website and on Google Maps, so I suggested this as a solution to Elaine to suggest to the Physicist: Could he give us the address so I could see it on Google Maps? The email chain went cold for a day, but then Elaine replied with an attachment he'd sent her of a screenshot of his attempt to capture the estate on Google Maps, using Street View—the image was of an ornate gate structure of wrought iron and stucco at the entrance to a tree-lined drive so straight and long that the house was hidden somewhere in the distance beyond the meeting of perspectival points. "He says this should at least give you a sense for the land," said Elaine on his behalf, "that's alfalfa all around, and there used to be canals." That screenshot, it occurred to me in my aisle seat while flying over the Tyrrhenian Sea, was still somewhere in my email.

When we landed in Rome, I took out my phone, reconnected to the cell network, ignored notice of another voicemail from Richards, and found the image in my email: the farm road, the white stucco gate structure, trees beyond it, alfalfa to either side, and, in the top-left corner of the image, the house's address, conveniently listed, which is finally how this whole day trip to Modena came to fruition, resulting in me here on the Frecciarossa heading back to Rome beside a set of twins still sleeping across from each other, like two waves in the same signal, each a station of disturbance, sleeping even after another Frecciarossa has just passed, its bulb of forced air causing our train to shudder just as ours caused it to shudder, both rocketing past with such speed there isn't even a second in their passing when you can catch the eyes of an opposite passenger and share a moment of lag, for there is only the blur of what can't be seen, the groups of windows clicking by like frames of film, throwing my reflection back to me in temporary relief—ghostly and calm, a visitation that immediately calls to mind the final moments of Don Fabrizio of *The Leopard* as he's slipping out of life on a hotel bed in Palermo, surrounded by mourners, one of whom is not a person but a presence, for it is Death herself: "It was she, the creature forever yearned for, coming to fetch him; strange that one so young should yield to him; the time for the train's departure must be very close."

←

WHEN MY TRAIN ARRIVED in Modena I walked without urgency into the station, blurring with my fellow passengers past ads for coffee and cars, the text of which I could barely read, but whose meanings were undeniable by virtue of their visual language, perfected by my culture, which it seems I can never escape.

Outside at the taxi stand I called the taxi company—the only thing about Italy I dislike—and requested a car in English, unsure if they'd understood me at all, then waited to see if they had. The streets were empty and eerie, facts only intensified by the devilish spirals of dust and dead leaves kicked up by the wind. A spotlight sun radiated over everything. I waited. I got a text. It was from Richards: "It is what it is!?!" I said to myself: This is a chance to help Richards. To make this all go away. I was close, I could feel it, and I was nervous, but I didn't resist it. On the other side of the nervousness would be something else. I hoped it would be closure. I waited.

Finally a cab arrived. I got in and tried to tell the driver—a man who looked like he could be from West Virginia, with his jarhead haircut and stocky frame—the address in Italian, but he only looked at me confused. I handed him my phone opened to the map and he nodded, then stopped, turned his head quizzically, looked at me, looked back at the address, adjusted the zoom on the map with a pinch of his fingers, looked at me again, his eyelids faintly pulsating as he focused on my face, reading me, if you will, then nodded again, said, *"Sì, sì,"* handed back the phone, slapped on the meter, and started on our way.

We crossed a main thoroughfare, shot down an alley, then skirted the main square around the city's Romanesque duomo, the sight of which, from inside the cab, shocked me with déjà vu. I didn't resist the sensation. Instead, I let it unfold further, until I suddenly remembered that I had been here before—not physically, but digitally. Way back as an undergrad in art school, my senior year, while working on a final project for Rage and Relentlessness: On Post-WWII Art, Film, and Literature in the German-Speaking World. Jules and I had managed to convince the professor, because it was art school, to let us do a joint visual project as our final instead of writing papers. We'd opted to do something on W. G. Sebald's first novel, *Vertigo,* which we'd read in class. The novel follows an unnamed narrator on a meandering journey between European cities, driven by association, curiosity, but, most of all, memory and its destruction. As mentioned, I took a liking to Sebald and looked forward to the project, though I didn't have a single idea what to do.

It was Jules who had the idea: we would visually re-create the novel's movements through space in such a way that, when encountered by the viewer, the work would simulate the experience of reading Sebald's notoriously fluid, dreamlike prose; it would be a single piece that, at its end, could only be a memory—that was how Jules described it to me. I asked him if he was stoned. He said he was, but only a little, then countered by saying I was stoned too, which I was, but that, more important, the idea would work.

Jules described the process as follows: first we'd make a precise time line of the novel's movements, but in reverse, so at the top of the order would be the novel's final image, "a silent rain of ashes, westward, as far as Windsor Park," and at the bottom would be the novel's peculiar opening section about the eccentric and syphilitic writer Marie-Henri Beyle, who, we'd learned in class, was actually Stendhal (Marie-Henri Beyle was his real name). With the reverse time line established, we'd then build a twenty-four-by-thirty-six-inch canvas frame, but instead of stretching a canvas over it, we'd cover it entirely with blue painter's tape. Next, explained Jules, we'd gesso the tape, turning it into a workable surface upon which we'd then paint gestural, expressionistic images from the novel, beginning with the "silent rain of ashes." We'd use acrylics so that the images dried quickly, but also because they were cheaper. Once the first image—that is, the last image—was set, we'd again cover the canvas in painter's tape and gesso, then paint the next image on the time line, which is to say the second-to-last moment in the novel. We'd repeat this process until finished, taking turns painting the scenes as we worked our way backward to the novel's beginning.

Once the painting was complete, we'd hang it in one of the dozen campus galleries and invite the class to a "viewing." Everyone would gather around the painting, which would begin with the same black-and-white Napoleonic image that opens the novel even before text, transposed in the style of Gerhard Richter's gray monochromes (which both Jules and I worshipped). Then Jules and I would take turns stripping away the layers of tape upon which the opening image was painted, gradually revealing the next image, then the next, on and on we'd tear the painting, slowly evolving it with the movement of the novel. In addition, we'd have recordings of particularly pregnant passages from the text played over a speaker whenever their corresponding image was revealed (my idea).

And that's exactly what we did. For four days we worked at a constant clip—tape, gesso, image, tape, gesso, image—until we were a little mad, living on delivery pizza and taking turns sleeping on a foam pad on the floor of Jules's studio cubicle. One of the final images I had to paint came from the novel's opening section about Beyle/Stendhal, a passage in which Beyle discusses love with one Mme Gherardi, described by Sebald's nameless narrator as a "mysterious, not to say unearthly figure," who may have been "a cipher for various lovers" and may have "never really existed, despite all the documentary evidence, and was merely a phantom, albeit one to whom Beyle remained true for decades." The passage about love comes from an account of a trip that, Sebald's narrator explains, "may have been wholly imaginary, made with a companion who may likewise have been a mere figment of his own mind." The passage marks the first three days of Beyle and Gherardi's journey, from Bologna to Lake Garda, where they spent the evenings cooling off on the water, floating on a barque (a word I had to look up), which is when Gherardi makes her claim that:

> love, like most other blessings of civilisation, was a chimaera which we desire the more, the further removed we are from Nature. Insofar as we seek Nature solely in another body, we become cut off from Her; for love, she declared, is a passion that pays its debts in a coin of its own minting, and thus a purely notional transaction which one no more needs for one's fulfilment than one needs the instrument for trimming goose-quills that he, Beyle, had bought in Modena.

Maybe it's because I can feel Annie getting ever closer as we scream down the line, or maybe, rereading this passage all these years later here on my phone, I don't understand it any more now than I did then, but my reaction is the same: I disagree. I can't say why, but I do, I reject it all the way down to the thinnest tips of my nerves. Regardless, the passage clearly warranted repeating, which meant I needed an image. What I painted on the "canvas" was Modena's cathedral reflected upside down, as if on the surface of the lake's water, to mimic the way in which we learn about Modena only after we've moved beyond it in time at Lake Garda. Instead of acrylic, I used thin washes of India ink in reference to the tool for trimming writing quills that necessitated Beyle's stop in Modena. To paint the image I'd first googled Modena, of course, then explored it briefly on Google Maps Street View, a relatively new technology at the time, the experience of which clearly incited the déjà vu I felt in the cab.

The painting was a huge success. For an hour Jules and I tore away the surfaces in front of our classmates and professor, moving gradually through the novel's spiraling journey across both space and memory as passages of the novel played out over a speaker, read in the deep baritone of a sculpture professor from Freiburg we'd asked to record and who enthusiastically agreed out of a shared love of Sebald, the haunting quality of his voice joining the incessant tearing of the tape in a strained but captivating experience. A crowd of passersby gathered as the viewing progressed. At times people would gasp, wince, or even wail a little when a particularly captivating part of the painting was destroyed, or if the act of destruction itself was particularly evocative. When it was over, there was only the wooden frame on the wall, but below it was an immense mound of blue tape, shredded and coiled like the peels of an alien vegetable, standing as high as the canvas's bottom rung.

The painting was gone. All that was left was the tangle of memory, embodied by the scrap pile, and yet the bare frame suggested as much about destruction as clarity, a sense of resolution and weight-lessness and potential that echoed the placid release of the novel's finale. The project received an A plus with distinction. Jules and I were written up in the student paper. The project's technique was Jules's breakthrough. He proceeded to expand and refine it over almost a decade, leading to his explosion into the art world. I'm honored to have been a part of his beginning.

Though I couldn't manage it in the taxi, I was determined to snap a picture of the cathedral on my way back and send it to Jules to see if he'd remember it, a simple gesture—sending a nostalgic message to a good friend—that in the past would've racked me with anxiety, but which now I looked forward to, as I looked for-ward to basically everything, even the unknown, or especially the unknown, which is what I was facing when the taxi dropped me at the familiar white stucco gate structure on a dusty road outside of town.

WITH NO FENCE extending out from either side of the stucco struc-ture, the gate was prohibitive only to cars, so I walked around it, over a culvert, and made my way down the long drive lined on both sides by tall Lombardy poplars, slim and feathery, like quills stuck into the earth. Save for the trees, the drive was nothing but a humble road of pea gravel, but somehow, like everything in Italy, just by virtue of its environs, it possessed a dignity above dirt and stone and looked more like a pale ribbon cut into the sea of alfalfa waving far out on either side. It was officially midday, the sun clear and omnipresent, my shadow small, bug noise raging in the air, the same sound of the warm months of my youth. For some reason I was surprised to hear it there, as if that white noise, that cacophony of chitter, was somehow beneath the dignity of this great peninsula. Still, I was grateful for the sound. It made me feel like a boy walking down farm roads, objectiveless and free in a green world that exploded out of nothing but the dirt, the Appalachian summer so hot you couldn't bother worrying about anything beyond right where you were. I listened with such intention that halfway down the path I began to hear the soft brassy notes of a trumpet and for a moment thought I was hallucinating. The notes grew louder, cool sounds of American jazz calling from the house that slowly emerged out of the green horizon line. A grand country house, three stories tall, with a fourth-floor portico, cream colored under a tile roof, with every window opened and flanked by shutters the same pale green as the undersides of leaves, with a large circle driveway of laid brick. A small terrace jutted from the second floor, shading the front doors, which were exceptionally tall, made of polished hardwood and left open like the windows onto a great hallway running through the house's center that opened again in the rear onto a long grass lawn whose green radiated like neon from where I was standing, on the other side. It all looked much better in color.

The music was quite loud now, but pleasant and soft, almost as if the trumpeter was playing from somewhere within the walls. I was standing outside in the sun, just beyond the entrance, taking stock of where I was, how I'd gotten there, how grateful I was for it all, no matter what happened next, when something fell on my head. I was worried I'd been shat on by an Emilian bird. I brushed a hand through my hair, but it came back dry. Something fell on me again, except this time it bounced down in front of me. I reached down and picked it up off the bricks: a pistachio shell, smooth and sharp as a manicured nail. I looked up and saw that looking down at me from the second-floor terrace, smiling and chewing on the roasted nuts, was the Physicist. "I'll be down," he said, then disappeared.

Though I knew he was an active guy who stayed busy in his free time with cycling (the kind done in skintight shorts and jersey) and swimming (done in a skintight Speedo)—the sort of stuff it seems all Italian men do as pastimes—I was still surprised to be greeted by someone so fit and put together. Even his hair, which in pictures looks like an unruly tangle of gray I'd always taken to be a nod to Einstein's famous coif—not unlike the countless men in the art world who dress like Warhol or de Kooning—was nicely cut, its balding pattern echoing my own, but with far more dignity, as again was true of everything in Italy. His gray beard was also trimmed tight, with perfect lines suggesting the use of a flat razor, which of course he must use, I thought, because he's Italian and classy. Even his jeans were classy, and his simple striped T-shirt, and his gray New Balance sneakers. He didn't look like a physicist is what I'm saying, except for maybe his glasses, with their thick black square frames. No, even these were hip. "It is time we finally meet," he said, extending a hand. "A pleasure. And welcome. I show you around."

To the left of the front door was a music room—a small square space lined floor to ceiling with vinyl records on three walls with a single large chair facing what I took to be a very expensive sound system set up between two windows. It was from here that the jazz trumpet issued. Listening, I thought I maybe understood at last what audiophiles are talking about when they use words like "depth" and "warmth."

It was impossible to stand in that room and not be reminded of the passage in the Physicist's book on time, in which he explains

Augustine's explanation of how the passing of time is internal, within the mind. He explains, on behalf of Augustine:

> When we listen to a hymn, the meaning of a sound is given by
> the ones that come before and after it . . . but if we are always in
> the present moment, how is it possible to hear it? It is possible . . .
> because our consciousness is based on memory and on anticipation.
> A hymn, a song, is in some way present in our minds in a unified
> form . . . And hence this is what time is: it is entirely in the present,
> in our minds, as memory and as anticipation.

"You like music?" asked the Physicist. Clearly my face betrayed my wandering mind. I apologized and explained I was thinking of the Augustine passage from his book, how the past is like a residue on the mind.

"A very smart dude, as you'd say, yes?" He laughed and walked back into the hall. I followed. Opposite was a cocktail room with pink satin couches, an old Victrola, and a spread of *amari* I'd never seen, much of which seemed very old. I was certain a real Warhol—a black-on-black silk screen of Marilyn Monroe—was hanging on the wall.

Off this room was a very large sitting room with a fireplace big enough to fit a Fiat. There was an expansive network of connected modernist brown leather couches meeting to form different seating sections, around which, everywhere, were stacks of books—novels, art books, textbooks, cookbooks. A small TV on a wooden pedestal. Cat palms bending out of the corners. We stood there for a moment before I noticed the ceilings were high, round, and frescoed in the rococo style.

We next passed into a dining room: an old table and old china cabinet with modernist chairs and black-and-white art photographs on the walls, all of people's hands. I found myself looking around for signs of a lace tablecloth. There was none to be seen. On the center of the table was a ceramic plate of hand-rolled tortellini, also ceramic. "In winter, we eat here," he said. "But in summer, outside. I show you." From there we stepped back into the hall, then out onto the terrace and to the right, where a long wooden table was shaded under a trellis thick with vine. He suggested we sit there, where at least we could catch a breeze, and I agreed of course and sat where he'd pointed to, at the table's end. He excused himself temporarily.

It all seemed so impossibly elegant. The terrace was made of large slabs of stone that made a perfect edge with the green yard, a perimeter dotted with lemon trees in terra-cotta planters, their green lacquered leaves faintly fluttering in the breeze. The grass, perfectly cut, stretched far back into the yard, a green sea from which rose tall old pines forming a shaded bower above a baroque fountain made of stone and shaped concrete flowing into a pond, the whole thing designed to look at once like an undisturbed space in nature *and* a space in nature that had been wrangled by man. Beyond the fountain I could make out a wire fence trimmed with planks of raw pine protecting a vegetable garden, and to its right a higher chain-link fence around a tennis court. I sensed—but could not see—a pool somewhere behind some willows.

When the Physicist returned he was carrying a silver wine chiller, not unlike the one brought to our room in Sicily. In it was a half bottle of the local Lambrusco, with its pressurized cork top, along with two bottles of Moretti, which he said would be best to drink while the Lambrusco cooled down. Along with the wine was a plate of Parmigiano-Reggiano, cut into craggy chunks, like golden gravel. "Aged twenty-four months," he said, "at a dairy just up the road." There were also slices of mortadella piled delicately like rare pink fabric. You could see perfect cubes of white fat suspended in cross-section. Decades-old Modenese balsamic vinegar, as thick and dark as chocolate, was drizzled over everything.

He opened the two Moretti, poured a third of each into small glasses—not unlike the glasses at the San Calisto—and handed me one, along with the rest of the bottle. "*Salute,*" he said. We toasted to meeting. He pointed out some landmarks on the grounds, then the alfalfa beyond, rehashing what I'd learned already about his family's successful past. Pointing to another pond to our right, he explained, "That used to be the launch bay into the canals. Canals once cut through the entire region. The farmers used them to transport crops. Very efficient." We were the only ones currently at the house, he explained. "Family will join me again soon," he said, "though family is smaller than it used to be." The breeze shook tiny white blossoms out of the trellis, settling around us like snow.

"I hope you are not angry with me," he said finally, wiping beer foam from his mustache.

"I was when you'd vanished, but not anymore," I said, not believing it—not what I said, but that I'd said anything at all. So often in my life, in my obsessive, punishing, relentless meditation on the future, I'd fantasize about conversations I'd hoped to have with famous artists, or an author, or my father, my father especially, frank conversations of fluid articulation, and yet whenever those fantasized encounters would arise in real life, the potential of the fantasies would fizzle off, and most often I'd feel something like dark, shameful embarrassment for thinking anyone would care to speak to me at all, let alone care about what I had to say—the great and painful echo of this, I now suspect, can be felt in my failure to write the novel—and yet, here I was, sitting across from the Physicist at his family's centuries-old outdoor table, speaking without fear, without worry, telling him I wasn't mad at him, not anymore. My guard wasn't down—it was gone (a symptom of the treatment). But that wasn't all; there was an intimacy too, a kind I've felt only with him and suspect I won't feel again, the kind of intimacy you build with someone when they entrust you with their voice. "Things are different now," I said.

"A change of heart? What have I done to deserve it?" he said, smiling, nibbling like a child at a piece of Parm.

"More like a change of person. I had an experience recently, a kind of treatment and—it sounds trite but—now I feel different about almost everything. I'm still figuring it out day by day, as different experiences arise. But since then I've stopped feeling angry about most things. Like how you disappeared. Before my treatment I'd fantasize about finding you and grabbing you by the collar and demanding you finish the job, saying something about how it ain't all about you—I mean, the book *is* all about you, but not in the labor sense—and then I'd say something about how people depend on their work in order to live, how you can't just leave them high and dry, then I'd say something about how, as a tenured best-selling soon-to-be Nobel laureate, you clearly couldn't understand what money meant to people like me, or what living with crushing debt is like, as I have, especially when it's owed to a giant publisher who employs a team of lawyers and a wild nag like Richards who won't leave me alone . . . I was very angry, very desperate. But things changed. Don't get me wrong, I'd really love for the debt to go away. It's the last thread still linking me to my past. But I don't want to make a point or something. I guess I just hoped that if I found you and asked, you might help me. Also, I am worried about Richards. He's got so much riding on all this. And he hasn't received the gift I have. I understand he's a total pain, but, yeah. I know you might say no to all this, I can live with that. But I'm here." I sipped some Moretti.

"You say 'Ri-shard'—you mean Richards?" He sipped his Moretti; it felt like an echo.

"No, that's not how it's pronounced. It's 'Ri-shard.' Kind of Frenchy, with no *s*."

He looked stunned, then a little happy. "Ridiculous. I always say Richards." And this made me happy. "At any rate," he continued, "I had no idea about your debt. I had some sense of tension between you and the publisher, but they of course did not tell me."

He was using an old professor's trick for talking to students: reveal a tenth of what you know, wait to see how the student responds, then adjust your candidness accordingly. That was fine. I had nothing to hide, nothing to protect. I'd come all this way. I'd tell him anything. I said, "I blew the advance money for a book I failed to write for them and now I've got to pay it back. That's why the publisher—still *our* publisher, I guess—was unhappy with me and didn't want me working with you. This gig is what was helping me work off the debt. The pages we turned in were erasing my balance. I wasn't making money, I was just getting back to zero. And if I don't get back to zero, because of the law in California where I live, it could really impact my wife. Even bankruptcy is out of the question. But none of this is her fault. I can't stand the thought of her paying a price for a situation I got in because I was a mess. I can't have that happening to Annie. She's suffered so much because of me already. I owe her everything."

"I see. My intention, you must know, was never to put you in a bad position. Or your wife. That is not my nature. I am sorry." He took his glasses off as he said this, looking at me softly, and with this single gesture I could feel in my jaw, forehead, lower back, toes, through all of me, one final grip of tension letting go, as if a signal had gone dark from some electrode in my head, one of those hair-thin implants they slide into the brains of rats, and it was suddenly gone; I could feel it because there was an absence there in my mind that caused me to breathe quickly and deeply, just for a moment, as soon as I felt it. Then I said, "I know. It's okay. I really appreciate it."

He shook his head, wiped his glasses. "I have to admit, I'm curious about the book you didn't write, though saying this in English, it feels nosy, as you say. English makes me feel rude sometimes." We both laughed.

"It was supposed to be about a great chemical spill that happened in the nineties in West Virginia, a small state in America where I grew up."

"Of course," he said excitedly. "The Great Monongahela River Chemical Spill of 1996. I remember it vividly."

I felt very confused. I looked down at my beer glass, wondering if there was something extra in it. He'd even properly pronounced the river's name. "I didn't know it made international news. It was hardly national news in the States. Only the ones who were there ever seem to know anything about it."

"Oh, no no—you misunderstand—I was there, in Pittsburgh. My apologies—I forgot we haven't gotten to this part of my story yet. I was a professor at the University of Pittsburgh from 1994 to 1999. It's on my CV in one of the files. My first big job. I remember the spill on the news. And the cold—the cold! Insane. I tried to drive bottled water down across the border with a colleague and we were stopped by the, what do you call them? Like your carabinieri, but not exactly . . ."

"The National Guard?"

"Yes, precisely, the National Guard. They told us to turn back. They claimed it was too dangerous to go across because of looting and riots, so we surrendered the water to them. I was certain it never left their trucks. So strange, that period of time. I didn't know that kind of thing happened in America. The naïveté! So strange. It was almost indescribable."

My eyes, as dumb as it sounds, began to well up. Since the beginning of that project, all the way back when I first conceived of the terrible idea of writing the novel, never once had I encountered someone outside the region who actually remembered the spill themselves. Those words, "almost indescribable," detonated within me, and I felt like the sun's already golden aura splashing down on everything became only more golden, and then, for the first time since sitting down, I recognized the brassy vibrato of the jazz trumpet still looping out of the music room, and on top of it the bug trill, could truly hear the waves of both, could hear—or maybe "sense" is the right word—the communicative impulse that spurred the expression of each abstract note, and I thought maybe all along the impetus behind the novel was nothing more than to hear someone else say they believed its story, that the disaster had happened, that it was horrible, scary and lonely and violent and strange, so horrible it could've changed the people who lived through it, changed them forever. All that just to hear someone say, *I believe you. I remember*.

I emptied my glass, poured in more, gathered myself. "Yes," I said. "It turned out it *was* indescribable, at least for me. I fooled myself for a while into thinking I was doing it. I'd drum up characters, but I could never get them to speak about it. Even third person didn't work. The voice would crumble without the presence of all the other voices. Too many stories, too many relations. To make matters worse, people often disbelieved the stories when I'd tell them in person, so while writing I'd try to make the book believable, which only served to kill the truth. My first book was an accident. I didn't write any of the stories. They already existed. I just kind of ferried them into a different form. It just happened. That's why it worked. But the second book—I was trying so hard to make something happen in my head. I was really trying to *be* a writer, you know? I thought a lot about this today. I used to think I was a painter and that caused me problems, then I wrote something and thought I was a writer and that caused me problems, so now I'm unsure if I ever was or wasn't either. Who knows? It doesn't bother me, not knowing. Honestly, I just miss how when I was young I made things without caring why. I had so many reasons for the book: to convince myself I'm smart, that I have talent, that I deserved my first book even though all I'd done was copy down stories that already existed, that I could be 'original.' I'm beginning to think originality is only an illusion of perspective. And I wanted the money, of course, so my wife and I could have a good life, a family. Terribly unoriginal.

"All that being said, I really did want to make something great. But that became tainted because I hoped if it was great, then people would stop hating me in the way I assumed everyone hated me. I was ill. I thought if I untangled the past and rewrote it, I could rewrite the future. I could arrive at a future I dreamed of, which is to say a dreamed-of 'me,' as opposed to the future I feared, the *me* I feared, which is of course the future I got. I failed. That's the long and short of it. But you know, since my treatment, I wonder if failure is nothing more than awaking into the present *as it is*— I'd become so obsessed with the past in hopes of manipulating my future that I got torn in two, one half going back, the other forward. But then you fail monumentally, wake up, and are left with your perspective. You're left with yourself. And I was no good. But that's not true anymore. I'm sorry for blathering. All this clarity, it's new, and I haven't figured out what to do with it yet, if it even makes sense to anyone but me." I realized the whole time I'd been rambling I'd been staring down at the beer in my hands, an old habit driven by shame, so instead I looked up and met the eyes of the Physicist looking back gently, with interest.

"No sorry. It is not blather. How many hours have you listened to me? And besides, it is my fault that you are here, though I am happy you are. It is good to meet. You are different than I expected, you know. Softer. Your picture, it is very—" For a moment he searched for the words, then finally gave up and mimicked my photo in exaggeration. He looked very brusque. We both laughed, drank, took bites from the board. "Were you once this way? Before your treatment, is it what you call it? Whatever it was it must have been something—the way you speak of it, it has me curious, of course, though it is not my business."

"I'm not usually afraid to speak about it. If anything, I feel responsible to share the story so it might help others. But with you, I have to admit, I fear explaining it. You'd likely find it preposterous. Or stupid."

"I make a living telling people that time, as they understand it, does not exist. Try me." He uncorked the Lambrusco with a dry pop and filled two glasses with bubbling red. We cheersed again. His Italian enthusiasm seemed less and less filtered by his English. Perhaps it was the food and drink. I took a moment to breathe, look around. So much green everywhere, so much movement—every leaf, the surface of water, clouds like rags across the blue above.

"On May twenty-second, a therapist gave me five grams of psilocybin mushrooms, then guided me through a journey that erased over twenty years of suicidal depression from my mind. I understand how it sounds—reckless, foolish, crazy, New Agey—but that's how it begins. The science is happening, and the technique seems sound—set an intention, then let the medicine untangle it in your mind. It's good enough for Johns Hopkins."

He straightened up, tilted his head. He asked that I excuse him for a moment, got up from the table, jogged into the house, and came back holding a knife and the rest of the Parmesan wedge.

"There is wine and cheese. The sun is everywhere. I am here. I am listening. Tell me everything you'd like."

I looked at him. He looked at me. I sipped the wine—berries and cellar air. I took a bite of cheese older than my marriage. Blossoms spun down.

"Perhaps I could show it to you? An approximation, I mean."

His brows bounced. "Please."

I took out my laptop and opened to the chart below. I began building it the morning after my treatment while everything was still vibrant in my memory. This was something I'd agreed to do for Denise, a "treatment report" is what she calls it. She'd explained that she requires one from every patient, not just because it's therapeutically useful to try to make sense of the experience and integrate its lessons, but because she gathers the reports as data. "Pretty soon I'll have a whole team to pore over them," she had said about her collection. "Who knows what might come from it." I was allowed to use any form I'd like, so long as I captured as much as I could. "I tried writing it out linearly," I explained to the Physicist, "but that failed. So this is what I came up with."

TREATMENT REPORT

NAME: ███████████

DATE: May 22, 20██.

DOSAGE: Psilocybin 5g.

NOTE: This is an approximate recounting. Much of it went far beyond language. Indeed, the failure of language to contain the experience was part of its immense, freeing power. Likewise, linearity doesn't really apply. I've tried to translate it into an order that our language and temporal reality can manage, but it's ultimately a fiction.

P.S. Read all "pain" as *very* painful.

P.P.S. Every dark thing, from snake to landscape to room, was TERRIFYING and clearly an expression of my depression. I went toward all of it and, just like you said it would, it vanished every time.

PHASE	VISUAL	EMOTIONAL	PHYSICAL	SPACE/TIME	LESSON/ EPIPHANY	AUDITORY
THE COME-UP (Duration: 10–20 min.)	Blindfold is on. Immediately a sinister cartoon face appears— a kind of evil Robin Hood. Then it fractals out into infinite repetition. Faces are interconnected, like a wallpaper pattern. They want to destroy me.	Rising fear.	I'm under a twenty-pound weighted blanket. Very cold, shaking, beginning to sob.	Beginning to fray.	I must let go.	Denise chanting, language unknown. A voice is rising out of her voice. A voice that isn't my own but is maybe Antony says: "It isn't about faces, it's about feelings."
	Faces dissolve into a great bright something . . .	INDESCRIB- ABLE TERROR!	Sobbing the hardest I ever have. My mouth stretches very wide while crying because another version of my body is rising headfirst out of my mouth, and then another rises out of its mouth. Repeat infinitely. Face rips in half. Body comes apart at molecular level. Ouch.	Collapsing.	Time to die.	Ibid. And then a great, all- consuming roar, as if inside a rocket blaster.
THE GREAT DEATH—or— THE BIG BANG (Duration: Unknown)	An immense explosion into the infinite. Very serene. All light, all energy—the workings of the universe revealed. Beyond language.	Absolute peace, freedom, joy, love. Cannot be described.	Body is gone.	Collapsed.	I die . . . and then am met with everything. Unity. Love is the one force. Other things intuited that I will never be able to explain but will never forget. Goodbye / Hello	All senses merged into one, as if in a single column of energy. Said aloud: "I get it now."

PHASE	VISUAL	EMOTIONAL	PHYSICAL	SPACE/TIME	LESSON/ EPIPHANY	AUDITORY
PHASE 1—or— THE MANY DEATHS (Duration: 60 min.)	A peach-colored light gathers. A dove flies through it. It is my grandmother.	Peach light = Annie's total love for me / Annie's spirit overlaying my spirit.	Annie's total love for me / Annie's spirit overlaying my spirit.	Ibid.	I will never be alone again, no matter the form "I" take.	All senses merge into one. Also, a rumbling.
	Light turns into green ceramic tiles, Mesoamerican in design, that become the body of an enormous snake (my biggest fear) with a Day of the Dead skull for a head. As big as a blimp. Skull is cackling at me, rearing up to eat "me." It is my depression.	TERROR.	TERROR.	No time?	I must let it consume me.	Sounds like I'm inside a tornado. Also the clicking of the tiles, the snake's cackling.
	Skull strikes, but instead of eating me, it crumbles apart and inside the skull, where the brain would be, is a baby's crib.	Joy and love. Understanding.	Gasping, warmth.	Ibid.	Screamed aloud: "I want to be a father! I can't wait to be a dad. I've always wanted this but feared I'd poison my child with my disease. But not anymore."	A joyous sound, origins unclear.
	All the color, all the light, as I die again, then again, then again, etc.	Fear, then surrender, then peace, joy, gratitude, understanding, love. Repeat.	A stellar explosion. Then the finest dust settles, gathers into matter, something like a star, the star collapses into a black hole. Repeat.	Collapses as "I" die, regathers as I regather, collapses as "I" die, etc.	"I" don't exist. Freedom of letting go. **A Dialogue:** "Denise, are you there?" "I'm here." "I think I'm coming back." "Okay, but know you have many deaths to go. That's okay. Let go and be healed. You're doing great. I'm with you."	More chanting. A sitar? At one point, drums.

PHASE	VISUAL	EMOTIONAL	PHYSICAL	SPACE/TIME	LESSON/ EPIPHANY	AUDITORY
	Colors begin settling into place, and then I realize I'm seeing ▮▮ ▮▮▮▮▮▮ and this became a young man sitting on a deck overlooking the sea, and then the whole thing happens in reverse, back to the beginning. *See watercolor triptych.	Awe.	Warmth, laughter.	▮▮▮▮	▮▮▮▮	Choral singing? Said aloud: "It's so simple, so beautiful."

PHASE	VISUAL	EMOTIONAL	PHYSICAL	SPACE/TIME	LESSON/ EPIPHANY	AUDITORY
	The universe as a Technicolor fabric rippling out in all directions, all dimensions—"I" am a part of it. Over it splashes waves of a black-and-white pixelated energy—the Mist. Then I feel horrible pain, the pain I'd have caused others had I killed myself. I watch it move through the universe, affecting Annie, my brother, my father. I am forced to feel all of it. Then I learn that I would've felt it until I was reunited with each of them in the whatever that comes after. Then the black-and-white pixelated force assembles into a glyph that represents my dead body. I do not look away. I stare back and everything dissolves into harmonious color. I sit up, take off the blindfold. I feel very lucid. Denise is sitting beside me.	Grief, pain, regret, and then a letting go into gratitude for my life. The sense of an ending.	After the encounter with my suicide I am settled back into my body. Lucidity as I sit up and remove the blindfold.	Back in the now.	After lifting the blindfold I begin to cry tears of gratitude. Said aloud: "I am so glad I didn't kill myself! I am so glad to be alive. I am so glad I didn't unleash that hurt into the world. Thank you, Denise. You saved my life." We hug. This is the end of the first phase.	Bright ecstatic music, origin unknown.

PHASE	VISUAL	EMOTIONAL	PHYSICAL	SPACE/TIME	LESSON/ EPIPHANY	AUDITORY
PHASE 2—or—HEALING THE BODY* (Duration: 90–120 min.) *Phase 2 followed a very clear pattern: Orbs, one after the other, would gather out of the material of the universe. Inside each orb was a landscape poisoned with the Mist. Each orb corresponded to a part of my body. Denise would massage this part of the body while I watched the Mist getting worked out, until finally the landscape was revived. Then I'd die and begin again. These are the landscapes I can remember.	A field of poisoned grass. The Mist gets kicked up out of the dirt, returning the field to a placid green.	Decades of built-up pain getting released. Humility and gratitude.	No blanket. Right leg filled with pain: pain gets worked out via massage; leg feels the best it's ever felt. Almost feels like leg is collapsed in a vacuum, then reformed.	Outside of spacetime.	Depression filled every inch of my body with pain.	Music from a variety of cultures. Languages not recognized. A good bit of classical Hindu, I think.
	An Alaskan shore goes from industrially decimated to thriving. Birds in the sky riding thermals.	Ibid.	Left rib cage: pain to lightness.	Ibid.	Ibid.	Ibid.
	A mountain cave full of animal bones crumbles, reveals an olive grove.	Ibid.	Left hip: pain to lightness.	Ibid.	Ibid.	Ibid.
	A sickly, logged redwood forest regrows in a steady rain.	Ibid.	Stomach: pain to comfort. Years of stomach issues because of depression dissolve away. Suddenly very hungry.	Ibid.	Said aloud: "Depression totally fucked my stomach. Wow I can't wait to eat!"	Ibid.
	Grove of oaks go from dead to full.	Ibid.	Face: pain to comfort.	Ibid.	Ibid.	Ibid.
	Oak roots reach across my face, into my front tooth. I go inside of my tooth. There is a stage. On the stage is a dentist's chair. I'm in it, very young. A dentist is pulling out my front right tooth with pliers. The baby tooth has gone necrotic. Inside the tooth: the Mist. I am screaming.	Pain, memory, understanding.	Front-right tooth: very old pain expelled. Then understanding and forgiveness.	Ibid.	This was the first time I felt betrayed by my father. But in this moment I feel his pain and helplessness as he felt it in that moment. Said aloud: "My father did his best." Gratitude.	Ibid.

PHASE	VISUAL	EMOTIONAL	PHYSICAL	SPACE/TIME	LESSON/ EPIPHANY	AUDITORY
	Alpine lake. Ash falls like snow. Healed by a gentle, steady rain.	Ibid.	Back: pain to comfort.	Ibid.	Said aloud: "I need to go hiking more. Hiking is a way to heal."	Ibid.
	A desert cave in the far-left distance. A campfire is burning. My father, as a teenager, is sitting beside it. He is very sad, very alone. His brother has just died. After a realization, the fire swirls up, consumes him, leaves behind a painted desert.	I feel his pain. It's awful. I learn from it.	Left arm: a theater.	I am experiencing my father's pain as he felt it in the past.	I will never be able to reach that version of my father, but that's okay. When I was born, I began to heal him.	Wind through dry branches.
	A burned vineyard comes back to fullness. The vines are all of the men throughout history.	A lesson being revealed.	Chest.	Outside of spacetime.	Said aloud: "Men are so afraid, especially of love. There is so much pain because of barriers to love."	A bow over strings.
	After my body has been rebuilt and healed, three orbs appear floating in the center of the universe. *Need to diagram ASAP.	*To be diagrammed.	Beyond the body.	Ibid.	*To be diagrammed.	A choir in a cathedral in an ancient city under snow.

PHASE	VISUAL	EMOTIONAL	PHYSICAL	SPACE/TIME	LESSON/ EPIPHANY	AUDITORY
	The fabric of the universe again: an infinite spool of Technicolor fabric made of love. An osprey appears and begins pulling on a patch of universe—of which I am a part—with its beak. With each pull, the Mist flecks off like pixelated static. Watching it, I know that whatever the osprey is doing, it's very wrong. Then I get it: this is how depression is created.	The wonder and disorientation after a secret has been revealed.	Ibid.	A moment of precise witnessing.	The great realization: depression is a malfunction of love. Somewhere in my life I lost the sense that my love reached people—that my dad could feel it, or Ben, or Annie. This made me feel like my love was returned as rejected feedback, which made me feel like a mistake. Also isolated. So simple. I'm failing to explain this, but I understand it now. And then depression's absolute *stupidity* exploded through me. After twenty years, it was gone. Laughter. I sit up into a second lucid state, lift my blindfold, say aloud: "I like who I am." I'd never said that before. Then I slide down the blindfold and collapse. This is the end of the second phase.	I can hear the trees rustling outside, bugs buzzing. Water through a stream.

PHASE	VISUAL	EMOTIONAL	PHYSICAL	SPACE/TIME	LESSON/ EPIPHANY	AUDITORY
PHASE 3—or— THE BED PHASE (Duration: 150– 180 min.)	As the music begins, I am torn in two, then broken into particles, before finally reassembling into my body, except I am not just in my present body on the therapy bed. I'm also in my childhood bed in West Virginia, my bed in Brooklyn, and my bed in Oakland, each version of myself getting healed across time. I am witnessing this *and* experiencing it, in each body, and in the mind of each of those sleeping bodies I am returned, wholesale, to a correlative memory from that time, e.g. my dad passed out on couch in WV. *Need to make breakout list of these.	Increasing calm, excited to live.	I'm in more than one version of my body at once, like I'm a deck of cards fanned open. At the same time, I can feel my cells realigning into harmony as the vibrations wave through me.	Existing in multiple times at once.	I was healed across time, the pain in past versions of myself coming undone, making the next version easier to heal, then the next, etc.	"The Orphan's Lament," Huun-Huur-Tu. Immense vibrations, like a million bees buzzing around me.

PHASE	VISUAL	EMOTIONAL	PHYSICAL	SPACE/TIME	LESSON/ EPIPHANY	AUDITORY
	I awake in my bed in Oakland. The room is gray and dark. But then the darkness begins to drag off every surface, as if a thick layer of dust—it is the last of the Mist—and it swirls up and away into a mirror hanging on the wall, leaving the room warm and bright. Then I die a small death and am reborn into the room again. It is dark, but less than before. Then the same thing happens—the dust lifts into the mirror, leaving behind sun, I feel great, I die—repeat over and over, until the final time: I awake into my room, warm and sunny at the start of the day. I feel Annie beside me in bed. I turn to her. And then I wake up.	When I awake in the dark room I feel exactly how I felt at my depression's peak: sad to have woken up, afraid of the day's pain, desperate to be gone. But as the darkness pulls away, I feel serene, free, and rested. Then I die, except now the deaths are gentle. I understand not to resist. I simply let myself come apart, come back together. Each time it gets easier and each time I feel better. I call this the 100 Deaths. At their end, I am so excited to live. I cannot describe this excitement. And then I wake up.	Rested in a way I did not know was possible . . . And then I wake up.	At the start of something / the end of something . . . And then I wake up.	Said aloud: "I cannot wait to take a shower, have a coffee, see Annie. I cannot wait to live." And then I wake up.	Faint music coming in and out, as if I'm in a great house in which someone is practicing piano. Also, somewhere in the distance, a lawn mower is running, even when I wake up.

The Physicist kind of giggled when I showed him the chart. I tried to explain briefly how there were roughly three phases, each with a different purpose and sensory experience. How my intention was to be healed of depression, so all the encounters were some expression of that. "Maybe it's best I just let you sort of scroll through it."

He agreed and began investigating the chart with interest, making warm noises to himself, shaking his head at parts, laughing even. When he'd point to a square, I'd explain it further, but mainly I tried not to watch him. Though I mostly did watch him. I couldn't help it.

Then he leaned back in his chair and pointed at the screen. "These here," he said. "These." He was pointing at the row of cells in phase 1 that I've since redacted, precisely because they recount the moment I witnessed his theory of quantum gravity in action. "Can you explain, in detail?" So I did, but can't here (lawyers).

"Remarkable," he said when I finished. "That's it. Precisely." He was very still, very calm, as if thinking through each move before he made it. "And this note about the watercolors, the man. Do you have them?"

"I do! They're in my backpack, pressed in one of my books." I found them in the bag and offered them to him: three small paintings done in indigo on rough, cold-pressed paper. I can't say too much about them. "They're sketches really, gestural. Not good. But I wanted to try to record it somehow. I don't think I succeeded, but it was fun."

He took the paintings, shuffled through them, then stared silently at each one. After a heavy exhale he again removed his glasses, rubbed his eyes. He took a long sip of Lambrusco, then refilled both our glasses. "I'm sorry," he said. "I've just remembered something, looking at these. I need a moment, then I will explain. But first, I'd like to keep looking."

"Of course."

He went back to the screen, the paintings still in his hand. Wind moved the tall grasses at the garden's edges. "And these," he said, pointing again at a row of cells, these in phase 2. "Where is the diagram you make note of?"

"I haven't done it yet—I tried a few times, but I couldn't get it right. Do you have a piece of paper?"

He ran into the house and returned quickly with a small memo pad and pencil. I drew and explained the following:

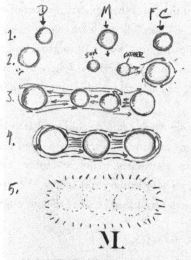

CASA MARIALUIGIA - Strageils Bonaghine, 55 - 41128 San Damaso MO Italia
Tel. +39 069 469354

See these circles as spheres of energy.

1. The three spheres are my dad (D), me (M), and my potential future child (FC).

2. As I conceived of myself as a father, my sphere sent energy—almost like how atoms exchange electrons—to the future child sphere. But something was wrong. I'd compartmentalized part of myself as "father," so my sphere split into two smaller spheres—son and father. My "father" sphere moved closer to the "future child," but my other half stayed in place. Because of this split, the energy I was able to send toward the child weakened because it was coming from a smaller sphere. This made me terribly sad. Likewise, I noticed my dad was very alone—I wasn't sending him anything and he was drifting.

3. When I realized this, my other sphere, the part of me I'd compartmentalized as "son," began exchanging energy with my dad's sphere, allowing my "son" half to grow, and as it grew it began to pull my smaller fatherhood sphere back into its orbit. My dad's energy was helping me rejoin into one sphere.

4. When I was finally whole again, I could see that the stronger the bond between me and my father, the stronger I grew, and the more energy I was able to send to the child sphere. Concurrently, the more energy I sent to the child sphere, the larger it grew, which allowed it in turn to send energy back through me, all the way to my father.

5. The result was a network of pure, bright energy moving harmoniously between three spheres. Conduits of love across time.

When I was done he sat back. "Have you shared any of this with your father?"

"Not yet. I don't know if I ever will. I don't think he'd understand."

"I see. And your potential future child—is that still potential or now certain, if I might ask?"

"Still potential, but I hope that one day it will be certain. I didn't even realize how much I want that to be the case until all this happened. Before this, I was so ill, I couldn't see it. It just wasn't possible. I couldn't imagine myself in that kind of future, not in the way I was. Or if I was imagining it, I was blocked from me realizing it, if that even makes sense."

"I understand, I think. I hope for you too that it is in your future." Then he bobbed his head and returned to the chart, reading through the rest. He seemed pleased with its ending, then sat back. Again a calm fell behind his face. He wasn't upset. No— it was as if he was being tugged between the joy of the moment and some other knowledge. The Lambrusco was gone, as was the cheese. Oil stains on the board where the mortadella had been. The Physicist looked out over the grass, away from me. He was shaking his head. I could not tell if he was tired or bored. I let our silence do whatever it needed to.

"*Grazie, grazie,*" he said finally. "Fascinating. Truly." He asked to be excused, went to the house, and returned with a bottle of Campari, two glasses, more ice, and a large bottle of mineral water. He made us each a glass. "When we were working on the memoir," he began, "the process was fine. I liked it, even with all the other work I had to do. You did very well. But then there was an issue. As I started proofing your renditions of my memories, they became my memories. Not just became—they destroyed *my* memories and replaced them. I couldn't get the originals back. Even if I listened to my recordings, they wouldn't return. Instead every memory was now filtered through your version of my voice. Even when I tried to remember in Italian, it was not my Italian but Italian as you would speak it. I might study physics for a living, I

might tell people there is only interaction, there is only impermanence, but even I get shocked at times by what can slip away. At
first, I thought it would be temporary. But month after month, the
feeling got worse. Losing those memories, I was losing me. I was
not ready for this. I panicked. That's why I went off-line. Or so I
thought. But that isn't all of it. I now see that there's more.

"You know, I learned about you on C-Span. On Book TV. The
ten years I spent in America, C-Span and PBS were the only chan-
nels I had, and I still watch them through the Internet whenever
I am homesick for the place I am not from. You were doing a
reading at the *LA Times* book festival and I liked the story you
read very much, but I especially liked how you sounded—you
reminded me of my friends from Pittsburgh. The same accent. I
could not get your voice out of my head after I turned off the TV.
You were speaking the same English of the place where I'd perfected my English. To write about physics—not so difficult. But
to write a memoir, I felt I *must* have you, because you shared my
speech. That's what I thought was my reasoning. That's how we
came to work together. But after I panicked and arrived here, I
began to have strange new memories. Déjà vu. Of course I'd been
here before—it was not like that—it was like, how can I say? I
began to remember the future." He stirred his Campari, wiped his
glasses again, pinched the bridge of his nose.

"The déjà vu kept happening, you see—flashes of it, every
day I've been here. I began to anticipate your arrival. And then
today you came! Us sitting here, these bites of food, our drinks,
the sun and falling blossoms—it was all as I'd expected. But then
you began speaking of your treatment, and it dawned on me then
that I had not been remembering the future. No, it was all from
my memory—the great realization. Ha! So much has been made

about it. Too much. To be honest, I hadn't even realized we were approaching it in our work until you began speaking here today. As your story unfolded, as I looked through your report, it came back to me so vividly, like I was again in 1978."

I worried even the wrong movement might scare him from going forward. I sipped my Campari only because he sipped his first.

"I arrived in San Francisco at the long end of a hitchhiking journey. May of seventy-eight. When I got to the city, I befriended some fellow young travelers like myself in the Haight. With them I rode across the Golden Gate to a house by the water in the town of Bolinas, a magical place. Early the next morning, the morning of my twenty-second birthday, I sat out on the deck, fog everywhere, so much fog I could barely see the waves on the beach, and ate a large dose of psilocybin mushrooms. As the trip intensified, the deck became two places at once. It was the deck overlooking the Pacific, but it was also here, this patch of earth where, even at twenty-two, I'd spent so much of my life sitting and dreaming. The fog acted like a kind of force—a teacher, if you will. It controlled what I could see. It directed my attention. When I would see this place, in Italy, it would transform from fog into falling blossoms, and at one point those blossoms took the shape of a man, a stranger who was sometimes a man from the future with a red beard and sometimes only falling blossoms that could talk. He told me how he'd seen the material of space itself, then described to me for the first time what would go on to become 'my' theory, except he didn't just explain it, he—the fog?—showed it to me simultaneously as he described it by enacting it upon me on the deck, in the fog. It was like watching a painting coming undone, then be repainted again. Except I was the painting! And I was a thing being imagined in my mind in Modena as the voice explained it to me. Except I wasn't in Modena. I was on the deck. Except I wasn't, because I'd become a painting. It was exhilarating. And very challenging. Everything you told me today about the things in your chart, I've heard before, from you. And these"—he held up the watercolors—"I have been these before. This experience made me who I am. But none of it belongs to me."

No wind now. But the blossoms were falling.

"Accepting this story means, of course, that you wrote my theory. Now, of course you could say you only saw what you saw because you'd read my books. But then I could say I only wrote those books because of what you told me, right now, all those years ago. Whose idea is it then? Mine or yours, or is it ours, or—another way—no one's? For decades I kept the story secret because I worried how the mention of psychedelics would land with the scientific community, let alone the tenure committees. A talking fog! Now I see that it's not the psychedelics I was afraid of—it was the story itself. It would be the end of *me* as I exist in that world. I wasn't ready to accept that. I tried to run from it but of course look where that got me. In many talks I have quoted my own sentence, 'we are the ones who complicate things with our confused fantasies about the supposed freedom of the future,' but clearly I didn't want to believe it. Now, what would happen if we put this story in a book, even if the book is about a man who tells you there is no difference between the past and the future? It would be rejected, certainly—no? How could it ever be believed by a public who worships the genius and believes that what we synthesize in a lab is more natural than what comes out of the ground, a public who believes nature is not *nature* but that which we have manipulated into being. It was difficult at moments to listen to your story, knowing it was the end of my

own, but impermanence is impermanence. To resist is suffering."
He brushed some of the blossoms off the table into his hand, then
tossed them into the air.

"I'm sorry," I said. "I feel like I've taken something from you."

"No, no—not necessary. Not true. Having said all this now, it is
good. *Va bene*." He smiled. "May I ask you something?"

"Please."

"This treatment, what it showed you, what it did—was this the
only way for you?"

"I'm not sure. I was very ill. With my depression—it was like I
was lost in a mist for twenty years. I couldn't see my life. The way
the treatment freed me from that, it seems like yes, it was the only
way. It genuinely felt like medicine, like healing. Like surgery.
But as for what I learned, what I saw, I don't think it's possible to
separate that from the healing. No, that *was* the healing. It wasn't
about the chemicals. It was about what was left once the chemicals
took everything away. What I will say is that much of what I've
learned, even some of the ways I feel, it doesn't all feel new to me.
I think parts of me always knew these things, and that there was a
time, way, way back, when that was my reality. Before all the noise
creeped in. Could I ask the same of you? What if you hadn't gone
to Bolinas? Could the realization have come some other way?"

"Impossible to say, of course. But realizations, discoveries, people mistake these things. They're not acts of invention. They're
moments when we finally see what's always been there. That
day in Bolinas, I was simply the interaction that disturbed what I
learned into visibility. All I did was share it."

"The paintings," I said. "I'd like you to have them. They're
yours," and he agreed.

After that we sat for a good while, saying nothing. It was warm, it was calm. He checked his watch. I stared up at the sky. From the house you could hear Louis Armstrong playing a trumpet in a studio in New Orleans almost a century ago.

"I suppose we should let some people know they can stop worrying, yes? Perhaps you could message our friend in California? As for *Richards*," he said, "I think it's best I call him."

I'VE FOUND that every time after I share the story of my treatment, I feel a little down. Nothing too big, but enough to notice it. Denise explained, during my integration session a week after my treatment, that this was common. She explained that the down feeling is likely because I'm telling a story that, in many ways, cannot be told. "So what you end up telling people isn't the story of your journey, but a translation. You're making it into something else." Hence the distance and disconnect. To resolve this, she first reminded me that I don't need to share it with anyone, but that if I do share it, to choose my audience wisely, and be sure to take some time afterward to reconnect with the experience as I experienced it—meditation can be great for this. So that's what I'll do tonight; I'll meditate before bed.

In the meantime, I do not resist the feeling. The night sky is paling with the ambient glow of Rome in the distance, the twins have woken up and are both sipping airplane bottles of Fernet and talking, and whatever gloom is in me will have vanished by the time I reach Annie. I will be nothing but ecstatic to kiss her, sit across from her, and admire her misaligned tooth. I'll tell her about my day, meeting the Physicist, his house, how I shared the story of my treatment, his reaction, then his story, and how he finally said, "We must keep the psychedelics in the memoir because we must honor them, but maybe we change it a little—make it faster, vague, treat it as sensitive. Don't go into too much detail—they'll never believe it." He said I'd have to make it up. "Imagine something great, then write it," he said, "so we can get you back to zero." Then he suggested we meet for dinner on Friday in Rome to discuss it, his treat, if Annie would allow it, and also to apologize for going rogue. I'll explain how he explained that he could call the restaurant where we have a reservation and make all the necessary adjustments, he's certain it won't be a problem, and I'm certain she'll be excited about this—surprised—but excited, and then I'll tell her how after we finished talking he insisted on driving me to Bologna to catch the Frecciarossa—"it's only down the road," he said—and on the way I asked if we could stop in Modena so I could take a picture of the cathedral for a friend, which we did, and I'll show her the picture on my phone, the very picture I sent to Jules while waiting for the train, and then I'll ask if she remembers Jules and I ever talking about our project back in art school, years ago, before I met her. Then I'll tell her about how, just before parting ways with the Physicist in Bologna, he said, "Goodbye, my ghost," and I corrected him and said "ghost*writer*," and how before that, while still in the Physicist's car, he'd handed me an old tattered envelope and said it might interest me to look at it, so long as I return it to him on Friday, and then I'd hand it to her across the table—the envelope I'm holding now, on the Frecciarossa—urging her to be gentle, and carefully she'll open its worn fold and find inside the pages of brittle yellowed notebook paper, scribbled all over in Italian written with blue ballpoint pen, which I can't read but which Annie can, at least somewhat, after all her study, and I'll ask her if she could tell me what it says, and she'll explain that it's dated May of '78 and looks like a kind of report or time line, then she'll explain how the handwriting is hard to make out, but it seems to be saying something about a conversation, and I'll say not to worry about it, I'll plug it into Google Translate tomorrow and figure it out. This will make me briefly anxious, not because I don't know what it says—I do—but because I know that once I read it, I'll lose something. But I'm okay with that. And then I think she'll say she has some things to tell me too.

I SLIP THE ENVELOPE into my bag and see *The Leopard* and *Rage,* my copy of *The Mermaid,* LD's first book, the much-lauded novel-in-stories, its burgundy cover with gold lettering. I open it to my favorite story, one of my favorite stories of all time, and wonder if part of my love for the story is because one of the characters shares my name almost exactly, a detail that never ceases to excite me in rereading. In fact, it seems I can never read about the character's fictional escapades as a writer in Central Texas without one of two things happening: either I project myself onto the narrative, thereby transforming it into a coded rewriting of whatever I've experienced; or, what more often happens, and what is certainly more strange, is I read his narrative and am suddenly certain it's about me (it can't be; it was written decades before I was born) and am returned with fondness to that late-middle-aged time in my life that hasn't even happened yet, amazed that LD was able to get it so right. I've always wanted to ask her if she's ever noticed the coincidence, but never have.

I'd once planned on mentioning it casually during one of our early dinners together. My plan was to use the coincidence of the character's name to segue into the real question I'd always wanted to ask about the story. At one point, the character boils down his entire writing practice into twenty words: "Whatever happens to you, you put it on a page, work it into a shape, cast it in a light."

I always wanted to know—did LD believe that? Is that what she did?

But when the time came during dinner, I couldn't ask. I was afraid she might feel like I was asking her to explain herself, so in a moment of panic I mentioned instead something I'd read just that afternoon in an essay on Walter Benjamin titled "Walter Benjamin," written by John Berger. Originally I'd been reading a novel I very much admired in which a quote by Walter Benjamin figured prominently, beginning with the epigraph. Benjamin, it seemed, was a name that writers liked to mention a lot, but I knew nothing about him, something I clearly needed to fix, I'd decided, if I was to be a "writer" too. I did some quick research, found which Benjamin book was the most important Benjamin book, located it at my shop in Oakland, bought it that morning, tried to read a number of different parts, and couldn't make heads or tails of any of it—not a single fucking sentence—finally gave up, and felt very dumb. Then I remembered my new copy of *Selected Essays* by John Berger (a quick search on my phone shows me that the book was edited by Geoff Dyer, a name that meant nothing to me then). The book was a going-away gift from Jules, who knew I'd admired Berger ever since reading *Ways of Seeing* in our freshman seminar (for what is the point of a freshman seminar in art school if not to read this book). I knew from flipping through the table of contents of *Selected Essays* that there was a piece about Walter Benjamin, so I read it in hopes that John Berger would say something about Walter Benjamin that I could actually understand, and he did, kind of.

And maybe tonight, as Annie and I walk home lazily through the gaslit labyrinth of the Eternal City, I'll share all of this with her before describing how at last, during the dinner with LD, I'd said,

"I read this exciting thing today that Walter Benjamin said, about how his dream was to write a book entirely out of quotations, and I feel like that's exactly what I'd like to do next."

"Interesting," said LD, not even looking up from her mapo tofu. "Who quoted it?"

I didn't know what to say because I hadn't said that I'd found it as a quote in a Berger essay.

"I ask because I know you weren't reading Benjamin and I know that because no one reads Benjamin and anyone who tells you they do is a fucking liar. The only way any of us know anything he said is by finding it elsewhere in quotation. And that's perfectly okay. That's how all of this works. One long daisy chain of echoes. Also—it's pronounced 'Ben-yuh-mean,' not 'Benjamin.'"

My face flushed. I wanted to jab my chopsticks into my eyes.

She took a sip of her Tsingtao and looked straight at me, a gaze of such severe honesty and pity that I was certain she'd located the somewhere behind my face from which all my observation comes. "It's okay. Really. Stop being embarrassed. No one knows how to pronounce it until someone tells them. Someone told me a century ago, and now I told you, and then someday you'll have to tell someone and hopefully you won't make them feel embarrassed when you do. That's the only way anyone knows. Now say it out loud: *Ben-yuh-mean.*"

"Ben-yuh-mean."

"Benjamin."

"Benjamin."

"Good. Now you sound like you know what you're talking about."

Acknowledgments

THIS BOOK, AND MY LIFE, would not have been possible without the belief, generosity, guidance, and support of the following:

Reagan Arthur, Sarah Bolling, John Gall, Rebecca Gardner, Hafizah Geter, Henry Glavin, Louise Glück, Gabe Habash, Jocasta Hamilton, Dana Hawkes, Rita Madrigal, Isaac Meadow, Emily Murphy, Tim O'Connell, Chris Parris-Lamb, Jordan Pavlin, Emily Reardon, Will Roberts, Rob Shapiro, Jeremy Sherman, Brian Tierney, all the excellent people at Knopf and the Gernert Company, my friends, my family, and especially Ryann Brewer.

Endless gratitude to everyone at the following institutions that have sustained and supported me in invaluable ways: the Bread Loaf Writers' Conference, the Stanford Creative Writing Program, and the T. S. Eliot Foundation; special thanks to the T. S. Eliot House, where large portions of this book were written—few places have come to mean so much to me.

I've never properly thanked Michael Green, my first great teacher. Thank you, Mr. Green.

All quotes attributed to the Physicist are from either *Seven Brief Lessons on Physics* or *The Order of Time* by Carlo Rovelli, published by Riverhead in 2016 and 2018, respectively.

The quote on page 128 is a slight misquote of W. G. Sebald quoting Walter Benjamin in an interview with Michael Silverblatt on KCRW's *Bookworm,* aired December 6, 2001. The exact quote of Sebald quoting Benjamin is "there is no point in exaggerating that which is already horrific."

The quote on page 252 is from "Triumph Over the Grave" by Denis Johnson, published in *The Largesse of the Sea Maiden* by Random House in 2018.